Still Blue

a novel

by

Ron McMillan

Still Blue

One

Bangkok, 2015

Tuk's mother called out to him three times before he emerged from his bedroom, badly tied necktie hanging askew from open shirt collar.

'Do I have to wear this thing?'

'Come here,' she said. 'You're worse than your father. He turned up for our wedding with his tie in his pocket because he didn't know how to put it on. Your grandfather had to do it for him.'

Tuk waved a finger at photographs on the wall.

'How many times have you told me that story?'

'You've heard it before?'

Prominent amidst a gallery of mismatched frames was a faded, formal wedding day portrait. The groom was ill at ease, shirt collar too tight, tie crooked, but Tuk had always thought his mother seemed almost as uncomfortable. They looked too young to be getting married, and it was many years of uncelebrated anniversaries before he worked it out: the wedding took place only seven months before he was born. When he was in high school, friends made him cringe by commenting on how attractive his mum was, and the photograph showed a real beauty, make-up applied with taste and subtlety beyond her years, hair heavy with spray, hands folded self-consciously across her tummy. Next to her, dad gave the impression he would rather be somewhere less formal, preferably still with the one love of his life by his side. Tuk tried to ignore the gap in the display where a photograph had hung for years, his mother refusing to take it down until he removed it himself. She didn't talk to him for days afterwards.

It took her only seconds to cinch the tie so firmly Tuk unwittingly mimicked the expression on his late dad's face.

She stepped back to admire her work. 'You have to be on time today,' she said.

'So you keep telling me.'

'You have no idea how many favours I had to call in to get you this interview. Did I tell you how many applications they received?'

'Almost as many times as you told me the story about dad's tie,' said Tuk.

'Nearly three hundred applicants! It took them a week to cut them down to a shortlist. Only ten interviews, all scheduled for today. You're on the list, but only because-'

'-because you've worked for the company for so long. I know, Mum.'

'Your CV wouldn't have made the top one hundred, never mind the top ten.'

'Are you trying to make me feel better? If you're right, what's the point in me turning up?'

'Don't be like that. You know how much I want you to get a proper job.'

Tuk squinted at the reflection in the cloudy mirror next to the photo frames. 'I know, but-'

'No buts! You worked hard for your degree, but since graduating, all you've done is play music. If you don't hurry up and get a real job, you'll never find one. And you'll end up like-'

'Like dad. I know.'

'So do this for me. See. You already look like a marketing professional. Except for the haircut.'

Tuk suddenly noticed she wasn't dressed for work.

'You're not going into the office? You never miss a day.'

'My line manager gave me the morning off. He said it was for your sake, but it's because I'll be useless when I know you're coming in. You have to get going.'

Tuk struggled into leather dress shoes he hadn't laced up since graduation day. When he went to pluck the guitar case from its spot near the door, his mother's hand came to rest firmly on his forearm.

'Oh no you don't. Not today. The guitar stays.'

'Mummm, you know I always-'

'-You can live without it for a couple of hours.'

'We have an audition later.'

'You can come back for it.'

Her eyes flicked to the old-fashioned digital clock beside the mirror, which said 07:41. 'Go. Good luck.'

She shook her head at the closing door in a mix of frustration and affection, glanced at herself in the mirror, and disappeared into the bathroom. At the precise moment the bathroom door closed behind her, the apartment door cracked open and an arm slipped in to spirit the guitar from the room.

Motorcycle taxis made Bangkok's permanently clotted streets almost bearable to ordinary Thais. However much motorists poured scorn or even hatred upon them, the ability of bike taxis to thread between lanes of stalled jams and take over at the head of traffic light queues meant thousands of people got where they needed to be much quicker than the proud fools sitting alone in oversized SUVs and high-powered luxury cars that spent much of their journey at a standstill.

The motorcycle taxi stand next to the apartment block where Tuk had lived his whole life was only seconds from Yaowarat, one of Chinatown's busiest roads, where the rumble of traffic hardly dimmed even in the wee small hours. In the commuter rush, service from the stand was in constant demand, so Tuk was surprised to see Uncle Mu look up from his newspaper. But not as surprised as Uncle Mu seemed.

He eyed his watch. 'Tuk! What are you doing on your feet at this hour?' He spotted the necktie. 'Oooh, appointment, eh? And no sign of your mum yet – don't tell me, you're taking her place on the run to the office.'

Tuk shook his head in disbelief. 'What's a man with your investigative talents doing riding a motorcycle taxi? Exactly right. Mum's office please.'

Uncle Mu fished a plastic helmet from the bike's front basket. Tuk jammed it on and did a pretend fix with the grubby strap. It would protect him from none of the dangers involved in any kind of traffic accident, but it would keep them both safe from predatory cops on the make for cash penalties that involved no paperwork. Uncle Mu had done this precise trip hundreds of times with Tuk's mum on the back, having worked the same stand for so long he could remember Tuk's dad. He knew not to mention him.

It was only when Tuk held on with his knees as they pulled away the penny dropped. Uncle Mu wasn't there by chance any more than he guessed where Tuk had to go this morning. His mum had set him up in case he got cold feet and chose not to go. The possibility had occurred to him.

One of Uncle Mu's regular shortcuts took them through Khao San Road, the backpacker district that grew out of an early guidebook mention of a couple of Chinese-Thai budget hotels. Tuk relaxed on his pillion perch, guitar case safe on straps keeping it secure behind his shoulders, in no danger of clipping traffic even when Uncle Mu split lanes through gaps so tight they required him to rotate the handlebar mirrors inwards.

Pavements were filling for the day with stallholders setting up their wares and with swarms of backpackers, some wearily searching for places to stay after long overnight trips from around the country, others heading off for the islands or settling down to breakfast at rickety tables and stools serving as kerbside eateries.

Khao San Road's global reputation meant it had more westerners per square metre than anywhere else in Thailand; from his moving perch Tuk enjoyed surreptitious glances at statuesque young women who seemed to think bikini tops were perfectly *de rigueur* in the middle of a city of ten million people, sixty kilometres from the nearest beach. He caught a glimpse of a pretty European girl with blonde shoulder-length hair sucking greedily at an oversized coffee mug. Hungover, he thought.

All around her, stalls touted thumb drives filled with bootleg music and movies, embroidered hippy-style clothing including the almost inevitable elephant-print, shapeless baggy trousers held up by a string at the waistband (a stall holder was at that moment crossing the road pushing a rail on wheels filled with the things in a selection of sizes and colours), tie-dyed shirts and blouses, beads, costume jewellery, barbecued meats on sticks, syrupy sugar-laden pancakes, whole green coconuts with the tops sliced off to get to the sweet juice and the added attraction of soft white pulp within. One backpacker hostel was studded with rattling window mounted air conditioners draped with signs advertising cheap drink offers for the evening trade and language lessons and visa deals and travel to the islands and tattoos of every style, machine- or bamboo-needle-applied.

Jo awoke cautiously. On a shaky pine table next to the bed, empty painkiller blister packs sat in a puddle of condensation from a plastic water bottle on its side. However many painkillers she had taken, it wasn't enough to dull the ache from the previous night's excess and the air conditioner rattling only a few feet from her head. She peeled back the thin sheet and recoiled in horror. The cover on the lumpy mattress was marked with blood. She sat up quickly enough to send pain lancing between her temples. From a gauze adhesive bandage attached to her left breast seeped the source of the blood.

Dani indicated the need for another cappuccino to the teenager with the snaggle-toothed smile, then opened a second finger to change the order to two mugs. From behind the young waiter, Jo emerged, barefoot and smiling. Behind the brave attempt to appear cheerful, she looked every bit as bad as Dani felt.

'What are YOU smiling at,' said Jo.

'You. Me. Both of us pair of drunken loons,' said Dani. She pointed at Jo's chest, where blood marked her favourite Cold Play T-shirt. 'And that.'

'Aw Christ! How many bottles of rotgut whisky did we drink? I can't remember anything after the second one.' She pointed at her shirt. 'When did this happen? Wait. Was it only me?'

Dani grimaced. She pulled down the neckline of her own shirt to reveal a gauze like her friend's, also on her left breast, but with little or no blood to show for whatever they'd had done.

'Aw no,' said Jo. 'How did it happen? Whose mad idea was it?'

'You don't remember? After the third bottle of Sangsom I got it into my head we needed something to celebrate our trip, and you thought it was the greatest idea you'd ever heard. The guy at the tattoo shop did his best, said we were too pissed, told us to come back tomorrow, but I was having none of it, waving my money and my tits in his face, telling him we'd take our business down the street.'

'Total blackout,' said Jo. 'Don't remember a thing. God my head hurts.

Wait! What is it? The tattoo, I mean. What did we get? Did we both get the same? My mother's going to kill me.'

'Yours says *Fuck The Pope*.'

'It does not!' Jo picked at the edge of the gauze but it was too painful. All around them, people stared at her showing off her breast and bra on a pavement full of backpackers and restaurant workers.

'Relax,' said Dani. 'That would kill both our old dears. We got the same. Two cute wee flags, the Saltire and the Thai one, with *"Scottish and Proud"* underneath. I was off my face too, remember, but I think the guy did a nice job. At least I hope he did.'

Two

Uncle Mu pulled to a halt in front of the office tower Tuk knew so well, even though he hadn't gone inside since his mother brought him to be spoiled by her colleagues on school holidays. The uniformed security man at the elevator lobby desk waved him past with barely a glance. This was an old-fashioned company whose employees, like his mother, often remained on the workforce for years, so it was quite possible he recognised Tuk.

The matronly woman at the reception desk on the seventeenth floor certainly knew him. When he began to tell her who he was and why he was here, she squealed in excitement.

'I know exactly who you are, young man,' she said. 'We haven't had the pleasure of a visit from you for a long time. I see you brought your guitar.'

'I have an audition later,' said Tuk.

'Of course you do. I will take you to the interview room. It's good you are punctual. Our managers take timekeeping seriously - but I bet your mum told you already. Maybe you would like to leave your guitar here with me....?'

Tuk stared at her blankly.

'Perhaps not,' she said. 'This way, young man.'

Tuk knew the room well. As a child he had spent many hours playing at or under what they rather grandly called the boardroom table. Back then, an impressive selection of toys waited in a cupboard for visiting kids to keep themselves entertained while mum or dad went about their business, and Tuk recalled using pamphlets and folders to create construction sites and quarries for a fleet of diggers and jeeps. Today he was left to browse a whiteboard filled with overlapping graphs and marketing gibberish. On either side of the board were motivational posters and stiff portraits of staff groups trying to seem interested. As far as Tuk could make out, most of them were having to fake their enthusiasm. A long shelf groaned under the weight of matching files and printed materials doubtless there to assist staff in living up to the happy clappy bullshit on posters assaulting their vision whenever they looked up from the table.

Two managers arrived unannounced and sat across the table from Tuk. They wore suits of an identical company blue with embossed name badges high on their left lapels. Maybe the badges allowed them to bypass normal courtesies and relieved them of any need to introduce themselves. Eyes down, they read through some pages of A4; Tuk assumed it was his own work history.

The slightly more senior man spoke first:

'Your CV is, well, interesting,' said Manager One.

'Thank you,' said Tuk.

'A little thin,' said the manager.

'Mother said to keep it relevant.'

'Ah yes,' said Manager Two. 'Your mother has been a faithful servant to the company since before our time.' The two men exchanged inquisitive glances as convincing as the efforts of daytime soap opera actors. 'How long? Twelve years? Fifteen?'

'Twenty-seven years,' said Tuk, feeling foolish. They didn't want an answer.

'I beg your pardon,' said Manager One.

'Twenty-seven years. In November. My mother has worked for this company for nearly twenty-seven years.'

'How nice,' said Manager Two, eyes on the CV. 'You graduated with a degree in business studies, let me see, seven years ago.'

'Six-and-a-half,' said Tuk.

'Six-and-a-half. Yes. Maybe you can tell us more about what you have been doing for those, ahem, six-and-a-half years. It says here "self-employed".'

'I think you'll see it says *self-employed musician*.'

'You take the work seriously.'

'I do. It is important to me.'

Manager Two gestured towards Tuk's guitar case, propped against the wall behind him. 'I see you brought your guitar,' he said. 'Are you going to play us a song?'

'No,' said Tuk.

'I was joking,' said the manager.

'I wasn't.'

The other man tried to fill the awkward silence.

'If we could just get back to the reason for the interview. How about you tell us why you think you would be a good fit for our marketing department?'

'How would I know? The last time I was here was about fifteen years ago, when I played under the table with diggers and jeeps.'

The expression on the face of Manager One said he was getting testy. This wasn't the attitude they expected from the family member of a long-serving colleague.

'You applied for a job,' he said. 'You must have an idea what it entails.'

'No.'

'No, what.'

'No, I have no idea,' said Tuk.

'So why did you bother applying,' said Manager Two.

'Because my mother-'

-'Because *mummy* wanted you to apply. Maybe you'd have been better off singing us a song. Hey! Where are you going?'

Tuk found Tod at his favourite pavement restaurant on Khao San Road, the place he freely admitted gave him the best possible selection of foreign eye candy to admire. With one foot, he dragged a stool from under the table and pushed it towards his friend and told him the good news about the gig.

'What do you think?'

'OK,' said Tuk.

'OK? Our first gig on the islands, one of the biggest Full Moon Festival parties in the world? The stuff of travel blogs and TripAdvisor threads by the thousand – not to mention it involves a boat trip, which makes it our first overseas show! This only came up at the last minute, and we got it, so long as we can catch the train south tonight. We're only lucky the other band got fired and my friend here knows the resort owner in Koh Phangan. C'mon, Tuk, am I ever going to get a smile out of you?'

'You wouldn't be smiling if you had to go home and face my mother.'

'Sorry, pal. I should have asked about the interview. Was it as bad as you expected?'

'Worse. A lot worse. Two stuffed shirts who weren't interested in me in the first place, and didn't bother to hide it. I walked out on them. Imagine the loss of face that's going to mean to my mum.'

'Bummer, man. But maybe she'll be happy for you, getting a gig like the Full Moon Party. It might be the start of something big for us. You never know who might hire us after this. This could lead to an expansion of our professional horizons.'

Tuk squinted at his friend, suspicious. 'What do you mean? Oh no, don't tell me-'

'Don't be like that, man. We can't play the blues all day every day.'

'Disguised behind all the excitement about a gig for drunk foreigners, you've signed us up to play covers?'

The downcast shift in Tod's expression told him he was right.

'You know how much I hate covers! Hotel California and Country Roads and the greatest hits of U2 and the Carpenters. My worst ever day just got worse. I'm off.'

'I'll see you at the station, right? You'll be there, seven o'clock?'

Tuk paused to put his guitar case on his back.

'I'll be there. It'll get me away from my poor mother. Twenty-seven years she's worked at her company, for what?

13

Like everything else she ever did, she did it for me. This is how I reward her, and just when I feel like I've sunk to a new low, you present me with a covers gig.'

'Lighten up, man. There's always tomorrow - and a full moon gig on the lovely party island of Koh Phangan. And don't forget it'll be heaving with nice foreign ass, you wait and see.'

As he watched his friend walk away disconsolate, his gaze fell upon two European girls who had been watching them with interest. He plucked his beer from the table and walked over to join them. So what if he wasn't invited. One of them seemed to have blood on her shirt.

Uncle Mu pulled to a halt in front of the office tower Tuk knew so well, even though he hadn't gone inside since his mother routinely brought him along on school holidays to spend time being spoiled by her colleagues. The uniformed security man at the elevator lobby desk smiled and waved him past. This was an old-fashioned company whose employees, like his mother, often remained on the workforce for years, so it was quite possible that he recognised Tuk.

The matronly woman at the reception desk on the seventeenth floor certainly knew him. When he began to tell her who he was and why he was here, she squealed in excitement.

'I know exactly who you are, young man,' she said. 'We haven't had the pleasure of a visit from you for a very long time. I see you brought your guitar.'

'I have an audition later,' said Tuk.

'Of course you do. I will take you to the interview room. It's good that you are punctual. Our managers take timekeeping very seriously - but I bet your mum told you that. Maybe you would like to leave your guitar here with me....?'

Tuk stared at her blankly.

'Perhaps not,' she said. 'This way, young man.'

Tuk knew the room well. As a child he had spent many hours playing at what they rather grandly called the boardroom table. Back then, an impressive selection of toys waited in a cupboard for visiting kids to keep themselves entertained while mum or dad went about their business, and Tuk recalled using pamphlets and folders to create construction sites and quarries for a fleet of diggers and jeeps. Today he was left to browse a whiteboard filled with overlapping graphs and marketing gibberish. On either side of the board were motivational posters and stiff portraits of staff groups trying to look interested. As far as Tuk could make out, most of them were having to fake their enthusiasm. A long shelf groaned under the weight of matching files and printed materials that doubtless served to assist staff in living up to the happy clappy bullshit on the posters that assaulted their vision whenever they looked up from the table.

Two managers arrived unannounced and sat across the table from Tuk. They wore suits of an identical company blue with embossed name badges high on their left lapels. Maybe the badges allowed them to bypass normal courtesies and relieve them of any need to introduce themselves. Eyes down, they read through some pages of A4 that Tuk assumed was his own work history. The slightly more senior man spoke first:

'Your CV is, well, interesting,' said Manager One.

'Thank you,' said Tuk.

'A little thin,' said the manager.

'Mother said to keep it relevant.'

'Ah yes,' said Manager Two. 'Your mother has been a faithful servant to the company since before our time.' The two men exchanged inquisitive glances as convincing as the efforts of daytime soap opera actors. 'How long? Twelve years? Fifteen?'

'Twenty-seven years,' said Tuk, feeling foolish. They didn't want an answer.

'I beg your pardon,' said Manager One.

'Twenty-seven years. In November. My mother has worked for this company for nearly twenty-seven years.'

'That's nice,' said Manager Two, looking down at the CV. 'You graduated with a degree in business studies, let me see, seven years ago.'

'Six-and-a-half,' said Tuk.

'Six-and-a-half. Yes. Maybe you can tell us more about what you have been doing for those, ahem, six-and-a-half years. It says here "self-employed".'

'I think you'll see that it says self-employed musician.'

'You take that work seriously.'

'I do. It is very important to me.'

Manager Two gestured towards Tuk's guitar case, propped against the wall behind him. 'I see you brought your guitar,' he said. 'Are you going to play us a song?'

'No,' said Tuk.

'I was joking,' said the manager.

'I wasn't.'

The other man tried to fill the awkward silence.

'If we could just get back to the reason for the interview. How about you tell us why you think you would be a good fit for our marketing department?'

'How would I know? The last time I was here was about fifteen years ago, when I played under the table with diggers and jeeps.'

The expression on the face of Manager One said he was getting testy. This wasn't the attitude they expected from the family member of a long-serving colleague.

'You applied for a job,' he said. 'You must have an idea what it entails.'

'No.'

'No, what.'

'No, I have no idea,' said Tuk.

'So why did you bother applying for the job,' said Manager Two.

'Because my mother-'

-'Because mummy wanted you to apply. Maybe you'd have been better off singing us a song. Hey! Where are you going?'

Tuk found Tod at his favourite pavement restaurant on Khao San Road, the place he freely admitted gave him the best possible selection of foreign eye candy to admire. With one foot, he dragged a stool from under the table and pushed it towards his friend and told him the good news about the gig.

'What do you think of that, then?'

'Pretty good,' said Tuk.

'Pretty good? Our first gig on the islands, one of the biggest Full Moon Festival parties in the world? The stuff of travel blogs and TripAdvisor threads by the thousand – not to mention it involves a boat trip, which makes it our first overseas gig! This only came up at the very last minute, and we got it. We're only lucky the other band got fired and my friend here knows the resort owner in Koh Phangan. Fuckit Tuk, am I ever going to get a smile out of you?'

'You wouldn't be smiling if you had to go home and face my mother.'

'Sorry, pal. I should have asked. You weren't looking forward to that interview. Was it as bad as you expected?'

'Worse. A lot worse. Two stuffed shirt managers who weren't interested in me in the first place, and didn't bother to hide it. I walked out on them. Now imagine the loss of face that's going to mean to my mum.'

'Bummer, man. But maybe she'll be happy for you, getting a gig like the Full Moon Party. It might be the start of something big for us. You never know who might hire us after this. This could lead to an expansion of our professional horizons.'

Tuk squinted at his friend, suspicious. 'What does that mean? Oh no, don't tell me-'

'Don't be like that, man. We can't play the blues all day every fuckin' day.'

'Disguised behind all the excitement about a gig for drunk foreigners, you've signed us up to play covers?'

The downcast shift in Tod's expression told him he was right.

'You know how much I hate covers! Hotel California and Country Roads and the greatest hits of U2 and the Carpenters. My worst ever day just got worse. I'm off.'

'I'll see you at the station, right? You'll be there, seven o'clock?'

Tuk paused to put his guitar case on his back.

'I'll be there. It'll get me away from my poor mother. Twenty-seven years she's worked there, for what? Like everything else she ever did, she did it for me. This is how I reward her, and just when I feel like I've sunk to a new low, you present me with a covers gig.'

'Lighten up, man. There's always tomorrow - and a full moon party on the lovely party island of Koh Phangan to look forward to. And don't forget it'll be heaving with nice foreign ass, you wait and see.'

As he watched his friend walk away looking disconsolate, his gaze fell upon two European girls who had been watching them with interest. He plucked his beer from the table and walked over to join them. So what if he wasn't invited. One of them seemed to have blood on her shirt.

Three

Tod was right about the power of the Koh Phangan Full Moon Party to attract tourists by the thousands. The setting of a best-selling novel that spawned a hit movie featuring Leonardo di Caprio meant awareness of the island among young travellers exploded. Never mind the movie was filmed on a different island, hundreds of kilometres away.

With their home already a magnet to movie fans and a hot internet topic, Koh Phangan islanders played a master marketing stroke by making it **the** place to hang out at Full Moon parties. To the delight of its hospitality sector, the island now had the equivalent of twelve extra New Year's Eves attracting hundreds, sometimes thousands, of extra visitors to the island, full houses so predictably regular you could set your lunar calendar by them.

From a stage crafted from bamboo above the high-water mark on the soft sandy beach, Tuk and the band worked their way through a set heavy on rock and roll and, whenever possible, Chicago and Texas electric blues. Tod had managed to persuade the organisers that *City Limits* were the wrong band to deliver slushy pop shit, so they got away with a promise to keep things moving at a tempo to encourage a lot of jumping around – which sold hundreds of extra drinks served up from huge vats of ice at premium Full Moon prices.

The beach in front of the stage, all the way to the surf and beyond, was filled with lithe young partygoers of every skin tone imaginable, from Scandinavian blonde pale to what Tuk imagined might be Brazilian ebony of African origin. From centre stage, playing to every pretty girl in the noisy crowd, Tod did plenty of Jagger-esque strutting and writhing of his own. Tuk adopted his usual stance, off to one side, restrained in his body language, only letting himself go just a little when he launched into spirited solos inspired by the work of guitar heroes like Stevie Ray Vaughan, Buddy Guy, Albert Collins and Gary Moore, every one drawing screams of appreciation from people all over the beach who wouldn't recognise the names or the music of any one of his heroes.

Immediately in front of Tod, Jo and Dani kicked sand high as they jived, barefoot, Dani's eyes fixed on the singer. At the pavement café on Khao San Road the day before, Tuk barely noticed them while listening to Tod trying to justify moving the band into more mainstream music gigs. But when his friend arrived at the train station a few hours later with two pretty European girls in tow, even he was amazed at Tod's ability to charm the birds off the trees. Seats in different parts of the train and changes to buses and a busy ferry meant they hardly crossed paths over the course of the journey, but when *City Limits* took to the stage, there they were. Now, Tuk couldn't help but notice Jo was spending much of her time staring at him. He watched an exchange of words inspire fits of giggles. If he was able to lip-read English, he might have shared their glee.

'How often do you think he gets to sleep on his own,' said Dani, eyes fixed on Tod.

'He'll get no sleep tonight if you can help it,' said Jo. 'Horny cow.'

'It was his idea we came all the way here, so I say he's up for it. Let's sink a few more sherbets and see what happens. Forget our troubles, seize the day.'

Jo laughed out loud. 'Seize the singer in the tight jeans, you mean.'

'The big guy on guitar might not know what's hit him,' said Dani. 'Tod says his name's Tuk. Quiet, but a lovely bloke. He does seem kinda shy. Hey! Maybe he's a virgin. You might pluck yourself a little Thai cherry!'

A few hours later, the island was at last going quiet, except for the drunken chant coming from the beach hut attached to the oceanside balcony occupied by Tuk and Jo. The whole hut shook to the rhythm of Tod marking time with 'Go! Jonny go! Jonny go!' to accompanying squeals from Dani and squeaks from a cheap mattress. The rhythm took hold of the beach hut, setting the oversized hammock swinging like a metronome lagging just behind the beat of their friends' lovemaking.

'Your name is Tuk?' said Jo, twirling her fingertip on her hammock partner's chest. It was as soft and hairless as a baby's bum.

'Yes, Tuk. My short name. Thai names are very long, so we have short name. Mine is Tuk.'

'Does it have a meaning?'

'Meaning,' said Tuk. 'No meaning. Some Thai names have meaning, some are English words. Like Golf or Beer or Fast.'

'My name is Jo.'

'Joe?'

'Yes, Jo.'

'Same as Joe Cocker?'

'Who is Joe Cocker,' said Jo.

'Famous singer,' said Tuk. 'Old guy – no, dead guy.'

'Never heard of him.'

'Yes, you are too young.'

'Not much younger than you,' said Jo.

'My father liked Joe Cocker. Had many, how do you say, LPs?'

'Records? Actual vinyl? My dad has a couple of hundred of those. No wonder I never heard of the guy. You don't have a girlfriend?'

Tuk was instantly uncomfortable. 'Yes,' he said.

'Yes, you have a girlfriend?'

'No.'

'No, you don't have a girlfriend?' Orientals were weird.

'Yes, I have no girlfriend,' said Tuk, who was taken by surprise by Jo clasping his face between her palms and kissing him passionately.

At last, Jo felt him relax. Maybe he was just shy. Maybe he was a virgin? She gently prised her way out of her T-shirt. Tuk gazed curiously at the gauze dressing on her breast.

'Tattoo?'

Jo wondered if he could see her blush.

'Dani and I got drunk in Bangkok.'

'Got drunk and got a new tattoo?'

Now she was definitely blushing at their collective madness.

'I know,' she said, 'stupid, eh? I was so drunk I didn't remember til I woke up and found this.'

She gently peeled the gauze away. Tuk's eyes went to her breast, which she couldn't see because she was lying back on the hammock. She hoped he liked what he saw.

'*Scottish*,' said Tuk, '*and* – what means *P-R-U-O-D*?'

Four

Tuk and Jo stood atop a ramshackle pontoon attached to a temple on the bank of the Chao Phraya river. Only a few miles to the south, the Chao Phraya met the Gulf of Thailand at a rate of millions of tonnes per minute, waters collected from as far away as Myanmar and Western China. In downtown Bangkok, it flowed relentlessly, milky brown with silt and thick with vegetation and fish life.

Behind them the river served as a major highway, thrumming with traffic from flimsy rowboats to strings of hulking barges low in the water from huge payloads of timber going south or sand or gravel or other construction materials crawling inland. With astonishing skill and precision, little pilot craft front and rear helped thread lines of barges through the arches of bridges crossing the river at odd angles and irregular intervals. River cowboys at the controls of long-tail speedboats powered by roaring reconditioned truck engines balanced above their sterns wove through traffic with skillful abandon.

Tuk and Jo fed stale bread to a swarm of fish, gaping maws stretched to breaking point as if their lives depended on one last lump of dough. Beside them on the pontoon, tourists and Bangkok locals did the same.

'This would never happen in Glasgow,' said Jo.

'Why?'

'All those big fish, nobody trying to catch them? In Glasgow they'd be gone in a minute.'

'I don't understand,' said Tuk. He was getting used to not understanding Jo.

'Some tyke would come along with a stick of dynamite or a grenade. Boom! Whoosh! Cheap fish at the barras – the market stalls.' She saw the horrified expression on Tuk's face as, thanks to arm movements to illustrate explosions he got the gist of what she had just said.

'Only kidding!' she said. 'But the banks of the river would be filled with folk wearing dodgy waistcoats full of pockets and bad hats and waders, waving fishing rods.'

'We feed the fish to make merit from the spirits. Also, big university nearby, parents come to wish for luck for their children to get good job when they graduate. My mother came here many times.'

'Did it work?'

'She still prays for me to get a good job.'

Jo put her hand on Tuk's arm. He did his best not to flinch, which amused her. Open shows of affection, especially with a foreigner, were frowned upon, and she enjoyed teasing him.

'I get the same shit from my parents. "*When are you going to get a proper job? When are you going to do something with your life?*" My dad says I should be like him, an entrepreneur, go into business. Do something with myself.'

'Difficult for me too. My mother is so disappointed. I try to tell her I am happy to play the blues. It was what my father

26

wanted - it is what I want. She cannot understand. Tells me "*You never make money, you will never be happy.*"'

'Maybe we can show them,' said Jo.

'What do you mean?'

'I have an idea,' she said. 'Let's talk about it tonight.'

Saxophone Pub had occupied the same premises on a lane outside the huge Victory Monument interchange for nearly thirty years, and enjoyed a well-earned reputation for putting on quality live music nightly. With the centre of the upstairs floor taken away, the ground floor stage, walls and pillars peppered with time-tarnished saxophones and trumpets set into brick, could be viewed from an upstairs balcony on all four sides.

The effect was of both spaciousness and intimacy. A table-level counter on the lower floor defined the edge of the stage, creating the most prized seats in the house only inches from where performers worked their magic. Music varied from acoustic solo artists through pop/disco/big band, traditional jazz and even ska/reggae, with the late Friday night slot reserved for T-Bone, a band whose reputation was so established throughout Thailand they drew their own midnight audience shift change. New arrivals piled in to savour the sight and sounds of a tightly-rehearsed ten-piece ensemble, Jamaican colours and dreadlocks and all, who shook the building to its foundations with the rhythms of the Caribbean. All this was delivered amidst a distinct hint of herbal aromas inextricably associated with the region and its most famous musical exports, even though many of the songs were originals and delivered in Thai.

But the week's prime slot, Friday evening from 9 to 11, had been occupied for the past two years by *City Limits*, who attracted their own loyal fanbase, many of them office-workers who celebrated the end of their week with food and drinks and powerful blues-rock from Tod, Tuk and their two-man rhythm section. The band worked hard and rehearsed often to give the audience variety in their playlists. Sure, there were old faithful, familiar blues covers that never failed to draw applause from the crowd (think: Stevie Ray Vaughan, Albert King, BB King, Chuck Berry and Willie Dixon), but they came interspersed with songs from acts like the Stones, Elvis Presley, Buddy Guy and even the Kinks and Santana. Three, forty-minute sets went by quickly, and bums stayed in seats and drinks and food courses were regularly replenished throughout. Saxophone's management loved *City Limits* almost as much as they loved T-Bone.

During their first set, Tuk twice caught glares from Tod. He was distracted, wondering what Jo was doing prowling the ground floor, talking to managers, examining and taking notes from the menu, and openly counting things. People, tables, drinks, meals, everything noted down. In the short breaks between sets, she was nowhere to be seen, and only after they finished for the evening and while T-Bone's roadies engaged in the difficult task of rapidly setting up for a ten-piece band was Tuk able to track her down. Outside in an area normally occupied by smokers, flicking through her notebook, tallying totals, writing herself memos.

At a table on the open-air food court below a circular walkway teeming with pedestrians going to and from the elevated BTS train station, Tuk picked contentedly at a ferociously spicy *som-tam* seafood salad while Jo drank beer to try and put out the fire from one small taste of it. Between slurps of Chang and sharp intakes of breath she bombarded him with questions covering every imaginable aspect of a normal week in the gigging life of *City Limits*. Having assessed the evening's business at Saxophone, it was no surprise to her that the band's Friday night gig was the envy of the town's musicians, or that management were delighted with trade drawn by the band. She had done her sums, based on the average price of drinks and food dishes on the menu, and on her calculation of the number of customers in the bar at any given time, and how many drinks the average customer consumed. Dial in guesstimated food sales and a rough cost for staff over the course of the shift, and Saxophone, with the help of *City Limits*, was printing money. The surprise was how little the band received for one of the best gigs in town, especially considering the work took up the whole evening, meaning their fee covered all three sets and had to be divided among the four band members.

'Shite,' she said. 'That's not much.'

'Good money for Bangkok,' said Tuk.

She gestured to her notebook full of scribbles. 'This is exactly what I studied at college,' she said. 'Customer numbers, rate of consumption of drinks and foods, estimated hourly revenue, fixed and variable overheads and day-to-day running costs. I know all about this stuff.'

'You're shitting me!' Tod slammed chopsticks to the table of their favourite Chinatown *kwee tiao* noodle stall that appeared just after dark, set up in the lee of a gold dealership painted traditional gold-dealer red and gold. Tuk sat with his back to bars of hardened steel that would not be out of place in a high security prison. Soup still splashing across the tabletop, Tod was waiting for an answer.

'Nope,' said Tuk. 'It's true. After we left Saxophone last night, she sat me down for an hour and grilled me about life in *City Limits*. I told her our gig at Saxophone was likely to come to an end in the next couple of months. Maybe it's a sign. Time for a change.'

'Big change! And now she wants you to go with her to Glasgow? Where is that, anyway?'

'You're not that dumb,' said Tuk.

'OK, OK, Glasgow, England. Why would you want to go there? You'll freeze your ass off, man. And never mind the shit weather, what about the food? I told you about the time I went to London. Nothing but white bread and grey meat. Fuckin' horrible. Fake Thai restaurants run by Hong Kong Chinese selling sweet and sour shit.'

'I'm not going there for the food.'

'You've no idea how true that will be after you've been there for a couple of weeks. Alright, lucky you. What are you going for? Talk to me, pal.'

'Jo wants to open a bar. A blues bar.'

Tod picked up his chopsticks and gingerly extracted some fine rice noodles from what remained of the broth in his bowl.

'Just like that? She's a backpacker, stays in shit hostels on Khao San Road, eats fried rice and drinks the cheapest beer she can score from the 7-11. Where's she going to find the money to open a blues bar?'

'Her father will help her. He's rich, has property all over the city. He made her go to college to study Hospitality Management so she can help his business expand, make more money from the properties he owns. She knows what she's doing. Says theme bars are hot, and Glasgow's screaming out for a good blues bar - and I'd be her USP.'

'Help me out. What's a USP?'

'Exactly what I said when she first brought it up. Unique Selling Point.'

Tod gave up on his noodles and opted for a long swallow of Chang beer.

'Shit, man, we know you're good, but now you're unique? What's your mother saying to all this?'

'I didn't tell her yet. I haven't decided if I want to do it. There's something else.'

'Something bigger than you moving to England?'

'Scotland.'

'Scotland, England, what's the difference? Hang on. What's the something else?'

'Jo says we should get engaged to help me get a visa.'

Tod reached for the Chang bottle, discovered it was empty and waved it to the stallholder, who rushed for the ice box. Regular customers like these two were rare, and he made more profit on the beer than the noodles. The big guy wasn't much of a drinker, but his talkative friend more than made up for him.

'I can't believe I'm hearing this,' said Tod, 'and I have only one question. Are you sure this has nothing to do with Pim?'

Five

Tuk used his two keys to open the expensive locks on the flat door. Other doors in the corridor sat behind ugly iron grilles secured with dead bolts and padlocks whose size and faded brass glow would fool no determined housebreaker. His mum and dad swore they would never live in a home behind bars like a prison cell; they paid a friendly uncle to fit door jambs with steel cores and costly Japanese locks in a reinforced teak door with hinges built to withstand a crowbar for long enough to alert neighbours, several of whom were known to keep loaded firearms close to hand.

Despite the relative absence of gun crime, Thai licensing laws were hardly strict; large numbers of weapons sat in private homes all over the country. They also travelled around Thailand in the glove compartments of cars. Road rage was uncommon, partly because in Thai culture, outward shows of anger were frowned upon. But when things went bad, they got very nasty. A recent news report from the northern city of Chiang Mai talked of a European motorcyclist getting into a loud dispute with the Thai driver of a pick-up. The confrontation was brought to an abrupt end at a traffic light when, in front of dozens of witnesses, the pick-up driver shot the motorcyclist dead.

Meticulously maintained locks slid open with little or no noise, and he let himself into the flat. He was ashamed to think it might be better if his mum was not home. He was scared of her reaction to what he had to tell her.

The door was barely closed when his mum gave him a shock by leaping from her room.

'We did it!' she shouted at a volume none of their neighbours could have missed.

'What?', said Tuk, 'we did what?'

'You got the job!'

It broke his heart to see her so happy.

'But those two managers hated me. I walked out on them…'

'Those nobodies only shuffle papers, do interviews for the real bosses. They don't make decisions.'

'I don't understand.'

'**Their** manager makes the decisions. My boss. The manager I have worked with every day for years. He and I – well, I've been meaning to tell you, son-'

'Mum-'

'I told you about him many times, Khun-'

'-Mum-'

'-Khun Jiraporn is a nice man. Divorced, but a lovely man. He and I-'

'Mum! I'm going to Scotland. Jo and I are getting engaged, and we are going to open a blues bar in Glasgow.'

He knew exactly what was going to happen now, and he couldn't blame her. Through uncontrollable sobs, hands held up to her face, her voice shook with emotion.

'You embarrass me at my own office. Then you sneak off to the islands for another of your "gigs" and I hardly see you for days. Now Khun Jiraporn tries to give you a real chance at a steady career even after you messed up the interview - and you want to marry a foreigner and run away to play your blues in another country? I lost your father to that life! What about me? I'm your mother!'

'I appreciate what you and Khun, Khun-'

'-Khun Jiraporn. He and I-'

'-Khun Jiraporn. I appreciate what he did, and what you did for me, but I don't **want** to work in an office. I'm not running away. Not right now, anyway. We're only talking about getting married, nothing is decided, but it could help me get a visa for the UK. She's a lovely girl, mum. Please come and meet her. I told her all about you. She wants you both to be friends, and so do I. Please.'

Still wearing his guitar on his back, he left the flat. He carefully closed and double-locked the door behind him, but it didn't block out the sound of his mum's cries.

The last thing she said before he picked up his guitar cut him to the bone.

'How different things would be for us if you hadn't driven Pim away.'

Six

Two hours later, he was back, slumped on the sofa in the living room, conscious of how empty the flat felt without his mum there. He had crept home dreading the confrontation that surely awaited his return, but she was gone. She had an older sister near Sukhumvit who owned a hardware store that required his aunt's attention sixteen hours a day. To spend time with her, his mum had to sit on a stool behind the counter and share her sister with a never-ending stream of customers in need of any one of a thousand items kept in tattered cardboard boxes on overhanging shelves. Even as a child, Tuk dreaded visits to aunty.

Maybe she was with Khun Jiraporn. A divorcee, mum had said, but a nice man. Was she trying to tell him something about her manager friend before he blurted out the news that he and Jo were moving to the other side of the world? Mum had been alone for far too long. He hoped she had found someone to be with, and not just because it would make his departure so much easier.

The sofa faced an old clunky TV and the wall with the photographs telling the story of Tuk's family's life. Mum and

Dad's wedding photo with the crooked tie and awkward expressions; Mum proudly showing off her blossoming pregnancy – and a few months later, even more proudly showing off their infant son. Tuk growing over the years in mum's arms and on his dad's knee, short arms trying to negotiate the necks of a succession of guitars. And dad with the same Gibson ES335 Tuk carried everywhere.

The Gibson's arrival was a cherished memory rendered pin-sharp and in astonishing detail thanks to featuring in a dream that had graced his sleep a thousand times.

The sofa he sprawled across today was new, soft and comfortable, unlike the old one, whose sharp-cornered vinyl cushions stuck to his legs while he anxiously awaited the return of his dad.

It was eighteen years ago, which meant Tuk was about nine. Knowing what his dad was bringing home, he hadn't left the sofa or taken his eyes from the house door since he came back from school. When his young ears recognized the footsteps in the corridor outside, he sprinted to open the door even as his dad tried to insert a key into the lock. Tuk's heart sank. Apart from keys and the usual battered music case he always carried, his dad's arms were empty.

'You didn't get it?' He was crestfallen.

'Get what?' said his dad. The sparkle in his eyes gave the game away. Tuk pushed past to see along the corridor. There, a cardboard guitar case, leaning against the outside wall of the flat. His dad ruffled his hair with one hand while with the other he reached for the box.

'Is it really the Gibson ES335?'

'It sure is.'

'The BB King replica ES335?'

'Shall we open it and see?'

'Can I open it? Can I?'

'How about we do it together?'

Tuk remembered turning back to face the kitchen alcove, with its cheap furnishings and second-hand pots and pans. From behind a beaded curtain, his mother's expression shared none of their happiness.

Only now, all these years later, did it even occur to Tuk to wonder whether she was angered by the arrival of an expensive new instrument they could ill afford, or envious of how close a relationship he enjoyed with his father. Now, the love of her life had been gone for seventeen years and Tuk spent more time with the Gibson than he did with her. And today's news only made things worse. Of course she was right. If Pim was still in his life, things would be different. But what was the point of fixating on things he could never change?

On impulse, he reached into the back of a drawer full of bills and papers and came out with a 5x7 colour photo in a cheap plastic frame. Tuk and Pim, quite formally dressed for the wedding of Tuk's cousin, the son of the aunty with the Sukhumvit hardware store, who was now a telecoms engineer in Canada. In the picture they stood holding hands, body language speaking of comfort and no small amount of joy. A couple, their relationship so firmly established it earned a spot on the family photo wall. The photo had occupied the same space for years until Tuk finally removed it and stuffed it in the back of the drawer.

After his dad died, Tuk suffered the last eighteen months of elementary school in silence that would have been solitary were it not for the persistence of Tod. His friend stuck by his side, at first striving to bring him some cheer, later realising all he could do was be there for him. Grief followed Tuk like a cloud. It initially kept people away, only to present openings to one or two thugs happy to generate laughs at his expense. Any perception of fun based on the manner of Tuk's father's death ended abruptly when Tod earned a two-week suspension for knocking out four front teeth of a bully called Beer. The bully made a big deal of being an expert practitioner of Muay Thai, so when he refused to leave Tuk alone, Tod feinted a textbook front kick that Beer easily blocked to protect his midriff; even as he did so, Tod transformed the strike into a Tae Kwon-do front snap kick that buried the ball of his foot in the thug's mouth. From then on, Beer and his new implants swerved to the other side of corridors to avoid crossing paths with Tuk or Tod.

The move to lower secondary school saw Tod push his friend towards group activities, where the most obvious one, a guitar club, was an instant success. He and Tuk never missed Wednesday lunchtime sessions where enthusiasts would share chord sheets and licks and lessons and cassette tapes made from the radio, and where Tod often put guitar aside and worked on his vocal skills. Unknown to them at the time, they were laying the foundations for *City Limits*.

One Thursday morning during breakfast, the telephone rang. Tuk's mother answered and passed the handset on its long curly cord to her son before she headed for the door, where she waved goodbye; downstairs, Uncle Mu would be waiting to take her to work.

'Tuk?' said Tod.

'Who else could it be?'

'Funny,' said Tod. 'Bring your guitar today. Special club meeting.'

'What do you mean special?' But the line was already dead; Tod could talk all day without pausing for breath, but the moment he considered a conversation over, it was done. Tuk finished breakfast and went to his room to collect his old Yamaha acoustic, still in its soft case from yesterday's club meeting. On the way he passed a mirror where he caught a glimpse of himself smiling. Not a common sight, it could easily be explained by anything to do with guitars.

At school, it was obvious Tod was up to something. In the playground before the morning bell, he was nowhere to be seen, and during the morning break he pointed to his stomach and ran to the toilets. When at last the science teacher wrapped up a solid hour of pre-lunch tedium, they went together to the classroom where Wednesday guitar club meetings took place. Except this was Thursday. Tod waved Tuk through the open door to find, instead of four or five club members trying to get another week's use out of worn-out strings, there sat one pretty girl on a desk, legs swinging. Leaning against next to her was a gleaming new Tanglewood parlour guitar. Even its strings had the shine that spoke of never having been played.

'This is Pim,' said Tod. 'Pim, meet Tuk. Tuk is the guitar teacher I told you about.' Pim greeted him with a polite *wai*, which he instinctively returned.

When he eventually got over the shock of Tod's transparent scheme to get him to break out of his shell, Tuk couldn't believe his luck. Pim was beautiful, was serious

39

about wanting to learn guitar, and perfectly happy to spend time with Tuk in order to achieve that. At first, shyness on both sides kept things rather formal, but Pim gradually became more open to chit-chat, something Tuk had never developed a talent for. How lucky could he be? He not only found a female friend whose company he enjoyed, but her rich doctor dad paid him for her guitar lessons.

Money for guitar tuition dried up the moment Pim told her father Tuk was her new boyfriend, but it did nothing to cool a relationship that remained steady throughout the rest of their school years. All the way to the end of upper secondary they spent so much time together that friends often reached for the old cliché about them being joined at the hip. Tuk's mother was giddy with happiness, even if she quietly worried about how Pim came from such a different social class. To avoid tempting fate she never expressed such thoughts, but still she feared it couldn't last.

Mum was eventually proven right. Towards the end of their final school year, Tuk only agreed to attend university to study business because the two women in his life insisted music could never provide for him (let alone, whisper it quietly, for them both; at the ripe old age of eighteen, the teenage lovers were convinced they would spend their lives together). Pim was going to one of the capital's most prestigious universities to study medicine; Tuk barely scraped into a third-tier college business studies course, and during increasingly heated discussions, he openly declared university was a pointless stop-gap which would change nothing. He **was** going to be a musician; he **was** going to live his dad's dream. Pim's response, blurted out in the heat of the moment, sounded the death knell for their relationship:

'Because that worked out so well for him?'

Seven

Adhere the 13th Blues Bar, Bangkok.

Adhere the 13th was a one-of-a-kind establishment, odd in the way it was loved by Thais and foreigners alike and owned and operated by a couple from different parts of Thailand. Nong took care of the bar while her partner Pong, who was an astonishingly good guitarist, concentrated on playing and choosing the music that drew the customers and generated the online reviews praising it as the most welcoming music bar anyone ever visited. Even before the days of the internet, its reputation had spread, mostly by word of mouth via backpackers staying on nearby Khao San Road. Lately, thanks to Tripadvisor and other online review sites, its name had gone viral. 'Best small blues bar in the world', one Canadian blogger declared in a post later picked up and regurgitated all over the metaverse.

For reasons unknown, the Canadian's confident assertion drew a lot of attention in Korea, which helped add to a flood of visitors from South Korea and a subsequent torrent of Korean-language posts on travel review sites.

Tonight, evidence of the bar's popularity south of the 38th Parallel took the form of a skinny arrival in torn jeans and a sleeveless top showing off clumsy tattoos. Visitors to Adhere who wanted to join in the performances usually asked band leader Pong for permission, which was seldom refused; the Korean skipped formalities and, to the bemusement of the crowded bar, he unfolded a hinged rectangle of wood about the size of an attaché case, placed it none too gently on the floor in the narrow aisle between Pong on guitar and Tuk's mother's table (which tonight she shared with Khun Jiraporn) - and proceeded to perform a tap routine on his personal dance floor. What he lacked in technique he more than compensated for with enthusiasm, and he instantly had the support and encouragement of the entire bar, band-leader Pong included.

The sense of community that bound the bar and its many regulars meant cakes with candles burning were an almost daily feature of the aisle where the Korean danced. Special occasions in an open venue saw mixtures of partygoers and total strangers embrace celebrations; usually they were birthdays, but tonight was something a little out of the ordinary, even by Adhere's standards, being Tuk and Jo's informal engagement party – complete with a congratulatory cake on the bar top. From wobbly tall stools on either side of the fast-disappearing cake, Tuk and Jo fed each other sticky mouthfuls while Tod hovered around them with a compact video camera, so close he was in danger of getting cake on the lens.

He turned the camera to English Phil, a bar fixture whose gravelly voice led the house band, and who sidled up to the happy couple. He flapped a hand in the direction of the camera. 'Bugger off, Tod,' he said. 'You know I hate having my picture taken.'

Of course he knew. 'It's video, Phil,' he said.

Phil turned to Tuk and Jo:

'Do you have any fooking idea how lucky you are?' he said.

'I know,' said Tuk.

'Not you, ya daft sod. You, Jo. Do you have **any** idea how lucky you are? Do you have a fooking inkling how great a musician this fooking kid is? I love him like a fooking brother, like a fooking brother.'

Jo pointed to the cake, symbol of tonight's celebration.

'You can't have him, he's all mine, Phil-'

'-This fooking guy could get a gig anywhere in the world.'

'You don't have to tell me, Phil.'

'What's he going to do in fooking Glasgow?'

His speech was slurred and he obviously was having trouble concentrating, losing the thread mid-sentence, but he eventually went on:

'Mind you, Gallagher's dead, and Gary Moore's gone. No, hang on, they were fooking Irish. Alex Harvey and Gerry Rafferty, they were Scottish. So there might be a space in the market.'

'Dead,' said Jo, her face a picture of disbelief. 'Liam Gallagher's dead?'

Phil failed to spot her distress.

'So back to my question. What's he going to do in Glasgow?'

'Liam Gallagher's dead?'

A waitress with a tray full of drinks ducked effortlessly under Phil's arm as he waved it at the crowded bar.

43

'I mean,' said Phil, 'is there anywhere near as good as Adhere in Glasgow for Tuk to show his talents? I very much doubt it.'

Tuk waited. This was Jo's moment, and she had news they hadn't yet shared with his friends in Adhere.

'We're way ahead of you, Phil,' she said. 'Exactly what we're thinking about.' When Phil's expression remained blank, she went on: 'We have a great idea for when Tuk gets to Glasgow. You'll love it.' She turned to Tuk. 'He doesn't know yet, does he?'

Tuk intercepted three fresh bottles of Singha coming over the bar from Pong's partner Nong. He gave one to Jo, another to Phil, and they clinked bottle necks. 'Exciting idea, Phil, he said. It's the reason we go to Glasgow.'

Phil held up the fresh bottle as if he couldn't remember it arriving.

'What are you on about?'

'We're going to open a New Adhere Bar in Glasgow,' said Jo, triumphant.

Phil wasn't so drunk he couldn't see the hole in the plan.

'Where will you get the money to do that?' he said.

'My dad's loaded. He'll invest in it for me. I'm his blue-eyed girl.'

Phil still wasn't convinced. 'Your eyes are fooking green, love. And who the fook's Liam Gallagher?'

Eight

Even from inside the flat where he had lived his whole life, Tuk would hear Tod before he arrived, so distinctive was his car's exhaust note. From street level, where he perched now on an old Samsonite suitcase given to him by Phil (*'too fooking heavy for me now, so you might as well tek it, lad,'*) he couldn't possibly miss Tod turning in from Yaowarat.

This was it. After nearly six months of frustration and mistakes and bureaucratic delays, he was about to take what he knew was the biggest step of his young life. Anticipation of the unknown was a real buzz. Thinking about it made him feel good. On the flipside, it also scared him shitless.

They knew by now Jo had messed up by not remaining in Bangkok long enough to simplify the process for getting Tuk into the UK. Wealthy countries don't make it easy for citizens of poorer nations to get past the gates. She had somehow assumed being engaged to Tuk would make securing a visa a relatively straightforward process. Hell, she had a British passport, right? Not so. The first thing they should have done was go together to the office off Sukhumvit where visa applications were received and vetted. The issuance of visas used to be the responsibility of the British Embassy, until someone spotted a way to further monetise the process by allowing private enterprise to step in. Sure, prices soared, but diplomats' days were no longer spent dealing with Thais. Instead, locals hired for their English skills did the interviewing, shuffled the papers, processed the fees – and, all things being in line, issued the visas. If Jo and Tuk had lodged an application together (all it would have taken was a letter from Jo attesting to Tuk's plan to spend his time in Glasgow based at Jo's home address), the stamp would have graced his passport long ago. As it was, endless hours were spent battling their own private language barrier while they sorted out the paperwork Jo had to provide, and what Tuk had to do with it. Weeks turned into months. The sponsor letter Jo eventually sent disappeared in the post, meaning she had to send another one, this time by way of a document forwarding company that, at considerable expense, provided online tracking to ensure it had a chance of arriving at Tuk's home in Chinatown.

After she returned to Scotland, much anticipated video chats started out nightly but soon fell away in urgency and frequency – and warmth – until before long they talked at most once a week. The pleasure with which they conversed together in Thailand, alloyed as it was with sexual tension (Tuk had never had such a wild time with a woman as he did with Jo when they were together in Bangkok) was impossible to recapture on video chats. Jo was increasingly resentful of confusion created by Tuk having to talk in a second language, never mind he hadn't studied it other than by rote learning lyrics to blues songs. And she seldom managed to avoid raging at bureaucratic delays created by her own casual approach to helping secure the visa for Tuk. Worse, she seemed to place the blame for delays squarely at his door.

Early conversations turned with enthusiasm to Jo's plans for the new Adhere Bar in Glasgow. She shared sketches made by a graphic artist friend to illustrate how Jo imagined the new bar would be, drawings put together based on digital photographs of the exteriors and interiors of premises Jo visited. Real estate agents tolerated repeat visits and interior photographs from every angle because they knew all about the detailed needs of business proposals clients like Jo would have to present to banks to secure funding. What they didn't know was Jo had never spoken to anyone at any bank; the only person she needed to convince of the proposal's viability was her dad, and he was loaded. Tuk commented on the drawings and listened to grand plans, filled with excitement but frustrated not to be able to offer anything to help make it happen.

Meanwhile, his mum had gone silent, but friends, Tod included, kept asking how plans for the new bar were coming along. In truth, he didn't know.

City Limits held onto their Saxophone Pub gig for a few months longer than anticipated when the lead singer of a Chiang Mai band who were supposed to be replacing them had a hellish motorcycle accident that put him in Intensive Care for weeks and set him up for months of rehab before he could think about returning to performing. A bad break for the singer and his band, but a good one for *City Limits*, and in truth, not an unusual set of circumstances in a country where road accidents, often involving motorcycles, were a leading cause of death among young Thais. Tuk knew another fine blues musician who had nearly died in two different motorcycle crashes. Both times, fund-raising concerts attracted fellow musicians and music fans who dipped into their pockets to meet medical bills. And that guy could count himself lucky. In the last few years alone, three good friends of Tuk's had died on the roads.

The weeks passed faster than he had thought possible, even if he had to endure total silence when he got back to the home he shared with his mother. If she was home, she stayed in her room, and by the time he woke in the morning, she was gone to work. Not a word shared. If they crossed paths in the living room, greetings were cordial, but brief, enquiries dealt with in the fewest number of words practicable. He started coming home as late as possible to increase the likelihood she would be asleep.

Tod lent a sympathetic ear to reports of his friend's misery and came up with the idea of buying some new cupboard units to replace the shabby furnishings that had been in their kitchen alcove since before Tuk's dad died. Tod drove them to IKEA, where they eventually found examples of kitchen cabinets with weird Scandinavian names and directions to faraway industrial shelving where unassembled flat packs of the same units hid, sometimes so far beyond their reach they had to bring in a professional with a battery-powered forklift. Tuk stood feeling useless while his friend located the kitchen department, tracked down flatpack-laden shelf units, marshalled the forklift troops and got them and their purchases to a broad swathe of cash desks. Situated strategically between the cash desks and the exits were food stalls and cafeterias selling dishes he had never heard of. Tod insisted they had to stop for Swedish meat balls and giant mugs of coffee that he claimed was as good as much of the fare at any downtown Starbucks, at a fraction of the price.

Tuk was sitting at a cafeteria table waiting for Tod to return when his heart skipped a beat at the first time he had set eyes on Pim in five or six years. She was about three tables away, sitting so that he was treated to a profile he had known and loved since the first day she turned up in an empty classroom for guitar lessons. She shared a table with two young children upon whom she lavished motherly care. Also at the table was an older woman Tuk didn't recognise. The way the old dame doted over the kids while regarding Pim's every move with something close to contempt made her a certainty for the mother-in-law role. Tuk wasn't interested in what the stupid woman thought. He couldn't take his eyes off Pim.

Tod was about to pay for the food and coffees when he saw Tuk's eyes lock on a nearby table. He apologised to the nice girl behind the counter and had the food packed and bagged to take away.

When he got to their table, his friend remained frozen in place.

'Let's get outta here,' said Tod. 'Kitchen cabinets to build.'

'She saw me,' said Tuk. 'She saw me for a moment, then looked away and didn't look back.'

'Ancient history, pal,' said Tod, knowing full well he wasn't even close to the truth.

Tod's Beemer was a rat rod sleeper based faithfully on one from Los Angeles spotted on YouTube and built precisely the way he liked it. Tod was famously brash, yet almost universally popular. His parents had been schoolteachers until his dad inherited a fortune in property accumulated by his maternal uncle. Inside a year they had walked away from modest existences as teachers to concentrate on a ready-made empire, which they built up steadily until their portfolio included residential and office and retail premises in some of the most prosperous areas of the capital. Despite their wealth, they remained grounded, and when they absorbed their only son into the management of the empire, they insisted he treat everyone, from company CEOs to garbage collectors, as equals.

It meant he didn't depend upon the modest funds generated from *City Limits,* his share of which he split with Tuk and the ever-changing members in the band's rhythm section. Tuk was at first embarrassed, and although eventually he came around to taking what he saw as more than his share of the band's income, he drew the line at any suggestions from Tod to fund recording studio time for the band to make an album. They were content to perform live for now. Who knew how much that might change, but in any case Tod had developed a pet passion for film-making, and now enjoyed a third career as a director/producer of music videos and music industry short features.

The twenty-year-old 3-series gave the impression of being one tow trip away from the junkyard but was in fact a beast graced with a fortune spent in aftermarket tuning and suspension modifications. The interior, littered with fast food wrappers and squashed energy drink cans, would deter most thieves. The boom of a custom exhaust hiding behind a rusty end pipe rattled shutters on Yaowarat shops. He turned into the side road and blipped the throttle one last time before shutting the engine down in front of where Tuk sat on a suitcase, guitar strapped to his back. Tod glanced up at an apartment window he could pick out from years of visits. Sure enough, Tuk's mum was there, forlorn at the prospect of her only chick fleeing the nest. Tod felt for her, but his concern today was for her son. He leapt out, determined to make this as easy as possible for his friend.

'Yo, man, why the sad face? Ready for the big adventure, right?'

'You saw her. She'd lock me in if she thought it would keep me here.'

'Difficult goodbye, eh?'

He leaned into the car to release the boot and pushed Tuk's suitcase beside a half set of golf clubs and two bags of gym gear; Tod spent a lot of time working out and in martial arts gyms. Tuk got into the passenger seat with his guitar transferred to his lap and paid no attention to the video camera attached to a bracket on the dashboard, wide angle lens set to film him. Tod loved his video projects, and it was impossible to predict when he would next decide to start filming. Tuk reached around for his seatbelt, which came away from the door pillar and fell to the floor. He leaned to the volume control on the stereo, which was playing Albert Collins at a level that shook the car windows. The button came off the stereo and joined the rubbish on the floor. From the side mirror he could see his mum, and even from here he could tell she was crying. Tod threw the car in gear and burnt rubber all the way back out to Yaowarat.

'She didn't make it easy for you, huh?'

'If she was only angry with me, I might be able to understand, but-'

'-she's still pissed off with your dad for dying on you both.'

Tod changed CD. Elmore James played *The Sky is Crying.*

Tuk glanced in the mirror, but the apartment building was long gone.

'Still pissed off, all these years after he died?' Tuk spoke in disbelief.

'I know, man. Some people grieve for a long time, but your Mum, she's like a gibbon, or a termite. Gibbons and termites mate for life, bro'. Whole goddamn life, one partner. Imagine that - wait, maybe that's you, now you're planning on getting married. Anyway. D-Day at last. Been talking to your fiancée? How's she doing?'

'Alright.'

'Alright? Hasn't seen you for six months and you're landing tomorrow, and she's just alright?'

'Talking on the computer isn't easy.'

Tod took his hand off the wheel and his eye off the road to mimic jerking off. The BMW swerved and nearly took out a motorcycle taxi with a pretty girl on the back.

'Skype sex failing to light the fires, huh?'

Tuk shook his head. Even if he was not about to grace the question with an answer, he was going to miss his incorrigible friend.

The grimy shophouses of Chinatown gave way to the shiny offices, condo towers and five-star hotels of Sukhumvit until they sprinted along the elevated highway towards Suvarnabhumi airport. A helicopter might have had trouble matching Tod's average speed, and before long, he pulled into a no stopping zone outside the main terminal building.

'I can't come in, man,' he said. 'I don't do goodbyes.'

'You have to come,' said Tuk. 'I need your help.'

'I can't come to Scotland. I didn't bring my passport - or my raincoat.'

'I don't know what to do,' said Tuk.

'Go to Scotland, be with your girl. Piece of cake.'

Nine

Having never before in his twenty-seven years set foot aboard an airplane, Tuk went on to spend twenty-two hours on two flights connecting three airports, each on a different continent.

Tod relented and came with him to the check-in counter, but only because Tuk really did need help and, Tuk suspected, because he wanted to film his friend up close during his emotional departure. The lovely young woman on the ground staff at the check-in counter seemed to enjoy being the focus of Tod's attention to the extent she had no objection to him flitting around in front of her, video camera capturing everything. Tuk foresaw a pitch for her mobile number in Tod's plans.

The possibility he might not be able to carry his guitar onto the aircraft hadn't even crossed his mind. Before they left the BMW in a short-stay car park, Tod dug from its boot a tattered bag containing his sweaty gym kit and added to it a second pair of sports shoes for a bit of bulk. At the check-in counter Tuk got a hand carry label for the gym bag which they later transferred to the guitar case. He would still have to get it past airline staff at the departure gate and at the door to the aircraft.

Tod kept the video camera running while he advised him to present himself at the gate only when the last call was being made for all remaining passengers for the flight to Dubai. If he met with trouble at the door of the plane, his only hope was to seek out a Thai staff member and turn on the charm. Tod even coached him on entreaties to employ, plaintive pleas easy to memorise since they were true. The guitar **was** Tuk's last remaining possession of his late dad's, and as such it was w-a-y too precious to be crammed in the frigid hold with the checked luggage. That the flight crew would be desperate to avoid a costly late departure could only work in his favour.

It worked. When he finally appeared at the gate, impatient ground staff hustled him across the bridge to the aircraft, where Tuk immediately spotted a stewardess with a Thai flag on her name badge. Even though he wasn't facing resistance to keeping the guitar in the cabin, he sought her out. Without even hearing any pleas, and despite the latecomer holding an Economy boarding pass, she set off to place the guitar in a closet used for the coats of Business Class passengers.

After take-off, when the stewardess found him stuck in a middle seat between two big westerners, she put smiles on all three faces by taking Tuk to an empty aisle seat with plenty of leg room. A few minutes later, his tray table was lowered to receive a Jack Daniels and Coke he hadn't ordered. His wrinkled brow made her laugh behind her hand, the way any proud Thai mum would have taught her.

'You are Tuk,' she said. 'I've seen you play at Saxophone Pub many times.' She raised her chin at the drink on the tray in front of him. 'When people send you a drink, it's always Jack Daniels and Coke.'

She saw Tuk squinting at the long name on her badge. 'Call me Lek,' she said. One of the most common nicknames in Thailand, it meant "Little". Her beautiful figure made Tuk think she must have sprouted after she was given the name. He didn't have the heart to tell her she wouldn't see him playing at Saxophone anymore.

The next time Lek dropped off another unrequested JD & Coke, she also gave him a bottle of water, an eye mask and a pair of earplugs. 'I see you're flying to Glasgow,' she said. 'You'd best try to get some sleep on this flight, because Dubai airport is anything but peaceful.' He thanked her with a respectful palms-together *wai*.

While he sipped at the second drink, he negotiated a dizzying selection of inflight entertainment, donned the eye mask and settled down to sleep to the Rolling Stones classic, *Let It Bleed,* playing softly through the earplugs. That the album was one of his father's all-time favourites meant he nodded off smiling.

When he peeled back the mask the cabin was bathed in harsh light streaming through freshly opened window shades. Lek helped strap his guitar carefully into the empty seat beside him. He felt pressure in his ears which he worked out must mean they were dropping towards Dubai. Lek fingered a bright new label dangling from the case handle.

'You were either very clever or extremely lucky to get this on the aircraft.' She placed a manicured fingernail on the new label. 'You shouldn't have any trouble on the Glasgow flight,' she said.

If he wasn't on his way to join his fiancée in Scotland, Tuk could easily have fallen in love on the spot.

Dubai International was like nothing he had ever seen before. His first experience of Bangkok's Suvarnabhumi airport was an eye-opener, but at least in Bangkok he could stop almost anyone and ask for directions.

Dubai airport felt like it might be ten times the size. He followed moving crowds of passengers up impossibly long escalators and through a security check zone with a line of X-ray machines stretching into the distance. After having to empty his pockets and take off his trouser belt and shoes to send them through the machines on a plastic tray, on the other side of the X-rays he collected his guitar and found a place to regather his composure along with parts of his wardrobe. By allowing himself to be led by the crowd he found a Departures board listing flights to dozens of destinations he had never heard of; the display was being stared at by people from all over the world, many of them in full traditional dress, some bleak and black, others exploding with colour. A fellow traveller wearing a Hawaiian shirt, sun bleached shorts and flip-flops spotted his confusion and volunteered to help. Within seconds he ascertained the gate number for the Emirates flight to Glasgow. He gestured along a corridor of five-metre-tall windows with shiny airliners nosed up to the other side of the glass. 'Thataways,' he said. 'It could be a long walk.'

He was right. Tuk spent twenty minutes at a leisurely stroll before he came to the correct gate, where he found a seat and stared into the post-dawn glow towards a distant city centre dominated by one improbably tall tower soaring from the heat haze like a giant hypodermic.

The Glasgow flight was a little shorter, and with the time broken up by movies even more boring than the inflight meals, it passed quickly. He enjoyed hearing accents reminiscent of Jo's voice and was surprised to see that some of the fellow passengers whose speech pleased his ear were Asian, perhaps of Pakistani or Indian heritage. It further pleased him to think Glasgow might have its share of Asians who, judging by the fluency of their Scottish speech, must have integrated well. He realised it was possible they were born and had grown up in Scotland, and for a moment allowed himself a vision of one or two kids of his and Jo's, growing up fluent in Scots-English and Thai. He had never imagined having kids of his own, and the vision pleased him. Maybe he was growing up. If there was one thing guaranteed to make his mother proud, it would be grandchildren.

People turned to peer out as the jet lost altitude and Tuk moved to a vacant window seat to get a first glimpse of what was to be his new home. It could hardly be less like tropical, jungle-covered Thailand. True, having only flown out of Thailand once in the dead of night, he had never properly seen his homeland from the air, but road trips covering thousands of kilometres had exposed him to the jungle landscape as seen from rural highways traversing mountain ranges in the East and North of the country. There, after the plains devoted mainly to rice, sweet corn and sunflowers receded, hillsides were taken over by nature run amok, dense tropical foliage with few signs of roads or other tracks through the jungle landscape.

Despite being fatigued to the point of dozing off, he was fascinated by what he saw of Scotland in the final half hour on approach to Glasgow. Farmed fields dotted with sheep and cattle, encased in stone walls at times crumbling into muddy animal tracks. Where flat land gave way to hills punctuated by outbursts of grey stone, man-made walls of rock persisted except on slopes covered in neat rows of farmed trees, laid out in lines as precise as old rubber plantations in Thailand, but with arrow-straight trunks reaching high into the sky. Water flowed everywhere, mountain streams linking lakes of differing sizes, some even near the tops of hills, and rivers gushing through valleys and bigger lakes towards the sea which, from several thousand feet up, never felt far away.

Final approach was from the sea to the west of the country, and followed a river that at its mouth, was far broader than the Chao Phraya, but which rapidly narrowed; compared to the congested river in the Thai capital it seemed all but empty of traffic.

The landing was so soft he didn't notice the wheels touching down, and after a short taxiway, they parked next to a terminal that struck Tuk, newly qualified to compare international airports, as miniature-model-like. Impatient passengers leapt for overhead luggage compartments and a friendly inflight staff member arrived with Tuk's guitar case.

Within minutes, he was in front of a tall counter, under the stern gaze of an overweight woman with reading glasses perched at the end of a rubbery nose. She stared at him, eyebrows raised in an unspoken question. He tried raising his eyebrows in response, but that didn't help. Finally, she spoke:

'May I see your passport, sir?'

'Yes,' said Tuk, unable to muster another word. Nerves seemed to have made him forget his English.

She accepted the passport and as she made it pivot by the corners between ink stained fingertips, he surprised her with a copy of the letter Jo had provided to back up his visa application. Getting back to the passport, she compared the photo to the man standing before her, and flicked through blank, unmarked pages until at last she paused where, for some unknown reason, the British Embassy in Bangkok had stamped his visa crookedly. On page twenty-seven. After twenty-six blank pages.

'New passport, sir?'

'I have only one.'

'This is a new passport.'

'Yes, new. I got only last month.'

She consulted the details page. 'Forty-seven days ago, in fact. Have you ever had occasion to visit the United Kingdom before today?'

'Nowhere,' said Tuk.

'I beg your pardon?'

'I go nowhere before today.'

'This is your first trip outside Thailand?'

'Yes, sir. Sorry – yes, madam.'

'Just a moment please.'

She signalled to a colleague, who came over to confer with her in low voices. The passport changed hands several times, the details and visa pages scrutinised with great care; a computer terminal on the countertop was referred to more than once and at least one telephone call was made.

She turned back to Tuk and with a thump that made him jump, stamped the passport.

'Welcome to Scotland,' she said. 'Your fiancée will be looking forward to seeing you.'

'I think so,' said Tuk. 'Thank you.'

Ten

Tuk came down the escalator towards the luggage carousel just in time to see his suitcase, one of the few pieces not yet claimed, disappear outdoors. He walked around to meet it coming back and shuddered when it appeared in a blast of wind colder than anything he had ever experienced. He made a mental note to seek out some warmer clothes.

Suitcase and guitar case on a trolley with one front wheel stubbornly refusing to travel in a straight line, he followed an Asian couple through sliding doors to the Arrivals area. It was almost deserted. A man in a shiny suit held up a board marked in uneven capital letters: *RABINDER SINGH, IBM.* Jo was nowhere to be seen.

A young man in a denim jacket with a grubby fur collar came around the end of the railing that marked the arrivals channel.

'Tuk,' he said. 'Jo is at work, so I drew the short straw. I'm Terry, by the way.'

The trolley ground to an immediate halt when Tuk instinctively went to greet the stranger with a *wai* that turned into a dash to save his guitar from launching itself to the floor.

'Short straw?' he said.

'Oh aye,' said the other man. 'She did say yer English was shite. Follow me.'

For a few seconds Tuk stayed where he was. He hadn't seen Jo in six months, and she didn't come to meet him when he arrived in Scotland for the first time? A few metres ahead, Terry turned and waved impatiently. Tuk followed him to the chilly outdoors. As an afterthought, when preparing to go to Bangkok airport he had worn a long-sleeved cotton shirt. Back home, he couldn't recall the last time he wore a jacket. Now he emerged from the terminal straight into another freezing blast of wind. Most people around him wore warm jackets or even long coats, but less explicable were entire families, mum, dad and two or three kids, walking around wearing matching soccer jerseys in either blue or green-and-white. The ones heading indoors might be anticipating a sunny overseas holiday, but what about the others returning from warmer climes, who chose to arrive wearing short-sleeved shirts? Maybe they were even more stupid than he was.

Terry strode on until Tuk ran the trolley into the back of his legs when he stopped suddenly next to a sign saying *Airport Express*. Sore legs and all, he was just in time to board a purple bus pulling up with a hiss of brakes. He left Tuk to deal with his luggage. On the bus, Tuk spotted the sign: *Seven Pounds*. This was a problem. The sole item on his to-do memo for Glasgow airport was to change money into British pounds, but the rude way he was dragged outdoors by this guy, straight from arrivals to the bus stop, meant he forgot.

'Can I pay US dollars?'

'Sorry pal. Pounds only, and I cannae gie ye change. Seven pounds exactly.'

He spotted the glance Tuk shot at Terry, who was settled into a seat.

'Hey, pal,' he shouted. Sort yer friend out, will ye? He seems to think he landed in New York.' He stared at a bare wrist as if he was wearing a watch. 'Ah've got a schedule to follow.'

Terry stomped to the front, dug a pile of money from his trouser pocket, and threw the fare into the slot. All without saying a word or glancing at Tuk, who found a space on the crowded luggage rack for his suitcase. The bus was almost full, but an elderly lady stood up and waved him into a window seat.

Guitar between his knees, he watched the scenery go by, still smarting at the treatment he was receiving from Jo and from the rude bastard she seemed to have sent to meet her fiancé. What was his name again? Terry?

After a few high-speed minutes on a crowded highway, the bus crossed a river via an overpass packed with speeding traffic before peeling off to follow a sign for Glasgow City Centre. As it slowed to navigate downtown traffic, the sights on the streets made him wonder if this might be his first taste of culture shock. Pedestrians, teenagers and adults, mostly male, some wearing football shirts, arms blue with the cold, held out from their sides as if being able to deal with the temperature made them special.

Girls who might still be in their teens, some of them pushing infants in prams, many of them smoking openly, bare arms dotted with tattoos. On a flattened cardboard box spread on a patch of muddy earth behind one bus stop, two unshaven men smacked their lips between swallows from a two-litre bottle of a clear liquid they apparently needed as much as they enjoyed. At one pedestrian crossing, a dutiful young man patiently led a much older man who tapped his way across the road with a white cane. Tuk wondered if the blind grandfather had any idea his grandson wore his hair fashioned into giant punk spikes, his handsome young face thick with Ziggy Stardust make-up and punctured by multiple piercings. Doc Martin boots with bright yellow laces almost reached the knees of black jeans so tight they might have been applied from a spray can.

Even the traffic was different. In Bangkok, never mind how it could rain like an incoming flood multiple times in a day, an unwashed car was the exception, and most vehicles sparkled in the sunshine, the only exception being public buses which operated twenty-four hours a day until they turned to dust. Bangkok cars tended to be no more than a few years from new – older models were more in evidence in country towns – but in Glasgow, mixed in amongst brand new Porsches, SUVs and Japanese and Korean sports cars and a fair sprinkling of late-model BMWs and Mercedes Benzes, cars might come from this year or from back when the Beatles were still a band. Some of the much older cars were beautifully restored or maintained; others would have made Tod's rat rod BMW look respectable.

'Come on, you,' said a voice. He woke up to see Terry march to the front of the bus, where he snatched Tuk's suitcase and left him with barely enough time to disembark before the bus pulled away. Terry took the suitcase along a crowded city pavement only as far as the next bus stop, where again he got lucky and stepped straight onto a waiting double decker. This time he paid for both of them before dropping the case on a rack near the front door. From behind a scratched Perspex shield, the driver waved Tuk past. Terry took the last remaining seat, leaving him to stand in the aisle, guitar case resting atop one of his shoes.

A young boy in the nearest seat stood and gestured to him to sit down.

'You can huv ma seat,' he said.

'I am OK, thank you,' said Tuk.

'Nah, gawn yersel' big man, huv a pew.' Fortunately for Tuk, he accompanied unintelligible dialect with clear sign language. Tuk sat down.

'You are gentleman,' he said to the boy who was now holding onto the back of the seat in front.

'It wisnae me. Ma mammy tellt me to gie you it,' said the boy as he plucked fluff from an unwrapped bar of chocolate fished from his pocket.

Tuk smiled at the woman who might be the boy's mother.

'You have to try and teach them some manners,' she said, 'in case –' she paused in mid-sentence as Terry slapped Tuk's shoulder and jerked a thumb towards the exit.

'–In case he turns into an arsehole like your friend,' she said.

'Not my friend,' said Tuk. 'But thank you.'

Back on the pavement, Terry waved a hand to where an iron gate lay open at the entrance to a tenement building.

'Give me your guitar,' he said. 'I'm not lugging this bloody thing up three flights of stairs.'

'No,' said Tuk.

'Eh?'

'No.'

'What did yer last slave die of? I met you off the plane and I paid yer bus fares, but I'm not about to carry your case up to the flat. Who do you think you are?'

'Give to me, please. Thank you.'

In Bangkok, electrical storms often caused power outages across whole districts that could just as easily last for hours as for minutes. Frequently, Tuk had no choice but to walk up to the eighth floor of his apartment building, guitar case in one hand, 40-watt Fender amp in the other. In the tropical heat. By comparison, this was a cinch. Guitar case on his back and the suitcase hanging from one hand, the steps were easy. A bit worn out from decades of weary footfalls and musty smelling with a distinct suggestion of cat piss, but no great physical challenge. When he got to the top floor, a door lay open.

He stepped tentatively inside – and there was Jo. His heart skipped and for a second he thought he might cry. He put down his belongings and opened his arm to embrace her. She leaned in to deliver the briefest peck on his cheek, leaving him standing there, arms wide. This was what he'd waited six months for?

'We have to get ready,' she said.

'I don't understand.'

She adjusted her watch on her wrist. It was Swiss, an expensive present from her father, she had told him, at least four times, but its strap needed work. 'We are going to see my parents.'

'Now?' Tuk wondered if this was her idea of a joke. Her humour often confused him.

'I am so tired,' he said. 'I have nearly two days, no sleep. I am just happy to see you.'

'I want them to meet you,' she said, as if it was a done deal.

'How about your parents. Do they want to meet?'

'Of course they do. Put your stuff in the bedroom, maybe give your face a wash and change your shirt.' She looked again at her watch. 'We leave in ten minutes.'

Eleven

Jo drove a new Mini not often seen in Bangkok, where Tuk associated them with spoiled daughters whose brothers probably drove Mercedes convertibles. Jo's car was bright red, with a glass sunroof that Tuk, huddled in a jacket loaned begrudgingly by Terry, couldn't imagine being opened very often. A temperature gauge on the dashboard said it was 16C outside, while the heater worked to blow hot air around the interior. In September. Was this what they called late summer in Scotland?

They argued about Tuk's guitar before leaving. He wanted to bring it, but she said he was being stupid. He didn't understand when she called it his comfort blanket, and emerged from the argument and from the flat none the wiser, without his Gibson.

At least they drove on the same side of the road as Thailand. After twenty minutes including a short spell on a busy highway during which Jo didn't speak a single word, they took to a roller-coaster slip road before coming to a halt at traffic lights. Before long they picked their way through a leafy residential area with broad streets, mature trees and quaint, arched streetlights that made Tuk think of gas lamps in Jack the Ripper movies. Uneven pavements lined with cars parked at odd angles, inside wheels mired in deep gutters. Occasional shambling figures wrapped as if for Arctic expeditions trudged behind dogs on leads, the poor animals having trouble finding anything worth sniffing. Beside them, tall garden walls of stone were shadowed by stout tree branches, leaves dripping fat drops of rainwater.

Jo swerved sharply into a gap bracketed by forged metal gates marking the entrance to a house reminiscent of the castles in books of fairy tales Tuk's parents read to him when he was young. Made from huge blocks of brown stone striped by water spilling from the edges of moss-lined slate roofs, it had extravagantly curved bay windows on either side of a set of stone steps bigger than his family home in Bangkok. Tall glass panes reflected the trees that dwarfed the garden wall, lit by motion-sensor security lights set off by the Mini.

Before they got out of the car, Jo reached into the back seat and thrust a small box at Tuk.

'Since I don't expect you got her anything, this is a present for my mum, from you,' she said.

'What is it?'

'You'll see.'

She led him along an uneven path of paving slabs made into trip hazards by the roots of plants and bushes passing below. On each side were lawns whose perfection of perpendicular edges and right-angles and smooth parabolic curves spoke of paid help. Skirting the grass was an array of roses, pruned to within an inch of their lives. She marched ahead of him, up the grand stone steps and rapped the etched glass panel on a pair of wooden doors suspended from yet more heavy metal hardware. She leaned on an oversized handle that might have taken a blacksmith a day to forge, and they were in.

He bent down to untie his laces before he noticed Jo had strolled ahead without pause, imprinting the polished wooden floor with wet prints from her Nikes. Dust rose in a cloud from a bristled mat when Tuk wiped his shoes carefully.

A teenaged boy appeared, hand outstretched. 'You must be the rock star all the way from Thailand!' He waggled a thumb at Jo, who disappeared into the house. 'I'm the wee brother. My name's Brendan, but everyone calls me Bren.'

'Hello, Bren, I am Tuk.'

'You didn't bring your guitar?'

'Jo said not needed.'

'Bloody spoilsport. Never mind, I've got a Strat and a Gibson SG. Maybe we can jam later, once we break loose from the oldies.'

Tuk heard the names of two desirable electric guitars and the word "jam".

'Sure,' he said.

Jo took him straight to a dining room, a formal affair with expensive antique furnishings and three walls of landscape paintings in heavy frames, floor covered entirely with a dense carpet bearing an oft-repeated, garish floral pattern. Carpets were a novelty to Tuk; floors in Thai homes were mostly tiled or laminate-covered, kept clean with soft-bristled brushes which when Tuk tried to use them, always left behind more bristles than they removed dust. The carpet in the dining room was striped with parallel indentations from a vacuum cleaner. He wondered at the pointlessness of trying to free microscopic dust particles trapped within the taut weave of machine-made fibres.

The fourth wall was devoted to religious art. An ornate crucifix dominated the central spot, flanked by shelves with photographs of two old men Tuk thought might be popes. Another painting was meant to be Jesus, who looked like a young George Clooney in a wig and a crown of thorns. Another idealised work of art might have been Madonna and the baby Jesus, with fair skin and blond hair.

The reason for him being paraded straight to the dining room became clear: formal introductions, first to Jo's parents, Mr and Mrs Brogan – *call us Robert and Nancy, please,* said Jo's mother (Jo shook her head; Tuk got the hint) – and to Brendan. Not Bren.

Both of Jo's parents had strange hair Tuk struggled not to stare at. Mrs Brogan's made him think of a wig on a Styrofoam stand the way it moved independently of her head like a too-big motorcycle helmet. It was a disconcerting mix of three shades of brown, perhaps chosen to match her formal dress, long sleeves and high collar and all. Mr Brogan's neatly-cut hair was a uniform flat brown, a dye job that wouldn't fool anyone, especially since it didn't match bristly grey eyebrows or painstakingly trimmed salt-and-pepper moustache. He spoke with his chin angled downwards and stared unblinking over the top of half-moon reading glasses. Combined with a three-piece tailored suit in pinstriped grey, the effect was of a senior banker who had only left his office under duress.

Tuk gave each a traditional *wai* that made Mrs Brogan squirm with delight and drew a sneer from her husband while he stood with his hand extended for the shake that never came. By the time Tuk saw the outstretched hand, he was too late. It had disappeared to be folded into a two-hand clasp below his beltline, like a military man at ease. Brendan cast formalities aside, shook his future brother-in-law's hand for the second time and hugged him enthusiastically.

'Never mind what folk tell you,' he said in a mid-embrace stage whisper. 'You can call me Bren.'

'Brendannnn,' said Nancy, as she reappeared from the kitchen carrying a tray full of food. She made three trips until the table groaned under dishes laden with meat and vegetables. It was exactly as Tod said: *grey meat and overcooked vegetables*, but didn't smell too bad. Jo tapped her foot against his. He took his eyes from the food in time to see Mr Brogan close his eyes and dip his head and take a deep, portentous breath while his wife made the sign of the cross and kissed a gold crucifix on a fine chain around her neck. Mr Brogan spoke in a pious drone.

'Thank you, Lord, for giving us food,
Thank you, Lord, for giving us food,
For the food we eat
For the friends we meet,
Thank you, Lord, for giving us food. Amen.'

In mid-verse, Tuk partly opened his eyes to find Brendan bobbing his head from side to side, eyes crossed, tongue waggling. He stopped in perfect time to escape being seen by his parents as the verse ended. Mr Brogan stood wielding a frighteningly sharp carving knife and a two-pronged fork.

'I hope you like silverside,' he said to Tuk. 'Nancy makes a lovely roast silverside.'

He probably wasn't expecting a response, since he immediately dropped three fat slices of grey meat in slimy brown gravy on the guest's plate.

'Thank you, Mr Brogan.'

'Jo says you have a Gibson guitar,' said Brendan. 'Is it a Les Paul? I have a Les Paul Custom and a Fender Strat SRV limited edition replica.'

'Nice,' said Tuk. 'My guitar is a BB King Replica, an ES335.'

'Who the feck's BB King?'

'Brendannnn,' said his mother in a low growl.

'Feck's not a real swearword.'

'Brendan,' said his father, the name cut short and sharp.

'Sorry,' said Brendan. It was obvious which parent inspired fear in the teenager's heart. He returned his attention to Tuk. 'Who is BB King?'

'He is my hero. Also my father's hero. My guitar was my father's.'

'He was a musician too?'

'Yes, I follow, how do you say, in his footmarks,' said Tuk.

'Tuk means "footsteps",' said Nancy.

'Lucky you're here, Mum,' said Brendan.

'Enough of your cheek, young man,' said Mr Brogan. 'So, Tuk, tell us – what are you going to do to make a living over here?'

Tuk's expression was blank. Robert tried again.

'Are you going to get yourself a proper job?'

'I'm sorry,' said Tuk. Jo spoke over him:

'Daddy, Tuk only just got here!'

'It's a fair question,' said Mr Brogan. 'I'm your father, and I want to know what your, your *fiancé* is going to do to support you. Lord knows you don't make much in your job at the art gallery.'

'It is the 21st Century, Daddy. It's not Tuk's job to support me. We will manage just fine. And anyway, we have a business idea. The one I told you about.'

Her father shared a shrug with his wife. 'Neither of them has a bloody clue,' he said.

'Language, Daddy,' said Brendan. A glower from his father made his stop right there.

'I am going to play the blues,' said Tuk.

'The brooz?' said Brendan.

'Yes, the blues. It is what I love. Jo knows.'

'Oh, isn't this just bloody marvelous,' said Mr Brogan.

'Thank you,' said Tuk.

'Mum!' said Jo, reaching for the package on the floor. 'Tuk brought you a gift from Thailand.'

'Oh, how lovely of you, Tuk,' said Mrs Brogan. 'May I open it?'

'Of course you can,' said Jo. Even Tuk could see she was trying to cut her father out of the conversation.

Mrs Brogan unpicked the wrapping like she wanted to save it for later use and extracted a green statuette of a seated Buddha.

Oh no, though Tuk. Fake jade tourist tat from one of the stalls near the Grand Palace or the Flower Market.

'Oh, goodness,' said Mrs Brogan. 'It's ehm, it's beautiful.'

'It's ornamental, Mum,' said Jo.

'Of course it is, dear.'

'What is "ornamental"?,' said Tuk.

'Like a decoration,' said Jo.

Tuk was horrified. 'Buddha is never only decoration.'

'Anyhow,' said Brendan, pointing at shelves filled with religious art. 'He can keep the Holy Fathers company.'

Jo covered her eyes with her hands as Mr Brogan glared again at her brother.

'Pass the potatoes, Brendan,' he said.

Twelve

In the room the Brogan household knew simply as "the study", Robert Brogan sat in his executive chair behind a roll-top desk designed to butt against a wall. In the study, the back of the desk faced the door. He told people he enjoyed the privacy it gave him, which was close enough to the truth.

When the study door opened without warning to reveal Jo, her expression showing every tell-tale sign of impending daughter meltdown, he hurriedly angled the screen of his laptop towards the keyboard. The *Married But Cheating!* website definitely merited privacy.

'Darling,' he said. 'What's wrong?'

'You know exactly what's wrong. Why did you have to put Tuk on the spot with talk about a proper job?' She hooked fingers in the air to suspend quotation marks around the last two words.

Robert stuck to his earlier argument. 'As your father I am entitled to worry about your future husband's plans for surviving now he's in Scotland.'

'But we talked about what he was going to do here. I even presented a carefully costed business plan!'

'Oh,' he said. 'The business plan. Listen, pet…'

'Here we go,' said Jo. 'I only get the *pet* bullshit when you're about to lie or break a promise.'

'I'll thank you to refrain from profanity in my house. And don't think you can talk to me in such a tone. Anyway, it was never a promise.'

'I was there, remember. You PROMISED.'

'I said I would consider it carefully, share it with Uncle Liam. I don't have to tell you I depend on his accounting skills to cast a professional eye over all proposals, to give the go-ahead to all of my investments. He crunched the numbers with great care.'

'And?' Jo was close to tears. Robert couldn't handle his daughter's tears. A voice purred from the laptop's speakers.

'Oooh, Daddy! Where did you go! Why don'tcha come to Gloria. What would you want me to do for you tonight? Surely baby's in the mood for some loving…'

He slammed the laptop closed.

'I'm not saying no,' he said to Jo. 'But at the moment I am doubtful. Uncle Liam estimates the upfront costs alone could be as much as a half million. And he says so-called theme bars are closing all over the country thanks to the recession. And that's before we even consider dealing with the organised crime hoodlums who will want us to pay over the odds for posting their security thugs on the door.'

Jo slumped in a chair off to the side of his desk. He made sure the laptop screen was firmly closed and went on. Maybe she was getting the message.

'The recession is killing the projections for my other investments. I'm just not sure I have the funds available for this idea. And theme bars occupy a field of enterprise I am inexperienced in.'

If he thought that was going to sway the argument in his favour, he was wrong. Jo was on the boil:

'I went to college precisely because you supposedly wanted me to join the family business,' she said, 'and you helped me choose Hospitality Management so I could bring fresh qualifications to help you diversify.'

She had him there. OK, he chose the course partly because it wasn't difficult to get into – face it, his daughter wasn't the brightest bulb in the candelabra – but if it helped her develop a skillset he could use to justify putting her on the payroll, all to the good.

'You promised,' she said, voice reduced to a keening wail, mascara tears running down her face.

Robert couldn't watch this. He closed his eyes for a few seconds; when he plucked up the courage to re-open them, she was gone.

He wondered if Gloria was still waiting. At testing times like these, a man needed friendly company.

Jo flounced along the passageway between the upstairs rooms. At the door to Brendan's, plastered with skulls and crossbones and signs warning of Nuclear Radiation, a deep electric bass whump-whump shook the floor. She didn't bother knocking, partly because she never felt any need to extend courtesy to her brother, but mostly because the police could use explosives to blow the door from the wall without anyone inside hearing them.

In a blatant act of self-preservation disguised as parental kindness, their father had paid for the room to be soundproofed to a standard suited to professional recording studios. Inside, the deafening din came from a stereo piped through one of her brother's guitar amps, electric blues rock joined by Brendan, sitting with his back to a wall covered in foam tiles, jamming along guitar hero style, eyes firmly shut. Beside him, Tuk lay swallowed by a giant bean bag with another guitar in his lap, sound asleep. In a sudden short break in the music, Jo thought she could hear him snoring.

Tuk fought with the seat belt as Jo took the Mini from the driveway at speed onto a road slippery with rainfall and dead leaves. Tuk had never learned to drive, though he knew from Tod's impromptu lectures how a manual gearbox was something to be exploited but not abused. He was fairly sure gear changes should not involve quite so much crunching of metal. Maybe she was angry with the car. Or was she angry with him for falling asleep, or was it what he said about the Buddha statuette? That was probably it.

'What's wrong, Jo?'

'Nothing. Never mind.'

'I am sorry about Buddha. Big mistake to say not a decoration. I'm sorry. But how can I know? In Thailand–'

'We're not in Thailand now. And anyway, the Buddha was no big deal.'

'I don't understand,' said Tuk.

She crashed another gear change as they pulled away from yet more traffic lights. Just like in Thailand, traffic signals seemed to spend most of the time stuck on red.

'The present we gave my mother is not important. Not a problem, I mean.'

'So why are you angry?'

80

'It's daddy,'

'Your father?'

'You know the idea, to open an Adhere Bar in Glasgow?'

'Yes.'

'We need him to invest in it. I spoke to him about it again when you were *jamming* with Brendan. Daddy is having second thoughts. Because of the recession. So now he might not give us money. Which would mean goodbye to a New Adhere in Glasgow.'

Tuk hardly knew what to think. What would he tell his mother, or Tod, or Pong or Phil at the real Adhere Bar?

'I'm sorry,' he said. 'Can we do something else?'

'Like what? We could make a fortune with a great blues bar with you as the star attraction, our USP. Now, if there's no bar, there's no place for you to play - and no fortune. What will we do?'

'I do same as always,' said Tuk.

'What does that mean?'

'I'll play the blues.'

Thirteen

Jo turned out to be a lot better at parking than changing gears. Back at her flat, she somehow got the Mini into a kerbside space only marginally larger than the car. When Tuk got out and closed his door, she used a remote to lock it and, without waiting, headed straight for the tenement entrance.

He felt like an imposter when he stepped from the bathroom wearing one of Jo's bathrobes. The light from the hallway helped him remember the layout and navigate the living room without falling over anything. In their bedroom, Jo lay on the far side of the bed with her back to him. The mattress creaked when he lay down beside her, but she didn't stir. He lay on his back, wondering what the hell he had gotten himself into.

Dim light seeping past heavy curtains prised him from a restless sleep. In the living room he found Jo in a scramble to get out the door.

'Good morning,' he said.

'I've got to get to my work. I told you I have a job at an art gallery in the city. I'll be back late.' She waved vaguely at the fridge and a counter where there was a box of corn flakes and a kettle. 'Get yourself some breakfast.' She held out a key on an enamel thistle key ring. 'This is for the front door. Don't lose it. Brendan will be here in an hour or two. He says he can help you.'

'Help me?'

'I never have a clue what Brendan's on about. He's a bit of dreamer.'

Suddenly she was gone, without so much as a goodbye kiss. Tuk made himself a cup of instant coffee of a brand he had never seen. Like everything else in his life right now, it tasted bitter, the stuff lonely blues songs were made of.

There was enough bread to make toast and cover it with salty butter and jam supposedly made from strawberries. He missed Thai food already.

Between bites he played his guitar. Even unplugged, its familiar feel and sweet sound brought him joy, until another door opened and Terry emerged wearing only boxer shorts, rubbing sleep from his eyes. Tuk had never seen him not wearing the fake-fur hood on his jacket. Now, he saw Terry had short, bleached blonde hair like a young Annie Lennox. Except nowhere near so attractive. When Tuk was in middle school, he and his friends gleefully divided themselves into two camps, one in love with Annie Lennox and the other obsessed with Janet Jackson. Tuk's worship pointed at Janet, even if he hid a secret love for Annie. Terry's hair needed its roots done, a tide of orange-red seeping from his scalp. When you threw in a bad case of acne and a yellow-toothed overbite, it wasn't a good look.

'Fuck me if it's no' Ellik Crapton,' he said. 'To what do we owe the honour, Mr Crapton?'

Tuk paused in mid-scale. 'You live in Jo's apartment, Terry?'

'Apartment? It's a three room flat, son. And it's not Jo's, it's ours.' He pointed to a flashy flat screen TV.

'That's a telly. My name is Terry. T-E-R-R-Y, or is that too difficult for you?'

'Arse,' said Tuk.

'What did you say?'

'Arse. Two letters R in Terry. I try to remember.'

Terry threw on some clothes and went straight out the door, leaving Tuk aghast that he hadn't washed his face or brushed his teeth. Was this considered normal here?

He was still noodling on guitar when the sound of a key in the door preceded the arrival of Brendan, who came in panting, with a bicycle on his shoulder. By the light from grubby living room windows, Tuk estimated he was about fourteen years old and trying hard to appear older. He wore hi-top Adidas basketball boots, torn designer jeans, a "distressed" leather jacket that smelled more of money than hard times and a shirt emblazoned with a MEGADETH logo screamed of bad taste in both music and leisurewear.

He surprised Tuk by shaking his hand again.

'I guess this makes me your manager,' he said.

'I never have a manager.'

'Or maybe I'll be more like an agent. Mr Ten Percent. No - fifteen. Memo to self: don't undersell yourself, Bren.'

'What are you talking about?'

'Did Jo not tell you I was coming? She says you need my help to find a gig, get you a place in a hot up-and-coming band, you and your, axe - your Baby Swing.'

'BB King,' said Tuk.

'Gotcha,' said Brendan, face lit up. 'Hook, line and sinker. Get your jacket – do you even have a jacket? – and we'll find bands in need of a guitarist of your calibre.' He stopped as if to consider something for the first time. 'Hey, I hope you're good.'

'Blues bands?'

Brendan came over all sheepish. 'There might be one or two out there, too. But….'

'But?'

'Well….this entertainment industry entrepreneur's instinctive understanding of the local music environment suggests a need to refocus on attainable goals to broaden one's professional horizons, apply one's skillset across the largest practicable marketable footprint.' He stopped, proud of himself. He'd been working on the pitch all the way from his parents' house.

'Please speak English,' said Tuk.

'Get. Your. Jacket.'

He let his bicycle flop against the sofa. 'Let's do it, man.'

'OK, man,' said Tuk.

'Hang on. You won't need your guitar.'

'I take it.'

'Are you expecting an urgent call to play a gig this morning?'

'I take it.'

Glasgow isn't especially known for its architectural delights, but after they got off the bus in the city centre, Tuk wandered in awe, staring up goggle-eyed at the buildings around them. In his mind's eye he pictured Bangkok which, apart from the trademark curves of Buddhist temples, could be split into two or three architectural styles, none of them particularly appealing. Chinatown where he lived was mostly shophouses, two or three floors high, sometimes with a second-storey overhang to protect the pavement walkway from searing sunshine or torrential rain. Mostly covered in a skein of painted plaster or cement, the closest thing they might have to an architectural embellishment would be wooden louvers on the upstairs windows designed to cut out heat and noise, neither of which tasks they succeeded in doing particularly well. Elsewhere, the Thai capital was becoming increasingly dominated by high rise buildings, offices curtain-walled, condos geometrically peppered with impractically tiny balconies devoted mostly to holding air conditioning compressors.

Scotland's largest city had its share of ugly modern towers, but the streets Bren took him down created a hilly grid among sandstone buildings only three or four floors high, centuries old and each one distinctly designed in ways doubtless favoured by the rich.

He learned some of this because Brendan, brainy and small-built, escaped abuse at school by hiding in the library. Having read or rejected all the fiction on the shelves, lately he had shifted attention to non-fiction. Which was how he was able to give Tuk a concise lecture on how 18th Century Scottish merchant scumbags built much of the Glasgow's grand architecture with wealth generated from shipping light machinery to Africa, re-filling the holds with tens of thousands of Africans for sale into slavery in the Americas, before bringing the fleets back to Britain filled to the gunwales with tobacco. Since the ships never sailed empty, vast sums of money were generated on every leg of a circular trade route. Despite the torture of imparting the story across a daunting language barrier, he eventually got the message through to Tuk, who appeared impressed for all the right reasons.

'So beautiful,' he said. 'But made from tragedies.'

Brendan cheered him up a bit by taking him to see what had become the city's most famous yet most unlikely icon, the statue in front of the Gallery of Modern Art. Commissioned in the early 19th Century and erected in 1844, the imposing statue of the Duke of Wellington had lately become noted, not for the Anglo-Irish aristocrat's many military campaigns or for his two terms as Tory prime minister. Since the 1980s the man-on-horse monument's fame derived from anonymous citizens' insistence on placing an orange traffic cone on the Duke's head. No matter how often the council took it down, it was replaced, sometimes within hours. Thais would never cock such a snoot at an aristocrat, but Tuk was more amused than horrified, and gladly posed in front of it for Bren to take a photo.

Four minutes on foot got them to Glasgow Central railway station, where Tuk seemed most intrigued by the people spending time under its vast ceiling of thousands of glass panes in dire need of soap and water; the homeless woman in an army-surplus greatcoat, her belongings bungy-cord-tied to a shopping trolley; people watching the list of delayed trains on notice boards stretched across the tops of the entrances to platforms; others debating whether or not to drop their money on a bland, overpriced caffeine hit from the nearest bland, overpriced franchise. He stopped to listen to the spiel from a man Brendan had seen occupying the same spot outside a pub entrance for years, searching for suckers to give him money "for his train fare", and who shrugged equably when Brendan pulled Tuk away.

After leaving the station by a back entrance they found their way to Argyle Street, where they paused to take in the window display of a ground-floor shop that dove deep into an old tenement building. Bobby's Classic Emporium had occupied the same location for decades, and was probably the only place in Glasgow where you could browse knives from pocket-sized to gleaming samurai swords and everything in between. Inside, bare fluorescent strips suspended unevenly on cobwebbed chains cast a green glow over the Emporium's wares. Air pistols, air rifles and fully-functioning crossbows with arrows in quills competed for shelf space with an array of mostly low-end musical instruments, many of them second-hand, from penny whistles to tubas, half-sized violins to double basses. Of more interest to Tuk was an oddball selection of electric guitars, from an antique Danelectro to samples from across the decades of Gibson, Fender, Ibanez, Gretsch and Yamaha.

After Brendan managed to convince the pushy man behind the sales counter of their unwillingness to let him see what was in the guitar case on Tuk's back, or to buy so much as a set of replacement tweezers for a Swiss Army Knife, he led Tuk to the real reason for their visit. The Emporium's famous corkboard.

'Step this way on the road to fame and fortune,' he said. 'Time for Bren to embrace his managerial responsibilities.' As he spoke, he belatedly realised Tuk wasn't catching one word in five. This was a struggle, but Bren was up to it.

They stood shoulder to shoulder in front of an expanse of corkboard, filled to overflowing with overlapping index cards and flyers and notices of all sorts and shapes. From computer-generated fancy colour graphic design nightmares to notes hand-scrawled on the backs of gas bill envelopes held in place by every type and colour of thumb tack or blob of blu-tack known to modern history.

'Heavy Rock Wedding band needs experienced drummer.
No wanker wannabes. Must have own van and drums.'

'Thrash Metal outfit need singer/bass player. Influences: Motorhead, Metallica, Slayer, Anthrax. We ROCK!'

'Athentic Lizzy tribbute band want leed gitarist 2 be Scot Gorrim (with own sunbirst Les Pall). No skinhead's or punk's.'

Brendan set about moving paper around the board, pinning notices on top of one another, to make clear space for his own addition, which, within a few seconds, took pride of place near the centre of the board's lower edge.

HOT ELECTRIC BLUES/ROCK GUITARIST/VOCALIST,** INTERNATIONALLY EXPERIENCED, NEW TO GLASGOW, NEEDS PAYING GIG WITH ESTABLISHED WORKING OUTFIT. CALL BREN: 0812 345 678 **BETTER THAN CLAPTON!**

'Blues/rock'? said Tuk, as they picked their way through a thicket of drum stands on the way out to the street.

'If we don't want my dad pushing you out the door wearing a suit to hunt for proper jobs, we have to expand our options.' He disentangled a mobile phone from a grubby handkerchief he pulled from his trouser pocket. In his other hand he clutched a miniature thatch of tags torn from the bottom of existing notices.

'You did well to bring your guitar. Enough idle chit-chat. Time to get to work, to take the mountain to Mohammed. Sorry, Buddha.'

Bren almost laughed out loud when this earned him the expected *what the fuck?* stare.

Fourteen

It was months since Tuk lied to his mum about needing to take his guitar on the day of the interview at her company, but he still felt bad about it. If he had said "rehearsal", it would have passed for a white lie, since rehearsals happened anytime two or more of the band sat down for more than a few minutes. But there was no audition and, truth be told, there hadn't been a formal audition in a very long time.

City Limits had been a band for the best part of a decade; in their first year at university together, he, Tod and two fellow students thought they might be able to generate some beer money playing electric blues with roots set firmly in the American South. Being heavily influenced by Stevie Ray Vaughan meant there were audiences happy to watch decent covers of songs made famous by Vaughan, songs the band copied, note for note, from DVDs of Stevie playing live at Austin City Limits.

Before YouTube and streaming re-shaped the broadcast and music worlds, Bangkok was one of the best places on the planet to buy bootleg DVDs or CDs. A specialist store in downtown, a short trek across an old steel pedestrian bridge from Pantip Plaza (famous for dodgy computer software) had music DVDs covering a bewildering array of artistes big and obscure. The new City Limits blues band sourced a lot of their repertoire from discs bought from the shop which for some unknown reason was called Rex and for another had its interior walls covered in Royal Stuart tartan wallpaper. Taking maximum advantage of Rex's eclectic selection, Tuk made sure they didn't stick only to SRV. They progressed to studying and interpreting the works of dozens of other, mostly black artists, many of whom, if they were not dead, had long ago fallen on hard times.

Within weeks City Limits went from playing for a beer each to being paid a few hundred Baht because their music drew customers who bought drinks or meals. Tod on vocals and Tuk on guitar and vocals were the constants; rhythm section members came and went. In recent years, hardly a gig took place without them being cheered on by a table filled with highly-paid city professionals, all former fellow students or one-time band members in the early days of City Limits.

Tuk had lain in bed last night, listening to the soft snores of Jo, thinking about the good times he had enjoyed with *City Limits* and wondering why he had left them behind and what he had let himself in for. The rest of the day, never mind how hard Brendan tried, started out badly, but fell away. Even if it did turn out Tuk had been right to bring his guitar.

Tuk hadn't realised it was Saturday, which explained why Brendan managed to ambush several bands in mid-rehearsal. Much later, the thought amused him. Bands. None of the outfits they saw over the coming hours could have competed with *City Limits* on their worst day.

A couple of years back, a regular member of the audience at Adhere, a friendly Englishman called Rick, gave him a CD to listen to at home. Rick told him they were an English band who had been around forever and who lots of people hated – but he was sure Tuk would appreciate them. He listened to excerpts from a greatest hits medley of *Status Quo* only once. The experience put him firmly in the "hate" camp.

The first rehearsal they interrupted was in a disused mechanic's shop next to a bankrupt petrol station on the corner of a major intersection where traffic roared. The band had rolled up the shutter, cranked up their amps, and played Status Quo three barre chord blues rock with relentless, brain-numbing monotony. Just like the real thing. Brendan had to convince them to let his man join them for a song or two before they allowed Tuk to plug in. Off they went on yet another *Quo* track, every dum-te-dum stroke of the rhythm guitarist deathly predictable. When Tuk misinterpreted the nodding head of the lead singer as time to take a few bars, he played an opening sequence inspired by Stevie Ray Vaughan before realising the rest of the band had stopped playing.

'Who the does he think he is?' said the lead singer. 'Carlos Santana? We're a Quo tribute band, same three chords every song, same dum-te-dum-te-dum-te-dum beat, the way Quo heads love it. Why would we need some twat showing off, playing pentatonics?'

The sound of the second rehearsal reached them before they stepped off a bus, more than a hundred metres from an annexe connected to an old church, its grounds complete with neglected gravestones, none of them close to vertical. Tuk stared at inscriptions going back to the 1800s as Brendan led the way to the source of the din. The building housed a funeral parlour, and inside, a heavy metal band were thrashing the life out of their instruments in the small area of the hall not filled with coffins stacked to the ceiling.

After Brendan made the introductions, the band kicked off on a thrash metal anthem at a volume to make coffin lids tremble. Tuk played along, anticipating and playing rhythm guitar chords, until the other guitarist confronted him amiably, sweat dropping off his spotty face, trying to get him to join in a screaming duet, guitars almost touching. Tuk backed off with an apologetic shake of his head.

They next stood on the doorstep of a boxy pebble-dashed council house, just about to press the doorbell, when something approximating music bled from an open upstairs window. A young female voice, accompanied by a single, strummity-strummity acoustic guitar (badly out of tune), doing her best and making a murderous mess of sounding like Joan Baez singing *Blowing in the Wind*. Neither of them went near the doorbell.

'Christ,' said Brendan as they walked back to where they might be able to catch another bus. He picked at the strips of paper in his hand. 'It never occurred to me we'd be out here listening to other folk auditioning for the right to play with you. But now I get it.'

Tuk's disconsolate expression was almost enough to make a grown man cry.

'Just one more,' he said. 'It's not far.'

It can't get any worse, thought Tuk. Of course he was wrong.

They didn't even have to take another bus. Instead, they picked their way through fast-moving traffic on a busy four-lane road. None of the vehicles seemed to make any allowances for pedestrians, but the closest they came to an accident was when a cyclist almost hit the deck trying to avoid colliding with Tuk.

'Arseholes!' he screamed over his shoulder, even while he wrestled to get both bicycle wheels travelling in the same direction.

On the other side of the main road, the setting transformed itself from neat middle-class suburbia to what looked like the fall-out from a bombing campaign. Open areas were striped by lines of trenches flanked by rubble like the world's least careful archaeological dig, foundations of housing no longer there.

One line of dilapidated shops remained standing, many shuttered and covered in graffiti. Dusty padlock-heavy grilles protected the windows of a Post Office hanging on for dear life, and next door was an off-licence, windows and entrance protected by more steel grates. A customer emerged with two polythene bags stretching under the weight of plastic two-litre bottles; before the door closed, Tuk got a glimpse of an interior lit by strip lights, sales counters protected by yet more metal grilles. This place was like a set for the Kurt Russell movie, *Escape From New York*, only more desolate.

The last of the near-derelict buildings was an Indian takeaway doing a solid lunchtime trade in chips with curry sauce; attached to the takeaway its sister restaurant, big sign on the doors telling would-be diners it didn't open until 5, vibrated to the sound of a band playing Thin Lizzy's *The Boys are Back in Town*. Tuk hadn't thought his heart could sink any further, but he was wrong again.

Inside, half the tables and chairs were lumped to one side, butting up against mauve, textured wallpaper and a corner shelf with a statue of Ganesha, the Hindu deity with multiple human limbs and the head of an elephant. Under his accommodatingly serene gaze, the band delivered a straight copy of the version of the Lizzy song from the *Live and Dangerous* album, minus the second lead guitar part played by Scott Gorham. *The reason we are here*, thought Tuk.

At least they appeared to take rehearsing seriously, to the extent of being in costume. Big boots, improbably tight shiny black leggings, even tighter shirts. The man who dominated the centre of an imaginary stage played a low-slung black Fender Precision bass that even had the correct mirrored pick guard. He had the right amount of silverware around his belt and across his chest, and wore a Phil Lynott-style wig complemented by a thin moustache. But there was no disguising he was Indian.

'*Get your knickers down,*' he panted, in a passable imitation of Lynott's Irish-accented ending to live recordings of the song. Still using the microphone and watching Tuk pull his Gibson from its case, his voice boomed in a broad Scottish accent:

'Can youse pricks no' read? We need a Scott Gorham wi' a Les Paul Starburst for a huge show in England, second slot only to a Springsteen E-Street band act at Newcastle's biggest festival of tribute acts. It could be our big break!'

'You haven't heard this guy play,' said Brendan.

'You turn up here with a Chinky hoping to do some noodling on his antique jazz guitar? What part of "Starburst Les Paul" or "Tribute Band" don't you understand, son?'

They picked their way across wasteland towards a bus stop.

'What is a "Chinky"?' said Tuk.

'Maybe Phil thought you were Chinese.'

'I don't look Chinese.'

'The same eedjit thinks he looks like Phil Lynott.'

Fifteen

Brendan only came back to Jo's place to get his bicycle, which they found lying on its side on the landing outside the door. From inside the flat came the sound of the TV.

'Bitch,' he said. 'This beautiful piece of craftsmanship is a brand new Cannondale. Hand made from aluminium in the USA, it cost my old man a bloody fortune. Never mind the likelihood of it disappearing to pay for some druggy's next fix, how difficult would it have been to just lean it against the wall instead of throwing it to the floor?'

He might have been considering going in to give his sister a bollocking, but in the end decided it wasn't worth it.

'I'll see you tomorrow, pal.'

He put the bicycle on his shoulder and took to the steps, still shaking his head in disgust.

Tuk remembered he had a key to the Yale lock. He opened the door to find Jo and Terry laughing aloud at a television quiz show, the remains of a pizza in a Domino's box open on the coffee table. He spotted they were sitting snuggled close together. It was the sort of thing a man might be forgiven for noticing of his fiancée and a stranger sharing their home.

'Ellik!' said Terry.

'Hello Jo,' said Tuk.

She waved at the remains of the pizza.

'We've eaten. What about you?'

Did he have any reason to be disappointed? He could have used Brendan's phone but hadn't thought of calling to tell her he was on the way back. Maybe he was as much to blame as she was.

'Not hungry,' he said.

She shrugged and thumbed the TV remote to unmute the sound. Conversation over. Tuk went around the end of the sofa and into Jo's bedroom. Yes, Jo's. Not theirs. In Scotland less than twenty-four hours, and already he knew that much.

At least she let him use her iPad and had shared the Wi-Fi password. He squinted at the clock on the screen and did the arithmetic. Two o'clock in the morning, Bangkok time.

Tod's face came alive on the screen within seconds of the call going through. Wide awake.

'What's this?' said Tuk. 'At home, all alone, no fresh conquest struggling to get to sleep on the bed behind you?'

'Hey, man. Good to hear from you. Howzit going over there? Loving the shit-awful weather and the indigestible food?'

'You were right on both counts,' said Tuk.

'Not surprised. What's new?'

'Not much. Only been here a day, remember.'

'You're trying to kid a kidder who's known you since elementary school. What's UP?'

'OK,' said Tuk, 'one or two problems here.'

'Already? I was hoping the exhausted face was because you'd spent the last 24 hours at it like rabbits with the much-missed love of your life.'

'There's a problem with the plan to open a blues bar.'

'Aw, pal, I'm sorry. What kind of problem?'

'You know Jo's father is supposed to have a ton of money, and she was certain he'd back the plan.'

'Don't tell me the ol' guy got cold feet?'

'Something like that. He says the market is depressed, his other investments aren't giving him the returns he needs because of a recession Jo doesn't seem to have heard about, so he can't spare the cash to set us up in a "theme bar" at a time when apparently theme bars are going bust left, right and centre.'

'Shit, man. Doesn't sound good.'

'It gets worse. I was out today auditioning for guitar gigs. You wouldn't believe the crap bands I saw rehearsing.'

'Worse than Filipino cover bands doing their automaton note-perfect shit in Holiday Inn lobby lounges?'

'I'll never say a bad word about the Filipinos again,' said Tuk. 'At least those guys sing and play in tune. Most of the time, I mean.'

'Whoah. Proper bad. What's next?'

'It's sooo expensive here. I need to make some money. I might have to find a job.'

'A job? Like your mum always wanted? If you weren't so far away, she'd be delighted, even if it meant your dream was coming undone. How's things with Jo?'

'I have to go,' said Tuk. 'We'll talk again if there's any news.'

'OK dude. You hang in there.' Tuk could tell his friend knew things were bad.

When he awoke, it was to an empty bed. The windows were closed – he had made sure before going to bed – but he not only could hear the wind outside, he could watch gusts send the curtains waving around the inside of the window. Poor construction work or just an old building screaming out for maintenance? Whatever it was, these people seemed content to live with it.

He spent as little time as possible in the frigid bathroom which, with its cumbersome, water-stained ceramic furnishings served by squeaky taps, made him feel like he was marooned in a museum. The water itself emerged in completely unpredictable torrents, either frostbite cold or bring-a-tea-bag scalding hot. One positive: when he brushed his teeth, the cold water tasted better than anything he ever experienced in Thailand.

'Nice outfit,' said Brendan when he stepped out to the living area in Jo's bathrobe.

'Nice bicycle,' said Tuk. 'A different one today. Brompton. Expensive.' And so small when folded, even Brendan could carry it under one arm.

'They have them in Thailand?'

'Only rich people.'

'It's my mum's. A Christmas present a couple of years ago. The only time she ever sat on it was in the living room next to the tree. After three eggnogs, she managed to fall off without turning a wheel. It comes in handy when I don't want these arseholes chucking my Cannondale out on the landing.'

They walked to the bus stop, Tuk with his guitar on his back, Brendan – *call me Bren, will ya* – with the Brompton still mostly folded but now turned into a trolley running smoothly on miniature wheels built into the carrying rack.

The day before, Tuk had changed some money at a city centre bank. Now Bren carried what he called their "float" in a Ziploc bank bag and took care of the fares. The folded Brompton was so small he was able to bring it to the seats they found in the middle of the bus. One-way streets sent them on a circuitous route around the West End, passing one grand structure Tuk thought might be a royal palace, but which Bren explained was a museum and art gallery, before describing to him some of its best-known attractions.

'Maybe we can see later,' said Tuk.

Bren wondered what had sparked the gentle man's interest. The world-famous Salvador Dali of Christ of Saint John of the Cross, the 1947 Spitfire fighter suspended at a jaunty angle in mid-flight over a stuffed giraffe, stuffed emu and two stuffed elephants, or the cartoonish statue of a slob-fat Elvis Presley, complete with neon halo, in his declining Vegas years. His money was on Elvis.

Tuk sat in the unemployment office holding his queue number, 39, faded and frayed from being rolled between his fingers a hundred times. Not long now, he thought, as the digital display told the holder of ticket 38 to go to counter number 7. An electronic chirp from his pocket confused him until he remembered Bren had loaned him a Nokia mobile so old it didn't even have a touch screen.

'Where are you,' said Bren. Urgency in his voice.

'Still waiting.'

'Did you have your initial interview yet?'

'Please say again.'

'Did you speak with anyone?'

'Ah, yes,' said Tuk.

'Yes?'

'Yes waiting for interview. My ticket is number 39. Number 38 now interviewing. I am next.'

'Quick! Get out of there. Leave, now.' He sounded out of breath. Pedalling hard on the Brompton?

'I waited for two hours,' said Tuk. 'I am next.'

'Good timing. Get out now. Walk around to the big art gallery. I will meet you there.'

The digital display switched to alert the holder of ticket number 39 that his or her presence was requested at counter 5. He looked at the ticket in the hands of the nice lady sitting next to him. Number 77. He gave her his ticket.

'I must go. Your turn at counter 5.'

Initial disbelief turned to delight.

'Thanks, son. You're a darlin'.'

She gathered together a cluster of faded carrier bags and waddled towards counter 5.

Sixteen

Bren consulted his iPhone while wheeling the partly folded bike back and forth in front of the grand sandstone building. He knew what direction Tuk would be coming from, so his spotted the silhouette, guitar worn like a backpack, Gibson neck pointing to a sky that was pleasingly blue for Scotland at any time of the year.

'Spanish Baroque,' he said.

'Excuse me?'

'Spanish Baroque. The architectural style. All the rage when this was put together about a hundred and twenty years ago. Glasgow's first ever municipal museum and to this day, one of the city's top attractions.'

Tuk's expression was blank. Nothing new there. Bren was being unfair. He folded the bike to its smallest form, clipped to it a carry strap boldly imprinted with the Brompton brand, and set it on his shoulder.

'Only way I'll get to take this inside,' he said. 'You'll need to check the guitar into left luggage.'

Tuk had something else he wanted to discuss before they went anywhere.

'Why the call. Suddenly you tell me, get out!'

'Oh, that.'

'Yes, that. Why?'

'I made a dumb mistake. I wondered if there might be a reason for not going to the Job Centre, so I called Jo. She nearly flipped. Your status here is as a visitor with no right to work. You don't have a work permit. If you told the Job Centre folk you were searching for paid employment, they'd be duty-bound to report you. You'd have been in the shit, big-time.'

'I cannot work?'

'Correct. No can do.'

'But I am engaged to Jo. She is British citizen.'

'Doesn't matter. Unless you qualify for a skilled job in demand – like in computers or I.T. – you'll never get a work permit.'

'I.T.?'

'Not important.'

'So I cannot get a job?'

'Not legally, no.'

'What can I do? I need to work to make money until I find a band. Wait – if I am in a band, can I work?'

'Probably not.'

'So why did Jo ask me to come to Scotland? Even if your father pays for new blues bar, I can not work!' Tuk had another dark thought. Last night, when Jo's dad asked him if he was going to search for a job, Jo already knew he couldn't work legally, but said nothing. What was she doing?

'She probably didn't think it through,' said Bren. 'Didn't think about it carefully enough. Bloody typical of my sister. Maybe she thought if the bar became a reality, daddy dear could fork out for an immigration lawyer to help fix your status, get you a work permit.'

What he didn't say was *Selfish, self-centred bitch, putting the poor guy through this shitshow.* There was no point in hitting a man when he was down.

'It's bad, but there are ways,' he said.

Tuk was doubtful. Bren went on:

'Lots of people work "on the black".

Tuk was back to mystified.

'Black like the guy who tries to be Phil Lynott?'

They made a small detour to get around a street juggler whose act had drawn a few appreciative tourists, a couple of whom put money in a frayed straw hat. Bren saw one of them bend down to move a pound coin onto the top of a five pound note to stop it blowing away.

'I have an idea,' he said. 'We'll leave the museum for another day.' Brompton still suspended from his shoulder, he led Tuk to the nearest bus stop.

Sitting on a stiflingly hot bus with no windows open, Tuk asked where they were going.

'If I told you, I'd have to kill you,' said Bren. He watched Tuk try to process that. 'It's a joke,' he said.

'But jokes are funny.'

'Aye, right enough, they're meant to be.'

They sat in silence while a discussion between two older passengers degenerated into a shouting match about a popular television soap opera. One of them thought it had gone to shit and would never get back to the days when Elsie Tanner and Ena Sharples played their roles with authentic Lancashire professionalism. For a change, neither Bren nor Tuk had a clue what they were on about. When Bren pushed the button for their stop and led the way to the door, the argument showed no sign of subsiding.

Tuk recognised the street and the house. The castle-like place where Jo and Brendan grew up, the Brogan family home. He slowed to a near-halt.

'Relax,' said Bren. 'There's nobody home. Dad's out squeezing the last drop from every banknote he can lay his hands on, and mother has her bridge club.'

'Bridge?'

'It's a card game. A squad of wrinklies spend hours playing cards and gossiping and drinking gin and tonic. At least when she gets home she's "too tired" to cook, so we get to phone for pizza better than anything the old dear cooked in her life. Don't tell her I said that,' he joked.

'I won't,' said Tuk in all seriousness.

He's catching on, thought Bren.

Ninety minutes and two more bus rides later, they set up on Buchanan Street. Grand architecture straddled a pedestrian zone full of people browsing upmarket shops. Tuk gawked for a minute at the big store with a corner window display contrived from a couple of hundred sewing machines so old they'd never find buyers in Thailand. Yet here they filled large windows in precise geometric patterns. Closer scrutiny revealed, in neat displays behind the machinery, piles of frighteningly expensive designer wear for women.

The walk from the bus stop was long enough to make them appreciate the lightness of the new Roland *CUBE* micro amp, the one beloved by buskers for its ability to operate on double-A batteries. One small amp, one cable from Bren's backpack plus Tuk's beloved Gibson was all they needed, even if Tuk was still reluctant. Shoppers stared as they passed, curious about what they were up to. Some saw the amp, guessed their intentions, and sped up to escape any danger of having to contribute money. Three teenaged boys wore matching school uniforms in dark blue with light blue piping around the jacket fronts and badges loading down lapels, ties wound into swollen knots whose blades curled out, too short even to reach the V of their sweaters. They sneered down patrician noses at Bren and Tuk, but kept their opinions to whispers and sniggers.

Bren woke up his mobile phone, checked the time and grimaced.

'I have to get my wee arse out of here. If I miss another dentist appointment my old man will kill me. You know what to do, right? People busk in Thailand, don't they?'

'Sometimes *farang* – our name for foreigners – do, but we call it something else.'

'A nice Thai word?'

'Yes, Thai word. It means "begging".'

'Some of the clowns you see out here aren't much more than beggars. One thing:'

'What?'

'The *CUBE*. If you take your eye off it for more than two seconds, some arsehole will be off with it.'

'Steal?' Tuk was shocked.

'I got it for my birthday. My next birthday, which isn't for three months. If you lose it, mother-dear will kill me.'

'So many reasons for nice parents to kill you,' said Tuk. He actually seemed sorry.

'If only you knew, squire. Good luck. I'll see you tomorrow at Jo's flat. If you make a go of this, maybe we can get a regular spot approved by the busker mafia.' He had an idea: 'Do you know The Proclaimers, *I will walk 500 miles*? Aw, never mind.'

'No microphone,' said Tuk.

'What do you need a mic for?'

'For singing?'

'Might want to stick to instrumentals.'

Feeling self-conscious, he warmed up with slow blues instrumentals. Some people seemed to eye him with curiosity, others with no interest whatsoever. Yet others fired resentful glares for making them take minor detours to clear the open guitar case Bren had placed a couple of metres out in no man's land, a few coins spread around its furry interior.

Tuk didn't even notice he had morphed from an aimless blues jam into a classic ballad. Tin Pan Alley was a hit for Jimmy Wilson in 1953, though most people knew the version by Stevie Ray Vaughan, which Tuk's dad loved. Not having a microphone meant Tuk opted to do it without vocals, which gave him the freedom to indulge musical tangents, and took joyful liberties with the original. He wound it down slowly and was pleased to get a spattering of applause from people who had stopped to listen. Some of them dipped into pockets or purses and dropped money into the guitar case. Different-shaped coins, even a couple of notes. *Nice.*

After a few more songs drew increasing attention and a fair sprinkling of donations, a punk rocker with multiple piercings and hair in a flame-red Mohican approached. Wary of Bren's warning about the value of his amp, Tuk rested one foot on the *CUBE*.

The punk pointed at Tuk's guitar.

'Gibson BB King replica, right?'

'Yes,' said Tuk. 'ES335 BB King model.'

'My uncle Jim's crazy about BB King. When BB died, uncle Jim went into mourning. Drives my aunt Joan crazy. She says there's no way my uncle will mourn her that way if she goes first.'

'Many people are sad,' said Tuk.

'My dad says BB was crap.'

'Crap?'

'You know, shite, rubbish, no good. My dad claims the wee bampot fae AC/DC is the best rock guitarist who ever lived, but my uncle Jim says that's because my dad doesnae huv a clue.'

Tuk made an informed guess.

'Angus Young, AC/DC guitarist, is very good player.'

The friendly punk wasn't convinced.

'I maybe play some more,' said Tuk.

'Good on ye, pal.'

The punk went off to rejoin three friends. Tuk checked the amp, still safe under his foot. With a sinking feeling he turned to the guitar case. It had been stripped clean, not a single coin remaining. One of the punks gave him a cheery two fingers, earning himself a slap on the head from the punk.

The punk came back to Tuk with his hands in a bowl, carrying all the cash his friends had stolen.

'Ah'm sorry, pal,' he said. 'That had nothin' to dae wi' me, honest. Ah cannae take thay bastards onywherr.'

Seventeen

Tuk was done with busking. Pleased about having already acquired a basic knowledge of bus routes in Glasgow's West End, he took a ride upstairs on a double-decker to a stop opposite a big park. OK, it wasn't Bangkok's Lumpini Park with its giant monitor lizards sashaying casually past couples enjoying romantic escapes and tourists desperate to get as close as possible to photograph the lizards, but on a sunny afternoon, the Botanic Gardens offered lush green grass locals went out of their way to enjoy. Today was about 19C, a temperature to make Bangkok motorcycle taxi riders like Uncle Mu reach for the winterwear. Glasgow at the same temperature saw young men lying on the grass with their shirts off, women stretched out face down, bra straps unfastened, searching for an even tan. Maybe they never knew when they would see the sun again?

He lay propped up on one elbow, watching four teenagers playing badminton. The game must have been unplanned, three of the four playing barefoot, two book bags and six irregularly spaced shoes forming a line for an imaginary net. One of the boys jumped up to intersect a lob and scythed the

111

air in a bold smash that met with nothing but air. All four collapsed to the ground in giggles. Tuk looked on, as envious as he was amused. When did he last laugh like that?

He must have dozed off, because wakefulness returned abruptly when a cheap plastic football caromed off his head and came to rest in his lap.

A boy of about four wearing shorts and a Polo shirt, and an older man in unmatched checked jacket and trousers approached. The boy was sheepish, the man amused, if a little apologetic.

'I'm sorry, son. My grandson has got a bit of the Jimmy Johnstone in him. The wild and uncontrollable bit. Say you're sorry, James.'

'Sorry, mister,' said the boy.

'No problem,' said Tuk.

'Granda Jimmy,' said the boy. 'Who's Jimmy Johnstone?'

The old man feinted as if he was going to grab the boy's cheeks between thumbs and forefingers, and he ran off laughing.

'He knows exactly who Jinky Johnstone was. I've told him all the stories a hundred times.'

Tuk held out the football, but Granda Jimmy peeled off his jacket, folded it with great care, and lowered himself slowly to the grass as young James came back and leaned on his shoulder. He pointed to Tuk's guitar case.

'What's in there?'

'My guitar.'

'Why do you have a guitar in a park?'

'It was my father's guitar. Now it's mine. It's my best friend.'

'Is your daddy dead?'

Tuk wondered where that came from. 'Yes, he is,' he said.

'My daddy's dead, too. Granda Jimmy's my best friend.'

'The wee guy could talk for Scotland,' said Jimmy, eyes watering. 'I can listen to him all day long. I get angry when I hear parents telling their kids to shut up, shut up, shut up. Me, I wish I had a tape recorder. Might get one to capture some of the gems that come out of this wee nutter's mouth.'

'I'm not a nutter,' shouted James.

'Of course you're a nutter, and you know you're a nutter, and that's why I love you.' He turned his attention to Tuk. We're off to our favourite café. I think you could use some company. Come with us. James can talk the wallpaper off the walls while we enjoy a good cup of coffee.'

'And a banana boat ice cream!' yelled James at a volume causing heads all over the park to turn.

'And a banana boat ice cream,' said Jimmy.

Outside the gates to the park they negotiated a complex intersection via a tangle of pedestrian crossings where drivers actually stopped to allow people to cross. Thai drivers treated foot traffic as the enemy, even on marked crossings with green flashing signs. Tuk thought he could get used to this. At the other side of the main road was a striking sandstone church with a tall pointed steeple. Jimmy said:

'You'd still think it was a church, eh?'

'Beautiful church,' said Tuk.

'Except now it's a couple of bars, a restaurant, a discotheque and a hall where bands play. I went to a wedding reception in the hall last month. Happiness and heavy drinking in what used to be a church full of holy willies? Fine by me.'

Tuk tried to imagine the place teeming with drunks – or with good live blues echoing out to the street. What he couldn't imagine was any Buddhist temple being converted to a venue for people to dance and get drunk. He had taken himself to an alien land.

Jimmy provided a running commentary as they walked along Byres Road. Pubs he drank in over the years, a lane full of trendy restaurants he could never afford, the avenue running uphill through one of the oldest universities in the world. *Probably where the badminton players came from,* thought Tuk.

He brought them to a halt outside what the old-fashioned, hand-painted sign said was The University Café.

'Bit of a legend, this place,' said Jimmy. 'Opened in 1918.'

'Granda Jimmy was here on the opening day,' said James.

'That's how old he thinks I am.'

'You told me you were here!'

Jimmy held his stomach with both hands and gave his grandson a guffaw that young Jimmy matched with a near-perfect imitation. 'Come on, ya wee rascal.'

Going inside was like slipping through a portal to Glasgow in the mid-1900s. Etched glass partitions enclosed narrow red vinyl benches and slender Formica-topped tables; walls boasting old photos of Glasgow through the decades, different portly proprietors with exuberant facial hair; flock wallpaper in fashion a half-century ago; and menus offering an alluring array of arterial threats posing as culinary treats. If it wasn't deep-fried, it was crafted with Italian flair and full-fat milk in the ice cream machine.

Jimmy seemed to know everyone. He checked to find out what Tuk wanted, tried but failed to persuade him to have something to eat, and they retreated to a red alcove.

James went off to hold loud discussions with bemused staff about how good the banana boat was going to be. After two milky coffees were served, Jimmy had a question:

'Back when James hit you with the ball in the park, you seemed down, son.'

Tuk didn't understand.

'I thought you looked depressed. Unhappy.'

Tuk struggled as ever with the language barrier while he gave Jimmy a rough understanding of the story so far. Meeting the Glasgow girl in Thailand and becoming engaged to her because she said it might smooth his visa application; how she was sure her father would set them up with a blues bar where Tuk could play and they could prosper and get married and have a happy life in a new homeland. Everything falling apart within days when the father refused to help, and in any case his so-called fiancée had hardly spoken to him since he got here. Now he was almost broke and needed to find a job, but he lacked a work permit his fiancée must have known about all along.

'Jeez-oh,' said Jimmy. 'That's the shits right enough.'

'Granda!' said James, who had slipped into the booth unnoticed.

'Enough of your earywiggin', said Jimmy, just as the banana boat arrived. 'Eat your sundae or I'll eat it for you.'

James spooned a lump of banana from beneath a cloak of whipped cream, ice cream and strawberry dressing. He had a question for Tuk.

'Do you have bananas where you come from?'

'Tuk's from Thailand,' said his grandfather. 'Lots of bananas and other lovely fruits we've never seen in Scotland.'

'Thailand? Like the restaurant we went to, the one with the deep-fried bananas?'

Jimmy explained he was friendly with the owner of a Thai restaurant.

'It's not real Thai,' he said. 'My friend who owns it is from Hong Kong, a Chinese bloke.'

'A Chinky?' said Tuk.

Jimmy fired a glance at his grandson, who was busy trying to lick strawberry syrup from the back of his spoon.

'Aye, well I try to stop this wee bugger using that word.'

'You're swearing again, Granda!' said James. 'I'll tell mum.'

'You won't do that.'

'Oh yes I will.'

'Clipe.' He rejoined the conversation with Tuk. 'My friend Raymond is always complaining it's near impossible to find help. To get people to work in his kitchen, I mean. We could have a word with him, if you like.'

When the time came to pay the bill, Jimmy waved Tuk away. 'Not a chance, son. This is my treat. Glasgow's given you a rough start. You're a blues singer. What's that song? …If it wasn't for bad luck…'

'…I wouldn't have no luck at all,' said Tuk. 'Ray Charles. I love that song.'

'Let's go have a word with Raymond, try to get some good luck to come your way for a change.'

Eighteen

The Lotus Blossom restaurant was having another good night, and Raymond Chang was in his element. He shook hands at packed tables and made sure complimentary fish cakes or shrimp crackers were distributed in his wake. New customers lavished praise on a menu he hadn't altered in at least two years and promised they would be recommending the Lotus Blossom to their friends. Music to the ears of any restaurateur, it was especially pleasing to Raymond, whose business had been on a knife edge for the last couple of years. Almost overnight, things were different. The introduction of the Lotus Blossom's greeter, Khun Tuk, had been a resounding success from day one, and Raymond knew he owed his old friend Jimmy a free dinner.

At first he was confused when regular customer Jimmy turned up in the middle of a Sunday afternoon with his grandson and an Asian bloke carrying a guitar and a little amplifier. Despite owning one of the better Thai restaurants in a city where competition for customers was ferocious, Raymond, second-generation Hong Kong Glaswegian, had never hired a Thai, and the Thai with the guitar couldn't even cook. He was tall for an Asian of his generation, a bit on the plump side, a touch shy but jovial and unfailingly polite with it, which made him the perfect candidate for a role Raymond had been toying with introducing for months. There was even a costume hanging in the office nook. This was his chance to mimic what he saw in the doorway of a London restaurant so posh the prices on the menu scared him out the door before waiting staff could get him seated. The better part of a year later, he was still embarrassed about not responding when one waiter called him a "cheap cunt" in Cantonese.

Five days since he hired Tuk, and the word-of-mouth benefit from having a Thai doorman/greeter in traditional costume showed no sign of wearing off. Now the Lotus Blossom was the only establishment with a smiling greeter speaking a mixture of Thai and English and decked out in a garish outfit sourced from the internet complete with jewelled plastic gold crown. The novelty of his appearance made passing trade browsing upmarket eateries on the West End's increasingly trendy Argyle Street pause, check out the interior, see the crowds, smell the coconut milk and the lemongrass – and come on in. An instant uptick in positive online reviews only added to the new trade, and now the Lotus Blossom, for the first time ever, was recommending diners call ahead for reservations lest they be forced to wait for a table. If he hadn't seen it with his own eyes, all in under a week, Raymond would never have believed it possible.

'Sawasdee kab,' said Tuk, palms together in the traditional greeting, for the hundredth time since his shift began. Scots seemed to eat their evening meal early, meaning he started work at five p.m., with every shift preceded by the same briefing from his boss.

'Keep at it, pal. Speak as much Thai as you can, be sure to give everyone who even thinks about slowing down the welcome bow and the palms-together *wai* thing. It's doing great things for my business, so there'll be a bonus in it for you. After the dinner rush slows, off with the costume and into the kitchen to help out. Pineapple rings, dishes and onions. Got it?'

Tuk had never done anything to inspire so much despair. Bowing and scraping in a ridiculous costume like nothing worn by any Thai in history made him hurt in parts of his body and mind that never hurt before. But he soon discovered the *wais* could be rewarded when diners left, a few Chang or Singha beers the worse for wear. A party of four who just dropped a small fortune on dinner and drinks seemed to think nothing of giving Tuk five – or even ten – pounds as a token of their appreciation. Waiting staff shared their own tip collection at the end of the night, and were uninterested in adding the new guy to the split. This meant Tuk got to keep all the tips that came to him at the door. The bowing and scraping was agony, but in truth it was only a little worse than busking, and he needed the money.

As trade slowed and he got the nod from Raymond, he went back to change out of the costume and hang it carefully in the office nook before nipping through swing doors to the kitchen, where a mountain of caterer-sized tins of pineapple rings awaited. For the next hour he alternated between deep frying pineapple rings and washing dishes and pots thrown at him by the two kitchen hands who underlined his place in the pecking order by yelling at him whenever they had anything

119

they wanted washed. At least he thought that was what they wanted, as they only seemed to speak Chinese.

One of the waitresses asked him to bring a tray full of dishes back from the main restaurant; it injected a hint of variety into an evening of such tedium he was beginning to rethink his hatred of cover bands. Right now, he'd play *Country Roads* and *Hotel California* on an endless loop if it got him out of the kitchen. *Think of the money, Tuk.*

He backed through the swing doors with the heavy tray of dishes and turned to find one of the cooks holding his guitar. The mutt was pretending to play it while crooning in out-of-tune Chinese. Tuk's beloved Gibson was smeared with wet fingerprints and food scraps. He put the tray down none too gently.

One hand outstretched, he said: 'Give me the guitar.'

The man spoke in Cantonese to his friend.

'Hey, Ah-wai! Can you understand a word this motherfucker says?'

'Not a chance,' said Ah-wai. 'Chinese kitchen and the prick can't speak a word. Sneers at us as if we're shit, too.'

Tuk was no fighter. He had never thrown a punch in his life, something made easier to understand if you knew Tod, whose side he had been nailed to since the first days of elementary school. Even as a kid, Tod's fighting ability was often on display for all to see, but as he grew up his *Muay Thai* (kick boxing) expertise became known throughout Chinatown and respected to the point of being feared all through Tuk's school days. After Tod summarily dealt with the bully Beer in lower secondary school, only a fool with a deathwish would have tried to bully Tuk. But Tod was a few thousand miles away.

The two Chinese cooks were still cackling when Tuk grabbed a shovel-sized wooden spatula from a pot of boiling soup. He jammed it under the chin of the man holding his guitar.

'Give. Me. The guitar. Now.'

Major loss of face time. The cook surrendered the Gibson without a hint of delay and as the spatula was dropped to the floor, smeared his wet hand under his chin. Tuk stood so close their noses almost touched. He spoke again, this time in Thai.

'You put your Chinky fingers on my guitar one more time, and it will be the last time you see them.'

Still rubbing at the burn under his chin, the cook considered responding, but thought better of it when Tuk showed no signs of backing off.

'Leave it, brother,' said his friend. 'The Thai prick can't take a joke.'

'Did he just call me a Chinky?'

Tuk had come to enjoy the cool weather and the fresh Glasgow air, so he routinely walked the couple of miles from the Lotus Blossom to Jo's flat. Maybe he was putting off getting back to a place and a relationship devoid of warmth or welcome. She had told him her father was being stubborn and had confirmed there would be no financial backing for a New Adhere Bar. Tuk beat himself up over how he had let such a tantalising but unlikely prospect draw him away from what wasn't such a bad life in Bangkok. Here he was now, too ashamed to open up to his friends in Thailand – let alone his mum – about the shit he had dropped himself into. Talk about stuck between a rock and a hard place. Even Brendan seemed to have lost his enthusiasm for helping. Ideas for gigging opportunities were drying up.

A familiar face sat in a doorway with a sleeping bag wrapped in plastic and a smelly dog for company. For the fifth straight night, the man asked him the same thing:

'Help a man out with a pound for a cup of tea or a sandwich?'

Tuk reached into his pocket for a five pound note he had received as a tip.

'Aw. Bless you man, you're a lifesaver.'

Tuk gave him a plastic bag with two takeaway boxes he had planned to take home. One was a mild coconut milk chicken curry and rice, but the other, fried rice, would be a treat for the dog.

'Enjoy,' he said, as the man dipped into the bag while his dog whimpered with excitement.

'Thanks, pal!' the man shouted after him.

The different wear on individual steps up to Jo's flat was becoming familiar. He dug out the door key halfway up the last flight, suddenly alert to noise from inside. Jo screaming. He threw open the door and rushed in, nothing on his mind but Jo's defence. There was just enough time to register Jo and Terry having sex on the sofa before he fell headlong over his own suitcase.

Nineteen

Tuk and Bren – he was back to demanding he be called Bren – sat on a pallet of tinned fruit in a storeroom off the Lotus Blossom kitchen. Tuk told him Jo had thrown him out.

'I was lucky,' he said. 'I come back, Raymond was here. He let me stay.'

'Just like that? She threw you out?'

'I arrive at Jo's apartment, she is having sex with Terry and my suitcase is waiting for me.'

'Hold on,' said Bren. 'Roll the tape back a bit. Terry Fielden was there last night?'

'Terry is there every night. He stays in Jo's apartment.'

'Aw Christ. Now I get it.'

'What?'

'When you met Jo in Thailand, she was on a holiday my parents gave her, a reward for dumping Terry. They hate the guy and wanted Jo to chuck him, and when she did, they sent her off on an all-expenses-paid holiday to help her get over him.'

'They don't know Terry lives with Jo?'

'If my folks knew he was back, they'd have kittens. Dad pays the mortgage on the flat for his wee girl who can do no wrong.'

'So now I wonder,' said Tuk, unable to finish the sentence.

'What?'

'In Thailand, Jo was pretending? Pretending to like me? Pretending to want to marry me?'

Bren mulled it over for a few seconds before replying. No matter how he put it, this was going to hurt.

'Jo changes her mind like other people change their mobile phones,' he said. 'Falls in love with people and ideas all the time - then a couple of weeks later she's head over heels crazy about something or somebody new. She probably wasn't faking it in Thailand, but the sad truth is it was never going to last. I'm sorry, man. Anyway. Change the subject. Your boss let you stay here?'

'Raymond. Raymond Chang. He is kind, but I must find another place. One week, he says, only one week.'

'Could be worse,' said Bren.

'You think?'

Raymond Chang turned up, eyes full of suspicion. Bren jumped to his feet.

'You must be Raymond! Just the man I need to see. I'm Brendan – Bren Brogan, by the way.'

'What are you doing here, Bren Brogan?'

'I needed a quick word with Tuk, and wanted to ask you if he could get an hour off tomorrow night. I'm helping him find places to play – his music, I mean. I doubt if he's told you, but the man's a bloody great guitarist. And I've got him a, well, a chance to let him shine onstage, show people how good he is. Won't take long, forty-five minutes, an hour, tops. Eight o'clock tomorrow night.'

This was the first Tuk had heard of an audition.

'You're talking peak time for us,' said Raymond. 'People to greet, work to be done in the kitchen.'

'Of course. Understood, but this is a special request. Just the once, honest.'

'I have customers who come here because they like the new atmosphere I created by hiring Tuk to give the Lotus Blossom a unique feel, a touch of Thai specialness. Now you want to take him away when we're at our busiest.' He seemed to think about it, to remember that Tuk was now effectively homeless. 'OK, one hour. Back here and in the kitchen at nine. I'm already taking a chance letting him sleep here, you know. There's a no-overnight-stays clause in my lease. That's why I can only take a chance on a few more days.'

Tuk hurried out the door the following night to find Bren waving at him from the back of a hackney cab. He jumped in and they took off.

'We take a taxi? Why do you ask Raymond for only one hour?'

'Do you think he would have given you two hours? The taxi will save us a few minutes.'

He was right. In under two minutes, a demonstrably unhappy taxi driver dropped them outside a bar on Sauchiehall Street with the name *Honky Tonk* lit up above the door next to a brightly glowing neon interpretation of the Rolling Stones' lips logo. Inspired by, not a copy, honest.

A doorman in black – shoes, socks, suit, shirt and tie – chortled at the sight of Brendan.

'Did you pull a fast one? Out the bedroom window and down the drainpipe? Does your mammy think you're tucked up in bed, son?'

Brendan pointed at the blackboard with the elaborate announcement in multi-coloured chalk.

'Open mic night, isn't it? My pal Tuk is up for that. Great guitarist, by the way.'

The doorman wasn't so easily diverted.

'What are you, twelve?'

'I'm eighteen!'

'Why didn't you say? If that's the case, come back when you're twenty-four.'

'Aw c'mon,' said Bren. 'Please. I'm helping my friend. His English isn't so good, and we're only here a wee while. He's got another gig in less than an hour.'

'Helicopter warming up? Crowd at Wembley already chantin' his name? If I catch you drinking anything stronger than cola, I'll have your nuts.'

He stepped aside for long enough to let them pass and shifted his attention to three girls wearing not much by way of clothing and enough make-up for a party of six, pushing ahead of them an eddy of sickly perfume. Bren guessed they were about fourteen. Sure enough, the bouncer waved them straight in.

Tuk's years as a gigging musician had given him an ability to assess a new venue within seconds of setting foot inside. He arrived without high hopes, but was pleasantly surprised by what he saw. Good line of sight for all the customers was a start. One of Bangkok's best live music venues had a thick square pillar supporting an upper floor, dead centre in front

126

of the stage. Directly behind it sat a table and two chairs popularly known as the Stevie Wonder suite. This place offered everyone an unbroken view of the musicians.

Even better, tables were arranged so that all seats faced the stage, meaning there was no playing to people's backs. He drew further encouragement from the sound system, which despite being a mish-mash of brands, was made up of decent equipment. A 24-channel Yamaha mixing console, matched Shure SM58 microphones, and quality Bose speakers for the PA system. There was even a bulky Fender amp with a single, 15-inch speaker, dedicated to the bass.

When they arrived, none of the equipment was being put to good use. A house band backed a female singer who belted out an Amy Winehouse number, some but not all of it in tune. *I told you I was trouble, you know that I'm no good.*

'You can say that again, darlin!' shouted a man at a table in the middle of the bar.

'She will in a minute – it's the name of the song,' yelled another drunk.

'How about *Rehab?*' shouted a woman with bleached hair.

'More like refund,' said a man at her table, to cackles of laughter, as the singer strangled the song to death with a long, warbling, unsteady final note.

Tuk wondered what Bren had got him into. The blackboard said "Open Mic", but this already felt like a karaoke session. He noticed his self-styled manager waving from the stage, where he stood with the house band's guitarist.

'You're on, Tuk!'

He slipped the guitar from its case and one of the band members helped him plug in. The lead guitarist spoke in a hurry. He wanted to keep the music going.

'Your wee friend says you want to do a slow blues.'

'Please. Slow blues in E.'

The guitarist gave the three-horizontal-finger "E" signal to the man on bass, who nodded. The drummer raised his eyebrows, lipread "slow blues" and replied with a raised thumb. So far so good.

The drummer played them in and Tuk took over, aiming to build up the volume from a teasing, melodic start. He didn't get far before drunk voices from one of the tables closest to the stage drowned him out.

'Hey, it's the big man from the Lotus Blossom!'

'So it is,' said his friend. 'Where's the fancy dress costume and the plastic crown?'

'Sweet and sour chicken wings over here when you're ready, big man,' said the first drunk.

Tuk opened up on vocals:

'Did you ever love a woman.'

'Rub a woman,' yelled the first drunk. 'I've rubbed a few!'

'Rubbed yerself, more like,' shouted his pal. 'On that internet.' The two drunks stood up and gyrated as they heckled in ever louder voices. One young man at another table gestured towards to Bren, as if he could do anything, but the disturbance destroyed Tuk's chances of engaging the room. After the shortest version of the classic he ever played and having ignored prompts from the band to take a solo, he unplugged his guitar and left the stage. Gathering the case, he made for an exit sign. The audience weren't bothered. Already taking centre stage was a favourite Elvis impersonator, gelled quiff, rhinestone suit, pendulous gut and all.

Twenty

A flickering sign drew him along a dimly lit corridor and out to a grimy cobbled alley of rubbish bins, beer barrels and skips full of glass bound for recycling. It was peppered with cigarette butts and crisp packets and reeked of piss. To his left, the lane dead-ended against a crumbling wall smothered in overlapping graffiti tags; to his immediate right, in the direction he thought might take him back out to the street, stood three young men wearing hoodies, smoking earnestly. From behind them emerged a fourth, fixing his flies while a stream of fresh urine made a zigzag between the cobbles at his feet.

Tuk swung the guitar case over one shoulder and made for the narrow gap between the smokers and precariously stacked beer barrels. The man with fresh splashes on the toes of his tan boots moved into the gap, forcing Tuk to a halt.

'Excuse me,' said Tuk, as he tried and failed to push his way through.

'What've we got here?' said the would-be alpha male.

'A foreigner with a guitar,' said the youngest of the four.

'Ah can see that.'

He stiff-armed Tuk and plucked the guitar case from his shoulder. Tuk snatched back at it just as one of the offsiders landed a right hook to the side of his forehead. The would-be knock-out merchant yelped and leapt back nursing sore knuckles, but by now the game was on, and in a matter of seconds Tuk was in a foetal curl on the floor of the alley, arms around his head while kicks rained into him from all sides. When he attempted to get up, a boot stamped on his left hand and another connected with the side of his head and he went face-first into the grime. Lights out.

'Hey, pal. Are you alright? Try and wake up. Speak to me.'

Tuk came back from the depths of a black hole, hurting all over and vision blurred, to find a man with bloody knuckles looming over him. Tuk brought his hands up, fearful of what was going to happen next.

'Easy, pal. Relax – I'm not here to hurt you. Do you need an ambulance? I've got your guitar.'

Tuk followed the man's gesture. His guitar, seemingly unharmed in its case, was propped up against the leaning tower of beer barrels. He moved his jaw carefully. Speech was still an option.

'Four men...'

'They're not going to be bothering anybody. You're safe, pal.'

A door flew open, hammered against the wall, and spat Brendan from the rear of the club.

'Tuk! What's going on? Hey you! Get off him! What are you doing?'

'Easy, I'm helping here.'

Bren got closer, saw the mess the thugs had created.

'Helping? I'm calling the police.'

'Bren,' said Tuk. 'I am OK. This man is helping.' He dipped his head in gratitude to him. 'Thank you.'

'No problem.' He put out his hand, which Tuk shook carefully. His right hand was fine; the left one was another matter. A dirty heel print on the back marked where one of the attackers had stomped on it.

'My name's Lewis,' said the man. 'I saw how badly they treated you in there when you were onstage; it was a bloody disgrace. I came around to tell you about a proper blues jam not far from here and bumped into four hoodie arseholes running out with your guitar.' He turned to Bren: 'I found your pal on the deck, out cold.'

Tuk allowed Lewis and Bren to gently lift him back onto his feet.

'Are you sure you're OK?' said Bren.

Tuk slowly lifted his sore hand again. 'I think so.' He turned to Lewis. 'Thank you for my guitar.'

'No big deal,' said Lewis.

'It is very big deal.'

Bren gingerly put the guitar on his back and they walked deliberately towards the mouth of the lane. On the way, they passed four young men in hoodies, two of them sitting looking sorry for themselves, one with a broken nose, the other with blood and teeth on the ground between his knees; two more stood unsteadily against a wall, trying to light shaky cigarettes with shaky hands. Lewis raised one fist and feinted a half-step towards them and they dropped their smokes and ran.

132

McDonald's on Sauchiehall Street was two noisy floors of crowded tables. Bren volunteered to go to the counter, after which he climbed the stairs to find Tuk and Lewis sitting next to half a dozen women wearing Farrah Fawcett wigs and 1970s disco outfits, clustered around a comatose friend who resisted all attempts to be revived; the hen party had lost the participation of its chief hen. Only one of them seemed a little fearful for the welfare of the bride-to-be, while others were lamenting how their piss-up seemed to be coming to a premature close.

He parked a tray at the edge of Lewis and Tuk's table and transferred four enormous drink cups and three portions of French fries.

'The chips are the only thing worth eating in this bloody place,' he said. 'Tuk – get your injured hand into the ice; it won't do any harm. It'd better not, after the snotty kid in the stripey shirt gave me all kinds of grief over selling me a cup without a drink in it. Would you believe he ended up charging me for a large soft drink that's not there? So take your pick, it's either not Coke or not Fanta.'

Lewis encouraged Tuk to get his sore hand into the ice. At the same time, he absent-mindedly used ice to wash blood from the backs of his own hands. Bren nodded at prominent calluses on clean knuckles.

'Martial arts?'

'Aye, ever since I was a kid. Different disciplines. I get bored easily.'

'Those four buggers never knew what hit them.'

'I gave them a chance to hand over the guitar, but they seemed to fancy the odds. Four against one. I hate bullies.'

Tuk was more interested in the blues jam he heard Lewis mention earlier.

'About two minutes from here, in the State Bar,' said Lewis. 'One of the longest-running blues jam sessions in Europe, they say. Don't know who "they" are, but apparently, they do say.'

Tuk raised his eyebrows at Bren, who shrugged his wee shoulders. 'Sorry, never heard of it.'

'Great pub, excellent house band, and the Tuesday jam draws quality musos from all over the west of Scotland,' said Lewis. 'It starts pretty late, so we could still make it.'

Twenty-one

Many drinking establishments in Bangkok dress themselves up as old-fashioned British pubs, but for the first time in Tuk's life, he found himself witness to the real thing. The State Bar on Holland Street made such an impression it momentarily took his mind off the pain in his hand and around the eye socket where the thug had punched him.

The bar counter, a tall fat island dominating the middle of the room and shaped like two horseshoes linked ends-on, was of dark-stained wood. It was meticulously wainscoted and encircled by twin fat brass rings, one at elbow height around the edge of the countertop, the other just off the wooden floor for drinkers' feet to rest while they attacked a bewildering array of offerings from tall taps on the bar or the fat row of bottles suspended upside-down in optics and arranged neatly on overloaded shelves. Above the drinkers' heads, a gantry supported by intricately turned wooden posts was studded with hooks from which shiny pewter tankards dangled, somehow pulling off the illusion of being free of dust.

Walls wore dozens of black-and-white photographs in plain black frames. Steam trains, men in top hats, women in flowing dresses reaching past their ankles, boats large and small under construction or sailing on the Clyde, horses and carts carrying flat-capped men perched high, reins in their hands, cigarettes or clay pipes protruding from untidy facial hair and being admired by grubby children, many of them barefoot.

Lewis sat them down at a table near a mirrored alcove that somehow accommodated a four-piece band complete with full drum kit. If the Victorian setting and the period Glasgow décor gave Tuk enough pleasure to put his pain in the shadows, the music emanating from the little alcove warmed his heart to its core.

To get to the bar to order drinks, Lewis gently negotiated a scrum of casually dressed customers, many wearing faded concert souvenir shirts shouting the logos and names of blues and rock bands of bygone decades. John Mayall's Bluesbreakers, Bad Company, AC/DC, the Stones and the Who were predictable; outliers like Family and Procol Harem less so. Every single person in the bar seemed to know Lewis and took a moment to shake his hand and exchange a few words before they returned their attention to a fine band playing a soulful cover version of *Smokestack Lightning*. As they wrapped up the Howlin' Wolf classic, one of the two lead guitarists, a trim figure in a neat trilby and a printed shirt advertising the State Bar Blues Jam he was leading, pointed one finger, pistol-like at a customer nursing a pint at the bar.

'Fraser,' he shouted. He did the closed fist side-to-side movement in front of his mouth to let the cognoscenti know some harmonica was in the works. 'You're up.' Heads around the room swivelled in anticipation.

The man with receding grey hair drawn with care into a miniature ponytail barely cresting the back of his collar manoeuvred his tall frame into a spot in the alcove. After the briefest exchange with the band, they struck up a Chicago blues shuffle in G, and Fraser launched straight into an opening solo Tuk recognised as the intro from the Little Charley and the Nightcats song, *Dump that Chump*. The guitarist in the trilby did a spirited version of the vocals, and Fraser pulled off a diatonic harmonica solo that would have made Rick Estrin proud. Conversation around the bar faded while the audience enjoyed the music. This was Tuk's kind of crowd.

When the band took a break, the singer in the trilby came over to Lewis, who did the introductions.

'Tuk, this is Jim. Jim, Tuk is from Thailand. We just met a couple of hours ago and I told him about the jam. Oh, sorry, and this is Tuk's friend Bren.'

'Pleased to meet youse. Tuk, I see you brought your guitar. Want to jam? Everybody's welcome at the State.'

'Thank you,' said Tuk, 'but…'

'..He'd love to,' said Bren, 'but some bampots just tried to steal his guitar, gave him a kicking for good measure – and jumped up and down on his hand.'

'Jesus,' said Jim. He shifted his gaze to the street outside. 'Not here?'

'Around the corner,' said Lewis. 'At the back of the *Honky Tonk*.'

'The lane where the working girl from Yorkshire was strangled a couple of years ago,' said Jim.

'Took the cops weeks to identify her,' said Lewis. 'No arrests, so far as I know.'

'Depressing,' said Jim. 'Are you sure you can't play, Tuk?'

Tuk showed him his swollen hand.

'Sorry to see that, pal. Welcome to Glasgow, eh?'

'My good luck it happened in Glasgow,' said Tuk. 'Lewis saved my guitar.'

Jim's eyes lit up.

'The wankers who beat you up and stole your guitar ran into the only man in Glasgow with three different black belts? Lucky's the word. I hope your hand gets better; we're here every Tuesday. It'd be great to see you next week. That is if you're not going up to Shetland for a few days.'

'Whoah, I almost forgot,' said Lewis. 'The Lerwick Blues weekend. It should be magic.' He added for Tuk's benefit: 'Lerwick's in Shetland.'

'Shetland?' said Tuk.

'Islands so far out in the North Sea they get a separate box on the TV weather map,' said Lewis. 'Lerwick Blues is only a two-day event, but it's drawing quality acts from all over the place.'

'Shetland?' repeated Tuk. He still had no idea where they were talking about.

'W-a-y out the back arse of beyond,' said Bren. 'Other side of the world.'

'It's not so far,' said Lewis. 'And the headline act is Tyler Gray. Some kind of comeback gig for him after he disappeared for a lot of years. No way I'm missing that.'

'Tyler Gray?' said Tuk. 'Really?'

'Who's Tyler Gray?' said Bren.

Tuk shook his head knowingly at Lewis. 'Two days ago he doesn't know BB King,' said Tuk, turning to Bren. 'Tyler

Gray is fine blues guitarist and singer. His album came a year before my father died. He loved Tyler Gray.'

Tuk let himself into the Lotus Blossom via a side door and promptly dropped his keys when Raymond scared the wits out of him by turning up out of nowhere. He bent to get them, gasped in pain, and leaned against the wall while he gathered his breath.

'You look like you went ten rounds with Mike Tyson.'

'Sorry, Raymond. I had a problem. Some boys tried to steal my guitar.'

Raymond drew him into the light of a bulb above the doorway.

'Christ. Did you go to hospital to get checked?'

'No hospital.'

'I've got the car here. I'll take you to A&E.'

'Thank you. I am OK.'

Raymond went into the restaurant and came back with two bottles of Singha beer.

'Sit down for a minute,' he said. 'As if your day wasn't bad enough, I've got more bad news.'

Tuk's heart sank. What now?

'I mentioned to your wee manager pal about how my lease doesn't allow anyone to sleep here? Someone called up my landlord – a property outfit in London I never see from one year's end to the next – and dobbed me in. I'm pretty sure it was the jealous bastards across the street with the fusion ramen place that's well on the way to going belly up. Anyway, the London mob are sending a "representative" to check there's no truth in the rumour I have someone staying here. They're coming tomorrow at eleven. The last thing they want is for me to be turfed out and the rent dry up, so I'm pretty sure we got the warning to make sure nobody will be here when they arrive. Just to be safe, you'd better be out by nine. Sorry. You've been good for my business, so here's an extra few bob to say thanks.' He handed over an envelope with a wad of twenty-pound notes, much more than Tuk was owed in wages.

'Thank you,' said Tuk. 'I am sorry I am late tonight.'

'Don't worry about it. I'm sorry to see you go. Anytime you're around, drop in for a feed. On the house.'

They shook on it.

Twenty-two

Davie's Caff, only two minutes from the much more famous University Café, was a throwback to the greasy spoon of old. One glass counter with tray-sized plates of Chelsea buns open to the elements, caramel wafers and tea cakes stashed behind glass away from sticky-fingered youths. One wall shelf piled unevenly with cigarette brands favoured by the working man and woman. And a husband and wife team struggling to keep up with orders from a steady stream of customers, many of them taxi drivers taking time out from plying their trade around a city that never seemed to have enough taxis.

Davie did all the cooking at a spitting hot plate set against the back wall. He was short, built like he was crafted from knitting needles, barely enough room on bony forearms for faded merchant navy tattoos, anchors and chains, a dagger surrounded by swallows, a lone dove lost on the web next to one thumb. He wore his coal-black hair in a 1950s duck's arse swept back with cream surely reinforced by cooking oil sitting heavy in the shop's air. An unlit filter cigarette nestled above one ear, white paper marked by the tip of an oily forefinger every minute or two; reassurance for Davie that nicotine was *right there*, if only he could get a break from frying up different kinds of sausage, fatty bacon (done to a crisp, of course), eggs (ditto: fried eggs never left his grill without yellow translucent crispiness around the bottom edges; discerning regulars appreciated how it took skill to cook egg whites to the consistency of chewing gum while keeping soft yolks ready for toast soldiers to explore), and the inevitable black pudding. Scots loved their black pudding, the blacker the better.

Davie's wife June, what Scots called "heavy set" (code for shaped like a fifty-five-gallon drum), wore her orange-red hair in tight metal granny curlers covered by a scarlet headscarf. Maybe in the evenings radiant curls were set free, but no customer had ever seen her without the headscarf. She cried greetings to regular customers and orders to Davie in a raw voice straight out of Glasgow's East End. She addressed everyone as "hen" or "darlin'" or "gorgeous". Davie was the exception; he just got his name, delivered in ever-rising tones whenever June thought he was slacking or, perish the thought, had forgotten an order.

Bren came back from the counter struggling with heavy mugs of tea and a solitary roll and square sausage on a chipped plate. He put one of the mugs in front of Tuk. The table pre-dated anti-smoking legislation by a couple of decades, its edges scored with tapered orange-brown scorch marks from cigarettes carefully rested to free hands for attacks on the café's treats.

'Are you sure you don't want something to eat?' he said.

Tuk was starving, but not in the least tempted by a floury roll dripping with butter wrapped around a thick slice of crispy burnt meat and gristle. The Scots seemed to love it, though, to be fair, in parts of Thailand, especially in the Northeast, locals thought you were mad if you turned your nose up at fried crickets. He shook his head in response.

'I wanted to see you before you left,' said Bren.

'To say goodbye?'

'Yeah, – but there's something else.'

'More bad news,' said Tuk.

Bren took a bite out of his roll and sausage, in the process smearing flour over half of his face. He chewed appreciatively, and slowly. *He's buying time*, thought Tuk.

'I need to tell you something about Jo. You won't like it.' He washed food down with a bubbling slurp of milky tea. Tuk hadn't touched his, he noticed.

'I don't like to talk about Jo,' said Tuk.

'You have to know this.'

'OK.'

'Terry phoned me on my mobile last night. I was surprised he even had my number.'

'And?'

'Jo threw him out yesterday. He's raging. Angry, I mean. He told me everything.'

'What is everything?' said Tuk.

Everyone in the café except Joan jumped with fright when a mug crashed to the floor, customers raising their feet above a thin wave of hot tea. A petite Asian university student was aghast, slender fingers still clutching the handle that had detached itself from the mug.

'Don't worry about it, doll,' yelled Joan. 'Happens aw the time. Thay mugs are foreign rubbish – made in England. Sit yerself down over therr. One mair tea, comin' right up.' She showed no sign of wanting to do anything about the broken mug, which the student cautiously toed under the counter before heading to where a friend waited, fingers pointing at the mug handle still gripped tightly in her fingers.

Bren turned his attention back to the roll and sausage, took a smaller bite. Added tea, swallowed. Deep breath time.

'Remember you asked me if Jo was pretending in Thailand? Pretending to want to marry you? You were wondering if maybe it was all fake?'

'I remember,' said Tuk. He picked up his tannin-stained mug, examined it suspiciously, and put it back down again.

'And remember I said she wasn't faking it, she just falls in love with ideas all the time, and changes her mind a couple of weeks later.'

'You think different now?'

'I don't think. After speaking to Terry, now I know. She **was** faking it. Terry told me. Jo called Terry from Thailand, all excited because she'd found her USP - a unique selling point - something she learned in college. They taught her every new establishment needed a USP to be successful.'

'I know. In Bangkok she talked about USP.'

'Well, she told Terry she'd found the guy who would be the star attraction at a blues bar in Glasgow. Her USP. You.'

'This is not news. We wanted to open a New Adhere Bar in Glasgow. I was her USP. I play in the bar, attract the customers, she is the manager. We talked about it, over and over.'

'You don't understand. She tricked you into coming to Glasgow so that all the talk of a USP would help her get money from my dad to open the bar she wanted to open. Not with you, with Terry. It was always about her and Terry, even

144

if my dad hadn't a clue Terry was still in the picture. He would never put money into anything connected to Terry, but Jo thought she could use you to hide Terry's involvement. Maybe she faked being engaged because it cost her nothing, might even help you with your visa, help her pull off the USP marketing pitch.'

'Maybe it is only part of the story.'

'How do you mean?'

'I was unhappy in Bangkok, wanted a new life, away from my mother pushing me to an office job. I made it easy for Jo to trick me.'

Bren felt sorry for the big guy. He knew none of this would make things better for Tuk, but hadn't anticipated it causing him to come over all reflective and blame himself.

'She was still a bitch, still treated you like shit.' He checked his smartphone, took an urgent last attack at his tea and folded the remainder of the roll into his mouth. He spoke through it, flour flying. 'Need to get a move on. The airport bus might be the only one in Scotland that actually keeps to a timetable.'

Inside the main airport terminal building, a noisy crowd of drunks mushroomed around the counter for a charter flight to Spain. For some unknown reason, they all wore ponchos, sombreros and fake moustaches. Even the women. Rotund families clad entirely in Rangers and Celtic football jerseys did their best not to be associated with them.

Tuk came back from a check-in counter carrying a boarding pass and his guitar.

'No problem with the guitar,' he said. 'The blues festival helps.'

'They know about Lerwick Blues? That's good. Everything else OK?'

'Not OK. I feel stupid. I believed everything Jo said. That's why I came to Scotland.'

'No point in letting it get you down,' said Bren, knowing of course it would get him down. If it was him, he'd be crushed. Never mind how much of a mug Tuk had been to turn up without a proper understanding of how his entry permit didn't come with the right to work, Jo had knowingly pulled the wool over the poor bastard's eyes.

Tuk found empty seats in a corridor filled with a moving crowd of excited travellers with see-through Duty-Free carrier bags. Vodka and Bacardi seemed to be the order of the day among young Scots, blended whisky more to the liking of their seniors, some of whom had thrown budgetary caution to the wind and splurged on Johnnie Walker Black Label or Hennessey XO.

'In Thailand, many old farangs - that's what we call foreigners,' Tuk said, 'Many old farangs fall in love with a much younger girl they meet in a bar. Prostitutes who pretend to love them. The old farang believes the girl, thinks he is such a lucky guy. Now lonely old man has beautiful young girlfriend, lots of sex. But it is a trick. He always loses. He gives her money. After she builds best house in her village, she throws him out like Jo throws out Terry and me. Old farang is alone. No money, no house, no wife. In Thailand we laugh at the stupid farang. Now in Glasgow I am the stupid Thai guy. If I go back to Bangkok, everybody laughs at me. Even my mother.'

'Aw c'mon man, it could be worse.'

'How can it be worse?'

'You had no money to steal, and like you say, you can always play the blues. Let's get you to the security gate. Before you know it, you'll be in Shetland.'

'Thank you, Brendan. I am sorry you cannot come.'

'I've already got a load of explaining to do. My folks have no idea I've been doggin' school ever since you got here.'

They walked together to where the entrance to the secure area forced people to say their goodbyes. They shook hands solemnly until Bren pulled Tuk into a hug before breaking it off and turning away to hide his tears. Tuk swung his guitar onto his shoulder and winced with pain from the injured hand.

A friendly man in a dayglo vest wrapped around the biggest stomach Tuk had ever seen pointed him to the correct gate, where people waited patiently for the aircraft that was running late. From the attitudes of those waiting, this was nothing unusual. He popped himself down in an empty seat with his guitar between his knees and watched children run erratic paths through hand luggage spread out on the floor.

Only then did he notice instruments propped against seats or wedged between knees. Two electric guitars, an electric bass, a possible banjo, and in one custom soft case covered in faded hand-sewn badges, an acoustic guitar and what may have been a mandolin. Its owner was a grizzled man in his fifties with an unkempt beard and a pleated grey ponytail down the back of a faded denim jacket. They exchanged nods just as a much younger man asked Tuk if he could take the empty place beside him and sat down before he had time to respond.

'Are you going to Lerwick Blues?' he said.

147

'I hope so,' said Tuk.

'I'm from Shetland, going back to see my family and to catch the music. Where are you from?'

'I come from Thailand. Bangkok.'

He pointed at a sticker on the guitar case. 'I saw the script on your case, and thought you might be Thai. I was in Thailand last year. Loved it.'

'I'm happy you liked it.'

'I was in Hua Hin for a wee blues festival. Magic. Did you ever go?'

'My band played in Hua Hin many times. Only a short trip from Bangkok on the minibus.'

'You're in a band? What is it called?'

'We are *City Limits*.'

'Like Austin City Limits? My all-time favourite YouTube videos are the ones of Stevie Ray Vaughan and Double Trouble at Austin City Limits. Must have watched them a hundred times. Cool name for a band.'

'Thank you. Are you going to Lerwick Blues?' It was the first time Tuk had attempted to pronounce the name of the Shetland town, and though he struggled with it, the other man seemed to understand. Maybe Shetland people were used to outsiders wrestling with "Lerwick".

'Sure am. Oh, do you mean to perform? No, just to watch. I might be the only living Shetlander who can't play a musical instrument. My dad says it's just as well, since I couldnae carry a tune in a bucket.'

With only about seventy seats and propellors instead of jet engines, the plane was a novelty to Tuk, whose sole experience of air travel to date had been trans-continental flights on giant jetliners from Bangkok to Glasgow via Dubai. Two seats on each side of a centre aisle felt more like a comfortable inter-city bus, and since nobody had booked the aisle seat, the Gibson was strapped there while he watched Scotland go by from his place next to the window. Inflight service was a choice between a slab of shortbread or a Tunnock's Caramel Wafer. The caramel wafer wasn't bad. He washed it down with two flimsy plastic cups of bitter coffee.

'It's not exactly gourmet cuisine,' said a woman who reached across the aisle to give him her Caramel Wafer.

'Thank you,' said Tuk. 'I was hungry.'

'You poor soul.'

By now he was used to smiling and nodding at things he didn't quite understand.

She gestured towards his guitar. 'Are you playing at the festival?'

'I don't know,' he said, which seemed to confuse her.

'Just turning up on the off chance?'

'Maybe some jamming,' he said, thinking *Helluva distance to come for a jam session.*

'There's a tradition of jamming at all the festivals in Lerwick,' said a familiar voice. The young man who earlier had said something about carrying a tune in a bucket spoke with his face pushed through the gap between the seats in front of Tuk. 'I'll give you directions to a couple of good pubs.'

'He's right,' said the woman. 'The Lounge and the Marlex for a start. My name is Vivienne.'

'I'm Davie,' said the young man, face still framed by the seat backs.

'I am Tuk.'

'Nice to meet you, Tuk,' they said, in near-unison.

Tuk started to have a good feeling about the latest leg of this madcap trip. Shetland people seemed friendly.

A spectacular final approach to Sumburgh airport made him wonder if the plane was about to ditch among white-topped waves thundering towards the shore until tyres chirruped to tarmac moments after painted numbers on an airstrip flashed into view.

A tidy terminal building smaller than a Bangkok elementary school was thrown open to passengers the moment the propellors stopped turning, letting them walk the short distance to the terminal. After the briefest delay before luggage crawled around the sole carousel in use, Vivienne and Davie led Tuk out to the waiting bus. Davie waved Tuk and Vivienne aboard as he paid for all three tickets and Vivienne encouraged Tuk to get a window seat on the right side, where she assured him he would get the best views of the coast. The bus waited long enough to ensure no passengers from the Glasgow flight were left behind before pulling away. The driver came to an unscheduled halt just outside the airport, where the grizzled man with the grey ponytail and the guitar/mandolin case stood by the side of the road. He waved them on, signalling he was going to thumb his way to Lerwick.

'He must like hitch-hiking,' said Vivienne.

'Either that or he has no idea how cheap the bus is,' said Davie.

Twenty-three

Laurel Hughson lived in a small world. She was born in the same hospital where she now worked, less than half a mile from the modest terrace house that had always been her home. Twenty-five years on a Lerwick crescent, and sometimes she wondered if she would ever leave.

She navigated the street on her Honda scooter with exaggerated caution, memories fresh from when the Halcrow boy, a green-and-white streak in his new football jersey, flashed from between two parked cars in pursuit of a runaway football. Laurel snatched the front brake at the same time as she took evasive action on a wet road. Skid, crunch, bang. Her much-loved scooter and a neighbour's car suffered superficial damage and she got a skinned knee, but young master Halcrow got away with a scare. It might teach him not to chase footballs quite so recklessly but probably wouldn't. That evening, his dad Bobby appeared at Laurel's door, full of apologies and gratitude for not running over his boy and repeatedly stating a pledge to pay for the repairs to both vehicles. Good, concerned neighbours in a tight community watching out for each other. Living in a small world was not without its positives.

Riding at not much more than walking pace gave her plenty of time to be reminded how most neighbours kept their homes immaculately clean, spotlessly maintained, paint fresh, gardens at times obsessively neat. The contrast when she got to the house she shared with her father was always depressing. Until five years ago, it was as pristine as any on the crescent, tended fastidiously by her parents, dad quite happy to work under relentlessly good-natured pressure from mum. Since she died of an aneurism at the same hospital where Laurel worked, it had decayed into a stain on the crescent, weeds sprouting, windows needing cleaned, paint peeling, front doorstep cracked and crooked, outdoor light dangling from a loose bracket. That Laurel couldn't face doing anything about the exterior of their home was a source of endless shame, but indoors she had other things to worry about. These days she never arrived home without a sense of dread.

The street was built by the local council in the 1940s. By the time her parents moved into the house, it was already forty years old and still had the original locks. Now, it had the same door and locks. Neither of them were locked in the daytime, which meant she only had to push down on the corroded handle next to the letter box and let herself in.

'I'm home,' she said in a raised voice she knew could be heard in the living room. There might have been a grunt in response. She opened the living room door to be met by several hours' worth of stale cigarette smoke and the nauseating funk of a full crystal ashtray on a side table next to her dad's armchair. He sat swallowed by the old chair, eyes fixed on the television tuned to horse racing. As far as she knew, George Hughson had never bet on a horse in his life. But still the horses ran, sound turned low. Company for the lone drunk who no longer bothered walking to the pub, so long as he could somehow get whisky to the house. Lately, a local taxi driver delivered a half bottle every day, charging a modest delivery fee. Laurel knew the guy and couldn't bring herself to resent him helping her dad stay tanked up without leaving the house. At least he was still at the half bottle stage, though for how long she couldn't guess. The slippery slope was getting steeper.

'You OK?'

'Fine.'

'Been home all day?'

'What do you think?' Ash fell unnoticed from his cigarette as he gave her a dismissive outward sweep of one hand. With his other hand he picked up the glass from the hearth. Straight blended whisky, well on the way to needing replenished. A few months ago he would have lifted himself and walked a few yards to the dining room cabinet for a refill. Now the bottle sat out of sight on the other side of the chair. He tried to take a sip but missed his mouth, splashing whisky down his shirt front.

'Shitfaced again,' said Laurel.

Again, the dismissive wave. He hadn't taken his eyes from the television for even a moment.

'Fuck off,' he said.

The neighbours doubtless heard the living room and house doors slam. It was a regular occurrence. Laurel jumping aboard the Honda, eyes filled with tears, hell-bent on putting distance between her and the house and the wee drunk in the living room, was no longer out of the ordinary. Except that today she made her escape with neither keys nor crash helmet. Bugger it, she would walk off her fury. Bobby Halcrow paused in the unloading of shopping from the family car for long enough to give her an enquiring stare, an invitation to talk if she needed someone to hear her out. She responded by way of a tiny head shake. *Thanks, but no.*

Twenty-four

When Tuk was a child, his dad set aside time to read to him, not at bedtime when dad would inevitably be out playing music for a living, but in the afternoon, after his son came home from school. These were precious moments he recalled fondly, and thanks to them Tuk became familiar with dozens of children's folk tales from Thailand and abroad.

Which explained why the view from a bus trundling up the largest of the Shetland islands made Tuk smile at the thought of Jack and the Beanstalk.

Central to the story's appeal was the shock involved in the appearance, a few hours after Jack's angry mother snatched beans from his hand and launched them from a window, of a giant beanstalk that grew overnight, reaching high into the sky.

To a youngster like Tuk, the premise was not particularly outrageous. In Thailand, some variations of bamboo grew three centimetres in a single hour. The notion of plants sprouting overnight wasn't particularly scary, even if the image of an angry giant glowering down at him from the top of a beanstalk was enough to terrify young Tuk.

Some thought the beanstalk story originated in frigid northern climes. Shetland was as far north as Tuk had ever been, and scenes outside the bus could hardly be less like the astonishingly fecund landscapes back home.

Apart from roadside tufts of grass protected by fences from sheep in lightly populated fields, nothing seemed to grow much above ground level. Hillsides wandered gently into the distance unmarked by a single bush, let alone a tree. Jack's beanstalk would draw a crowd in Shetland.

To the east, the North Sea pounded itself to foam on rocky shorelines and towering cliffs. Tides were deflected towards complex inlets with deserted sandy beaches fronting farmhouses far enough from the water's ever-moving edge to be safe from the highest of tides.

A sparse population clearly depended on a bus service operated by the friendly driver called Bobby, who was on first-name terms with many. Seemingly impromptu stops were made to let passengers disembark directly outside their homes, loud appreciative cries of thanks to Bobby not quite snuffed out by the pneumatic hiss and clatter of the door closing behind them. At one official bus stop inlet, the man with the ponytail and two instruments climbed out of an SUV, patted the roof in appreciation, and waved at Bobby, who nodded back as he engaged first gear.

After a uniformed airport worker friend disembarked outside a squat home set into a hillside cleft as if to hide from North Sea storms, Vivienne slipped into the seat next to Tuk. She waved at the view.

'What do you think?'

'Very nice,' said Tuk.

'Nothing like Thailand, eh?'

'Yes. Not like Thailand.'

'The lack of trees bothers folk, but they've been gone for centuries, used by our ancestors for cooking fires and keeping warm in the winter. Now, because of hungry sheep, they never get a chance to grow again.'

Tuk was pleased. He seemed to be picking up enough words to get the gist of long sentences. 'I come from Bangkok, a very big city,' he said. 'Crowded, many tall buildings, traffic jams, so many people everywhere.'

'It must be strange for you,' said Vivienne. 'Hardly any buildings, few cars, not many people, but we love it.' She pointed to a rare uphill slope ahead of them. One solitary van came the other way. 'When we get over the hill, we see Lerwick, the capital. The biggest town – the only town – in Shetland. About seven thousand people live there.'

'Seven thousand?' said Tuk. 'Only?' He thought about it for a moment. The apartment building where he grew up might house a thousand. He checked his phone which, far from Wi-Fi and without a UK SIM card, served mostly as a clock. Mid-afternoon UK time meant late evening in Bangkok. He worried his mum might be sitting in their apartment, sad and alone. He hoped Khun Jiraporn was keeping her company.

He climbed down from the bus at Victoria Pier in time to see the hitchhiker arrive in the bed of a pick-up truck shared with two sheep dogs who acted as if they were embarrassed by his company. The truck sped off in such a hurry Tuk wondered if carrying a person in the back was illegal. In Thailand, entire construction crews or families moving house or clusters of children with water pistols travelled in the back of

157

speeding pick-ups, and the resultant death statistics were a national horror story. Whether or not it was illegal, nobody seemed to know or care.

'Howzit goin', pal?' said the man with the ponytail and two instruments in one case covered in stickers and sew-on patches.

'I am fine, thank you,' said Tuk.

'Here for Lerwick Blues?'

'Yes. I want to see. How about you?'

The man patted his instruments. 'I'm my own one-man festival. Been playing all over Europe for nearly thirty years. I like to keep moving, and there's always a generous audience in wee towns when a festival is on.'

'You are playing outside, on the roads, the streets?' The word he was reaching for came, suddenly. 'Busking?'

'Aye, that's me, a provider of professional urban entertainment for the discerning pedestrian with pocket change to fling at a starvin' man with a guitar. Do you busk?'

'I tried one time only.'

The older man seemed relieved. 'It's not everybody's cup of tea. Listen – you're welcome to join me anytime you like – but no queerin' my patch, mind, strictly as a guest. Hang on, I know that accent – are you from Thailand? I go to Thailand every winter for three months. Beats the hell out of singing in the rain here, freezing my balls off for pennies.'

He didn't wait around for a response, which was just as well, as the only word Tuk got from his outpouring of impenetrable Scots was "Thailand".

He sat at one end of a bench facing out over a choppy channel separating the pier from what might be another island.

158

Teenagers busied themselves around little, red-sailed boats they slipped from a floating pontoon into frigid black water. At a prime spot near the mouth of the inner harbour sat a powerful-looking craft painted bright orange and blue. Prominent signage told him it was a lifeboat, named for people called Michael and Jane Vernon.

It was late afternoon in a strange location of which he knew next to nothing. He didn't know a single Shetlander, had no idea where he might stay tonight – a matter not unconnected to an embarrassing shortage of funds – and had no reason for being here, apart from a hunger to play the blues at a festival unaware of his existence. His mother hadn't heard from him in the best part of a week and even his best friend Tod would be wondering if he'd fallen off the edge of the planet. He was tired, hungry, lonely and depressed. What was he doing here?

Self-pity was intruded upon by the sound of sobs coming from a young woman at the other end of the bench. She was about two metres away, and he hadn't even registered her presence, let alone her despair. He listened to her sob for a few more seconds.

'I want to cry,' he said, loud enough for only her to hear, timed for when she paused for breath.

She held back on the sobbing, chest heaving.

'You do?' she said.

'I want to cry for I am alone in a strange country and I followed the wrong woman to Scotland – and I cry for my father who is dead for many years.'

'I'm crying because sometimes I wish my dad was dead.'

'I am sorry,' said Tuk.

'Are you here for the blues festival?'

'Yes. And no.'

'I don't understand.'

'I come because of the festival, but maybe I cannot play.'

'Why not?'

He held up his left hand, swollen and bruised.

'My big problem,' he said. 'Maybe cannot play guitar.'

'So you are not here just to watch? You are playing at the festival, but because of your injured hand you might not be able to? Where are you from?'

'I don't know.'

'You don't know where you come from?'

'I don't know if I can play. I come from Thailand.'

'I don't remember reading about you. If someone was coming all the way from Thailand, Colin and Susan would be making a big deal of it.'

'I hope to play. I want to play.' He knew how stupid he sounded. She changed the subject for him.

'Where are you staying? Do you have friends here, or a hotel room or a bed and breakfast reserved?'

'I must find. No friends.'

She took an old mobile phone from her bag and brought it to life.

'You're a bit late. The whole town's booked solid.' She held up a hand to Tuk and put her ear to the Nokia.

'Colin? It's me. There's a guy here on the pier, needs a room somewhere…. You think I don't know the town's full up? The man came all the way from bloody Thailand for your festival. OK, alright.' She ended the call and spoke to Tuk: 'Colin's one of the festival organisers. He is just around the corner. Says he'll be here in two minutes.'

'Your friend knows a hotel?'

'He'll know somewhere,' she said, as a young man on a bicycle with squeaky brakes came to a halt in front of the bench. The girl gave his bike a mocking grin.

'Wow, you're pushing the boat out for your esteemed international guest, eh?' she said. 'What's next, a red carpet all the way to a suite in his five-star accommodations?'

'My car's jiggered. It needs parts all the way from Korea.' He turned his attention to Tuk and handed him a business card with all his contact details. 'My name is Colin. I'm the co-organiser of the blues festival. Laurel says you need somewhere to stay?'

'My name is Tuk. Thank you for your kind offer.'

Colin was stuck for words. There was no offer.

'The town is totally full, bursting at the seams, no rooms anywhere. But I might know one option because you are a friend of Laurel. It's only a few minutes away, if you don't mind walking.'

'Does he have a choice?' said Laurel.

'Did you give me a choice?'

'Tuk gave Laurel a hands-together *wai* greeting. 'I am Tuk. I am happy to meet you. Your name is, ehm, Rauren?'

'Laurel. L-A-U-R-E-L. Like Laurel and Hardy, except I wasn't named after the comedian.'

'Very difficult,' said Tuk.

'To remember?'

'To say. To pronounce is difficult for Thai person.'

Twenty-five

Colin pushed his bicycle across the road, waving his thanks to vehicles slowing to allow them access to a broad lane with shops at street level and occasional upstairs retailers. He pointed out a Thai restaurant on one side, and High Level Music on the other. 'Great wee music shop,' he said. 'Instruments, CDs, accessories, the lot. They'll hopefully sell a lot of guitar strings and how to learn the blues materials in the next few days.'

In front of a Tourism Office, he turned left and Tuk and Laurel followed. Laurel asked if she could help with Tuk's suitcase or guitar. He shook his head in thanks, wondering where they were going. They walked past a bank, shops selling knitwear, a post office and, biggest premises of all, a bookstore. To their right ran steep, narrow lanes heading uphill; empty of commercial premises, residential homes climbed the lanes, buildings of rough grey stone. Bangkok sprawled over a giant flat coastal plain without a single hill. When Colin took them to the other side of a small crossroads and turned right, Laurel saw Tuk eye the new hill they faced.

'Don't worry,' she said. 'We're almost there.'

Whatever "there" was, she was good to her word. Less than two minutes later they cut left towards a row of houses built on the incline, their roofs creating a saw-tooth shape against the grey-blue sky. The end house had a passageway beneath, allowing them to access another street with houses laid out on the hill in the same saw-tooth design. Colin paused at a porch, rang the doorbell and pushed his way through the unlocked door, shouting as he entered: 'It's me!'

He led them past a shoe rack, a coat stand bowed by the weight of heavy raincoats and a tall ceramic pot with a variety of umbrellas and at least two ornately carved wooden walking sticks. One more door kept the weather out of a living room that opened up straight from the porch.

The first thing to strike Tuk was the heat. Stiflingly warm from a gas fire in a tiled fireplace under a mantlepiece holding a bewildering array of glass ornaments. Above them, a clock reminiscent of the old one next to the photographs in his home in Bangkok ticked loudly.

Standing between the fireplace and an overstuffed sofa were an elderly couple. The woman wore her white hair in two silver clasps, an ornately patterned woolen cardigan, hands overlapping in front of a pleated skirt, arthritic fingers wrapped tight in rings she had clearly held dear for a long time. The man wore a heavy checked shirt, baggy slacks and leaned one big, veined hand on a walking aid with three soft rubber feet making equidistant circular dents in the heavy carpet.

'My gran and granda, Sadie and Matt – this is Tuk.'

Tuk gave them both a respectful *wai,* clasped hands held high in recognition of their seniority.

'Hiya,' said Laurel, who turned to Tuk. 'Gran and granda is short for grandmother and grandfather. Because of the festival, there isn't a single hotel room or bed and breakfast to be had anywhere in Lerwick, so Colin asked Sadie and Matt if you could sleep here for a few days.'

'You are so kind,' said Tuk.

'Don't be daft,' said Sadie. 'We're awfie proud of what our Colin's doing for Shetland with the festival, so of course you can sleep here. So long as you don't mind the sofa.' She pointed at the big settee.

'You'll be fine on the sofa, won't you?' said Laurel.

'Very fine! Thank you so much, Mrs Sadie, Mr Matt. Thank you Colin.'

Sadie declared with certainty the need for a pot of tea and disappeared into the kitchen. Laurel and Colin stepped outside to talk. Matt was eager to chat.

'You are from Thailand?'

'Yes, Bangkok.'

'Oh, Bangkok. How about Patpong with all the girlie bars?'

'I know Patpong, but I don't go there.'

'Do the girls still do the amazing trick show with the ping pong balls flying out of their –' He stopped talking when Sadie came back in with a plate of biscuits.

'Tea's almost ready,' she said. Before she turned toward the kitchen, Matt spoke to her:

'I was just asking Tuk about Thailand. He's from Bangkok. Sure we had a lovely holiday there a few years ago.'

'Oh yes, best holiday we ever had. The Royal Palace and the Wat Po temple by the river with the reclining Buddha –

but my favourite was a tour of the floating market at dawn.' She jabbed a thumb at her husband.

'This one never even saw the floating market. All the way to Thailand to lie in bed nursing a hangover. Here's your key to the front door. Make yourself at home, son. What's wrong with your hand?'

Tuk gently flexed the fingers of his damaged hand.

'I had a problem in Glasgow.'

'Looks like some so-and-so jumped on it with their tackety boots. Did you see a doctor?'

Tuk shook his head, almost in apology. 'No, I –'

'We know just the man, don't we Matt?' said Sadie. 'The Henry boy who went to school with Colin, the alternative medicine fellah, does the whatchamacallit, acutincture thing wi' the wee needles.'

'She always has trouble with that word,' said Matt. 'She means acupuncture.'

Sadie gave her husband a mock scowl.

'Enough of your lip, smartipants. It's only been forty-seven-and-a-bit years since my dad walked me up the aisle to meet you at the altar, so there's still plenty of time for a divorce.'

She turned her attention to Tuk. 'Only kidding, son. But sometimes I do wonder.'

Colin and Laurel huddled in the porch.

'What do you think?' said Laurel. 'Any chance he can get to play somewhere?'

'What's with the pressure? You don't know him from a hole in the ground. He might be shite.'

165

'If you don't give him a chance you'll never know. He's a nice bloke, came all the way here from Glasgow because he wants to play the blues. What more do you need?'

Colin was unconvinced. 'Susan will shit herself. Everything's already fixed. There are no empty slots in the schedule – and he doesn't have a band, so I'll have to see if someone else will let him join them for a couple of numbers. It'll never happen without a rehearsal at least. We can't put an unknown quantity onstage.'

'Talk to your ex and see what you can do. Just don't tell her it's a favour for me or it'll never happen.'

Twenty-six

Sadie walked Tuk back down to Commercial Street, past the post office and up a precipitous lane with an unbroken double metal handrail running up the middle like a miniature elevated railway track. A few buildings later, she rang a polished brass doorbell next to a garden gate with an even more brightly polished sign: *Henry McVicar. Alternative Therapy.*

A young man came out to open the gate and led them into a boxy, flat-roofed extension that clashed horribly with the grand old bay-windowed home.

'Thanks for coming by,' he said, after Sadie did the introductions. 'What can I do for you?'

Sadie answered. 'The lad's got a sore hand. Needs you to work your pointy needle magic on it.'

Henry took Tuk's hand in both of his, held it under an angle-poise lamp for a better look, and examined it with great care.

'How did this happen?'

'I had a problem in Glasgow.'

'So I can see! Where are you from?'

167

'I am Thai. From Bangkok.'

'My favourite city in the whole world,' said Henry. 'I love Bangkok. I could spend a month walking around the Chinese medicine stores on Charoen Krung Rd. Do you know Charoen Krung? It's in Chinatown.'

'My home is only one minute from Charoen Krung. I lived in Chinatown all my life.'

'Oh, wow. I bet you know more than I do about my favourite shops.'

'You two stop your blethering,' said Sadie. 'Henry – get the man sorted. He needs that hand to play his guitar.'

Henry paused his examination. 'You're here for the festival? I didn't see you on the website.'

'I don't know if I can play,' said Tuk.

'Because of your hand? No wonder.'

'Also because nobody knows I am here.'

'You're wrong, son,' said Sadie. 'Our Colin knows you're here and I'm sure he'll help you.'

'You are sure?'

'If he doesn't, he can forget about Christmas at his Gran and Granda's house! Only kidding. He's the apple of his Gran's eye. Now, if he'd just get himself a proper job.'

'Your turn to stop blethering, Sadie,' said Henry, as he rested Tuk's hand on a sterile towel on top of a firm cushion. From a drawer he produced a folder of individually-wrapped acupuncture needles.

'Have you had this done before?'

'No,' said Tuk.

'Not afraid of needles, are you?'

'Not afraid,' lied Tuk. 'Please go on.'

Henry spent about ten minutes carefully placing six needles at different locations on Tuk's injured hand, some of them nowhere near the worst swelling or bruising. He made Tuk lie down on a comfortable sofa with his hand resting on a pillow, dimmed the lights, and told him to relax. Tuk closed his eyes, and when he heard the door close behind Henry and Sadie, tried to concentrate on happy thoughts. He was fairly sure happy thinking would not interfere with an Oriental traditional healing process he had no faith in whatsoever.

A gentle hand coming to rest on one shoulder stirred him from the deepest sleep he had enjoyed since coming to Scotland more than a week before.

'Glad to see you are still with us,' said Henry.

'Lucky for me Henry makes a nice cup of coffee,' said Sadie. 'You've been sound asleep for about half an hour. You must've been worn out.'

Henry helped him up to a sitting position and carefully removed the needles.

'Can't do any more today,' he said. 'Keep moving it, but gently. Take it easy at first, waggling your fingers like this,' – he demonstrated what he meant – 'but don't overdo it. Come back in a couple of days if it's not getting better.'

'Thank you,' said Tuk. 'How much do I –'

'Don't worry about it,' said Henry. 'Colin and Sadie are old, old friends. If I get back to Bangkok, maybe you can show me around Charoen Krung Road and tell me some of the names of the herbs and potions on offer. I hardly scratched the surface last time I was there.'

Late in the evening, stomach groaning from a dinner of mouth-watering smoked fish with lashings of buttery mashed potatoes, Tuk sat at a desk in the corner of the living room. Matt had encouraged him to use the computer and assured him the broadband service was fast, so he decided to try and get hold of Tod.

Matt used a browser Tuk had never seen before. As he muddled his way through it, he inadvertently hit a *back* button, setting off a noisy pornographic video. While he tried and failed to find the volume control to take away the sound of an improbably-stacked woman engaged in extremely vocal sex with an improbably-equipped man half her age, the sound of the living room door opening made his head spin. Matt leaned through the open door, wearing baggy pyjamas with *World's Best Granda* repeated across it in soft-flowing script.

'Sadie said I should come down to make sure you're OK. D'you like the website, too?'

'No!' said Tuk. 'I made mistake!'

'Sure you did. Don't be worrying about the volume. Sadie's as deaf as a post without her hearing aids in. Enjoy yourself. See you in the morning.'

After a few more minutes, he managed to log into Skype and make a call. It was answered almost immediately by the unmistakable voice of Tod screaming so loudly in Thai he was glad he had remembered to plug in the headphones.

'Tuk! My man! How the hell are ya?'

'I am in a place called Shetland. The Shetland Islands. Like Koh Phangan, with no trees and a lot colder. But the people are friendly.'

'Hang on,' said Tod. 'I thought you went to join Jo in Glasgow. How come you're somewhere else already?'

'Jo dumped me.'

'Jesus, Tuk, you went all the way to Scotland to get dumped? Man, that's a blues song in the making. But hey, it could be worse.'

'Now you sound Scottish,' said Tuk. 'They are always telling me things could be worse.'

'But trust me bro' when I say it could have been a lot worse,' said Tod. 'You nearly married the bitch.'

'Anyway, I don't want to talk about Jo. Now I'm in a little town called Lerwick where there's a blues festival this weekend, and Tyler Gray is the headline act on Saturday night.'

'Whoah, now you're talking. He's the guy you were always playing on CD, the album your dad loved? How many days is the festival? Have you got a gig?'

'Only two days. I'm trying to get to play, but it's not easy when nobody knows me.'

There was no point telling his friend about the state of his hand, though after the needle torture, it was actually beginning to loosen up. He remembered Henry telling him to keep moving it, and began the stretching exercises that were becoming easier every time he tried them.

'Aim high, man,' said his friend. 'Let me see what I can do from here. Email me the name of the town and the festival website and any contacts you have, and your old front man Tod will take to the web and see what he can do. You can't let a chance this good pass you by. But I'm sorry to hear about Jo. Does your mother know?'

Tuk pictured the sort of misery news of this would inflict upon his mum.

'No! And don't tell her. I'll call her when I'm ready to talk, just not now.'

'OK, my friend. Don't worry, man. I'm telling nobody. I have to go - I got this hot new hi-so chick wants singing lessons! I tell ya, the way she's been giving me the eye, there's a good chance she's gonna be teaching ME things. Email me the contact info and I'll get onto it after I finish introducing this babe to skills she never knew she had.' He rang off without another word. Before he forgot, Tuk reached into his pocket for Colin's business card to send over the details Tod needed.

Twenty-seven

Laurel had told him Shetland's annual high temperature was around 16 degrees Celsius. In Bangkok, that would be close to the annual low, suffered once or twice in December or January, sending Thais digging out long trousers and army surplus jackets to keep them alive on motorcycle trips across the city. Thai entrepreneurs with storerooms full of specialized stock must wait, desperate for cues from weather forecasters to set up roadside racks on wheels, heavy with thermal jackets and long trousers and woolen bonnets and mittens that would remain on sale for two or three days at the most. Now, from the pillion seat of Laurel's scooter and wearing a borrowed open-face helmet without a visor, 16C made his eyes stream with tears from the cold.

When Sadie was encouraging him to tuck into a breakfast plate heaped with enough to feed three grown men, she paused to take a short phone call on the clunky old rotary phone attached to the kitchen wall. She listened for a few seconds, nodded happily towards Tuk, thanked the caller and said a polite goodbye before hanging up.

'Laurel says don't go anywhere. She'll be here in half an hour.'

Thais are endlessly flexible when it comes to time. Half an hour could mean anytime this morning or even later, so Tuk was surprised and pleased when Laurel rang the doorbell and let herself in less than twenty-five minutes later. She wore a motorcycle helmet, carried another one strapped to the crook of her arm, and a plastic bag from which she extracted a woolen sweater that Sadie latched onto right away. She picked it up in two hands and examined it in the light of the living room window.

'This is a beauty. Unless I'm mistaken, it's the work of Isobel Laurenson – she was born a Jacobson on Bressay a few years before the war – it's from maybe the early sixties. I think I remember your dad wearing this. How is he?'

'Same,' said Laurel. 'I remember when he could fill it. Now it would hang on him like a barber's cape. It's to keep Tuk warm when we're on the scooter.'

'Good thinking, pet,' said Sadie.

She rode with expertise he recognised from thousands of kilometres spent as a passenger on the backs of countless motorcycle taxis. Some of the taxi riders back home showed astonishing skill in the most difficult of conditions. Others rode like they were drunk – which occasionally they were. Tuk made it a rule never to ride a motorcycle taxi after eight o'clock in the evening, because some of the guys still on the roads in the evening were returning to work after gambling away their day's earnings while slugging back industrial-strength rice liquor of the sort that saw tragically high rates of liver and kidney failure among young members of farming communities all over Thailand. Uncle Mu had warned him about the number of funerals he had attended in the provinces, friends and cousins and nephews dead in their thirties from cirrhosis of the liver or alcoholic hepatitis. Stay away from rocket fuel homemade hooch, was the obvious sub-text.

But he put such thoughts to the back of his mind and giggled with delight at the sights and sounds as Laurel (he still wasn't sure he'd ever be able to pronounce her name; the "l" at the end was the real test; many Thais struggled with "little", pronouncing it "littun") swept around town gracefully, exchanging waves and greetings with people she knew. They pulled up at a quaint coffee shop near the waterfront, took an outdoor table (it wasn't *that* cold, Tuk was coming to realise), and she sat down while he went in to practice his communication skills.

He returned with a tray, emboldened enough to attempt a Scottish accent.

'Here ye ur. One larrrge Americano, one medium cappuccino wi' extra chocolate and awrat by the ways.'

It warmed Tuk's heart to see the woman he first saw sobbing on a nearby bench laugh so hard she almost spilled her coffee.

Still smiling, she said: 'Tell me about the friend in Bangkok you talked to last night.'

'Tod is my oldest friend. The singer in our band, *City Limits*. We are friends since elementary school.'

'Was he surprised to hear you were in Shetland?'

'Very surprised. But happy I am away from that woman.'

He had told Laurel about the farcical move to Scotland, how he had come over in chase of a different woman from the one he thought he met in Thailand. How the lure of playing a central role in a blues bar in an unknown city on the other side of the world was attractive enough to make him walk away from family and friends and fellow musicians in Bangkok. How well-meaning pressure from his mum to find a steady job had contributed to his restlessness. And how he never considered the misery she had already suffered from having a struggling musician for a husband who died long before his time. Now he had taken the misery to a second generation and felt guilt-ridden. And stupid.

Instead of judging him, Laurel told him it was water under the bridge, time to move on. When he realised he hadn't mentioned Pim, it made him consider that she hadn't appeared in his thoughts once since he arrived in Scotland.

'What else did he say?'

'He says I must try to play with Tyler Gray, but I didn't say about my hand.' He held it up and flexed his fingers. The swelling was going down, the movement better. Perhaps it was time to re-evaluate his skepticism of traditional Oriental therapies. 'I said I will try.'

'Colin says the schedule is totally full,' said Laurel, 'He will try to get you a spot. But he did say it's not likely to be with Tyler Gray because he's the headline act, and you are….'

'I am nobody from Thailand. I understand. But still we try. Tod is using email to talk with Colin. Maybe something is possible.' He took in the sights. People enjoying the fresh air and delicious hot drinks and muffins bigger than their giant coffee cups; the water rippled by a cool breeze, the sky a colour of blue he had never seen before and a car ferry setting off for the island across the strait. 'I like your town,' he said.

'Probably because your luck might be changing.'

'What is the word? Fortune? Maybe fortune changes.'

'Do you have fortune tellers in Thailand?'

Tuk nodded enthusiastically as if to say *of course* while he took a big swallow of cappuccino.

'Drink up,' said Laurel. 'There is someone you have to meet.'

A few minutes later, they took to the road Tuk remembered travelling in the other direction the day before. Shortly after, Laurel said something that got lost in the breeze as they turned left and followed a scenic route along tiny lanes with unrestricted views of two giant oil tankers in the North Sea and rocky cliff faces speckled with bird life and golden beaches striped with seals and broad swathes of farmland dotted with sheep and the occasional herd of cows. Some of the roads were single-track with room for only one vehicle, irregularly flanked by little passing places where twice Laurel pulled to a halt to allow pick-up trucks to pass. By way of thanks, farmers raised a single finger from the top of the steering wheel while in the back, dogs stood with front paws on the edge of the pick-up beds, noses in the air in case they missed something.

The complete absence of trees still bothered Tuk, at least until Laurel pulled sharply into the gravel driveway of a cottage surrounded by moss-laden dry stone walls. And in the lee of the walls, trees. Actual living, waving trees. Someone must have put in a lot of work to make this happen.

The cottage wore its decades well. Small, deep set windows allowed plants to flourish in long, narrow pots on their ledges. Old-fashioned roof tiles heavy with lichen and sturdy gutters and downpipes directed rainwater into iron-banded barrels at the corners of the building. Antique farm implements – hoes, ploughs and other things Tuk would never be able to name – posed artfully around rock gardens dotting the edges of the path to an arched front door studded with antique hardware. A matte-black, anchor-shaped door knocker was positioned to clatter against what appeared to be a miniature panel from a ship's hull, mushroom rivets and all.

The opportunity to hear how the knocker sounded was denied when the door opened revealing a roly-poly grandma figure enveloped in a black and red silk gown from heavily bangled wrists to ankles with gold chain bracelets by way of button-and-loop fastenings and a Chinese collar. Pleats of silver hair interwoven with beads and ribbons flowed over her round waistline.

'Laurel!' she shouted, delighted.

'Hi Aunty Elma, this is my friend Tuk. He's from –'

'Thailand,' said Elma.

'How do you know?' said Tuk.

'I'm a fortune teller, son.'

'That's why we're here,' said Laurel. 'Tuk says Thais believe in fortune tellers, and I told him you were the best in Shetland.'

Elma looked Tuk up and down like she was measuring him for a suit.

'I spent many a month in Thailand, long before you were born. Koh Samui before they gave it tarmac roads and flash hotels and an airport and all the other shite that spoiled it for us beach-loving hippy types. Used to be paradise. I haven't been back since 1981. I don't suppose it's got better.' She shifted her attention to the sky, where dark grey clouds were forming ominous thunderheads. 'You'd best come in before the heavens open up.'

She welcomed them into her warm little home filled with Oriental and Asian art and hippy-influenced decorations of beads and raffia lampshades and silhouette portraits of Bob Marley and Jimi Hendrix. Teacups appeared and were filled to the brim with steaming watery tea. They sat at a polished black table covered in abalone inlay of dragons and constellations and butterflies and flora from another world. Despite its noticeable lack of dolphins, it made Tuk think of wall hangings in Khao San Road tattoo parlours. Which made him think of Jo and the crass, mis-spelled tattoo on her chest.

'Now you've given him a potted history of Thailand before he was born,' said Laurel, 'do you think you might get around to telling Tuk his fortune?'

Elma held the back of her hand to her forehead.

'Ooh, I just got an awfie strong vision there.'

'You did?' said Laurel. 'What kind of vision?'

'Of me putting you over my knee and skelping your cheeky arse.'

They laughed long and hard.

Elma stood, lifted Tuk's uninjured hand from where it lay on the table top, and urged him to follow her to the light of the window. She pored over the hand, caressing it and rubbing it between her thumbs, stretching and releasing the skin, comparing its callused fingertips to the fingers on the undamaged right hand. She spoke in a different, low voice filled with gravity. No more humour.

'You are a man who knows what he likes, and you are not afraid to go after it, even if it puts a strain on your relationships with others. Music is your life, correct? It's important to you?'

'Music? Yes, most important thing to me,' said Tuk.

'I'm thinking not the classics. Maybe jazz, or blues? I'd say blues.'

'Blues, yes!'

'You've had some pain in your life, and your music is an antidote to the pain. Something hurts you now, but music helps. Tell me what you need to know, what's important to you right now.'

Tuk did not have to be asked twice:

'Will I get chance to play at the festival? With good blues players. Maybe someone famous?'

Elma dipped her head to more closely scrutinise his palm. Out of Tuk's line of sight, Laurel nodded animatedly.

Elma raised and lowered her head, twice. 'I see you playing on a big, professionally-rigged stage, surrounded by excellent musicians - and in front, an audience loving your music.'

By the time Colin and Susan broke up late the previous year, they were already well on the way to getting Lerwick Blues off the ground.

Their first foray into concert promotion grew from an idea to bring local blues musicians together for an afternoon event, preferably outdoors. Shetland was rightly famous for the way it embraced traditional folk music thanks to how, from the 1960s, educator and fiddle player and band leader Dr Tom Anderson fought hard to have the music of the islands taught in local schools. Thanks to the cumulative efforts of teachers who prospered under Dr Tom's passion and enthusiasm, the islands today were full of kids and adults who spent much of their free time honing skills on different instruments. From this pool of talent grew acts devoted to every kind of music, from trad folk to country and western to blues to heavy metal and everything in between. Long dark winters were doubtless a factor; for half of the year there was never a shortage of time for kids of all ages to get together and rehearse.

Colin and Susan had so little trouble finding Shetland blues acts keen to be featured at their first ever promotion that the plan for an afternoon event expanded into a two-day miniature festival they called Lerwick Blues. What came next was a bigger surprise: word of mouth alone drew enquiries from bands and musicians outside Shetland eager to appear in Lerwick. Now, they had a packed schedule showcasing acts from all over the islands plus a handful of established names from the mainland UK blues world. There was even a headliner from America.

The event's rapid expansion presented them with a problem. For many years already, there had been a successful annual Shetland Blues Festival, run by a local blues enthusiast. Everybody in Shetland knew Jimmy, even if Colin and Susan had never talked with him. Now they had to ring him up (of course he was in the phone book) and ask if they could meet for a beer. He asked if they were worried Lerwick Blues was stepping on the toes of his Shetland Blues Festival, and they confessed to being bothered by precisely that. Jimmy laughed.

'No need to buy me a beer. Just go for it,' he said. 'Shetland can't have too many live music events. I'll be bringing my friends to yours.'

There was no longer any room for doubt or excuses. Lerwick Blues was on.

Staying on as co-organisers had worked out fairly well, even if occasional bumps in the road turned into heated disagreements. Now, as they walked along Commercial Street, was one of those times.

'C'mon, Suze, it's only for two or three songs,' said Colin. She was having none of it:

'For a nobody we've not even heard play a note? Are you off your head? The shows start tomorrow night. Every slot is filled. The poster has been up for months and the website has every act listed and a timetable set in internet stone. And you want to squeeze in a stranger?'

'It might be good PR, a man who came here all the way from Thailand –'

'Don't talk shite. He came all the way from Glasgow on the plane, and I hear he turned up so unprepared or broke you had to find him a place to sleep on your Gran's sofa. What's going on here? Is it because Laurel likes him? Is Laurel the only woman in town who hasn't yet been bedded by Mr high-and-mighty Festival Man Colin? Or are you and Laurel already…'

'No, we're not. And it's nothing to do with Laurel.' He was distracted by his mobile phone. Because of their work with the festival, it rang constantly. He answered it without bothering to check who was calling.

'Hello?

'Colin? It's Aunty Elma. I need a favour, son.'

He listened for a minute before saying, 'I'm awful busy just now, but I'll see what I can do.' He politely ended the conversation, disconnected the call and put the phone back in his pocket before redirecting his attention towards Susan.

'Surely we can get him a guest spot with one of the other acts, two or three songs.'

'There's something funny going on here, Colin Drummond.' She walked away, leaving him thinking this might work. She hadn't said no.

Twenty-eight

Laurel and Tuk set off for Lerwick having somehow avoided a rainstorm that left the roads damp and the countryside smelling fresh. Laurel piloted them back to town cautiously. Tuk, who was starting to recognise landmarks, was surprised by a right turn that sent them out to a headland. After a couple of minutes, they pulled up at a small parking area attached to the town cemetery. Laurel fished a pair of waterproof binoculars from under the scooter seat and led the way to the end of the Knab. This was one of Lerwick's best-known landmarks, partly because of the short distance from Anderson High School, attended by every kid who grew up in the islands. The Knab had romantic memories for teenage courting couples going back decades, Laurel's parents included. It brought her cheer to think of them walking this same path, but at the same time it pained her to think of her mum, dead much too young – and the ongoing misery her passing brought to her dad.

The Knab marked the southern end of the strait separating Lerwick from Bressay, a long, imposing island that provided shelter to the Shetland capital, turning it into an ideal port that, four centuries ago, used to be packed so tight with Dutch vessels visiting for the annual herring season it was said you could walk between points on the waterfront without setting foot on land.

Tuk wondered about the binoculars Laurel wore on a strap around her neck. She almost launched into an enthused lecture about the quality of wildlife around her homeland, but hesitated, knowing how difficult it would be to make herself understood. Tuk saw the hesitation and reached for his iPhone. He had been feeling stupid for not using technology to help him communicate, and now was the time to address the error.

'No SIM card, no internet, no Wi-Fi,' he said, 'but I have an app. Can use offline.' He showed Laurel. The translation app represented a lifeline for conversational details she ached to share. She typed into the app: *the wildlife here, birds and sea life, is amazing. We never know what we will see.* Tuk, impressed by the Thai translation, urged her to go on. *We often see seals, some sea lions, otters, dolphins, sometimes basking sharks and even orcas – killer whales.*

'Amazing,' he said. In English. She saw he was already interested. It was time for the binoculars to do their thing.

She pointed out birds floating like the pattern on a vast, undulating bedspread atop the sea off the headland, soaring around cliffside nests and perched on grassy tufts. She used the app to translate the names of shags, fulmars, guillemots, ravens and black-backed gulls. Seals lolled on rocky platforms at the foot of the Knab, and Tuk happily used the binoculars to scan waters further offshore, clearly hopeful of seeing more.

The rain at Elma's home a few miles away hadn't touched Lerwick, so with their jackets spread on the ground, they were able to sit in the lee of a drystone wall and make the most of the scenery.

'Are you tired?' said Tuk.

'I am tired. I'm staying at my cousin's house. She has three lovely kids who never sleep.'

'You live in your cousin's house?'

'No, I live with my dad.'

'Yesterday you said…'

'I know. My dad has his problems, mostly with drink. I am the only one there to talk to him about it, so almost every day my own dad tells me to fuck off. But there's only me and him left since my mum died five years ago. If I had a pound for every time he said that, I'd have the deposit to buy a place of my own.'

'I understand.'

Laurel wondered how he could possibly understand.

'My father died seventeen years ago,' he said. 'My mother is still angry. How do you say? Grieving? Still grieving. So unhappy. I try to help, but what can I do? But maybe I understand your father. Poor guy.'

Laurel wondered if Tuk had ever talked about this to anyone else and felt privileged he had shared it with her. She was also embarrassed that his first reaction was to feel sorry for her dad; something maybe she could learn from. She put her hand on top of his. For just a moment, to kiss seemed like the right thing to do.

'Hi there,' said a man struggling to keep a young dog under control. 'You must be the bloke from Thailand. I heard about you.' His pup, a young border collie, flashed black and white like a strobe in the sunlight.

'You're from Bangkok, they tell me. I'm a real foodie, and I did a wee southeast Asia tour last year. I loved the food in Bangkok, but was disappointed by Cabbages and Condoms restaurant. Overpriced and not especially authentic, I thought. Just as well it's for a good charity, or not so many people would go.' He tugged at the dog's lead. 'Stop it Jolly, you daft wee monkey! Sorry, have to keep moving or this guy goes nuts. Or even more nuts! Nice talking to you.'

Laurel and Tuk shared a grin.

'Cabbages and Condoms?' she said.

'Real restaurant, real condoms,' he said. 'Food is nothing special.'

They rode downhill towards Lerwick slowly enough to have a haltering conversation over the wind and engine noise.

'You made me think,' said Laurel.

'What kind of thinking?'

'About my dad.'

'Good,' said Tuk.

'I never just sit down and talk with him anymore.' She paused to exchange waves with an old woman walking an arthritic English Boxer. 'I always rise to the bait and we end up fighting.'

'In Thailand we say always keep *jai yen*. Cool heart. Stay cool. Everything is better.'

'It's an idea you might have trouble selling to Shetlanders, especially after they've had a couple of swallows.'

The sound of sirens bearing down on them from behind made her pull to the side of the road to allow an ambulance to roar past, siren blaring and lights flashing. Tuk noticed other vehicles did as Laurel had, allowing the ambulance to keep moving. In Bangkok, ambulances could sit in stationary nose-to-tail traffic, sirens wailing, going nowhere, in part because nobody moved out of the way. Thais are mostly gentle, kind, considerate people – and Tuk could never work out why one exception to the rule arose when it came to giving up a few metres of road in heavy traffic, even to emergency vehicles working to save lives.

Less than a minute later, they entered a curved residential crescent to find the ambulance pulling to a halt, paramedics running around to open the rear doors. They were stopped close to a house shrouded in smoke. All around them, people stood like statues, already in shock.

'That's my house!' cried Laurel. She took her scooter onto the pavement, sending people flying for cover, and skidded to a stop in front of the only driveway on the street with weeds poking through paving stones. Tuk stopped her from running at the house. He peeled off his guitar backpack and leaned it against a low garden wall. The houses reminded him of the street where he was staying with Sadie and Matt.

'I will go,' he said. 'Is it the same as Sadie and Matt house?'

'Yes,' said Laurel. 'Exactly the same.' She stood locked in place as her new friend dashed towards the burning house.

As he ran to the front door, Tuk had a flashback to an afternoon in upper secondary school in Chinatown. To a fire safety presentation by an officer from Golden Mount Fire Station. The boys in the audience played it cool, as if this was too stupid an activity to merit their attention. Some of the girls swooned over the ruggedly handsome fireman. Tuk was glued to the presentation. This stuff might save a life. He had seen his own dad die, and was determined not to miss anything that might help some other poor soul avoid an early demise.

He checked the door. A little smoke came out from under it, and from the brass letter box. He tentatively put one hand a few centimetres from the door's surface. Good news. No obvious heat coming from it. He put palm to door to confirm the there were no flames raging on the other side. It was warm, but not hot. He remembered to play it safe and leaned on the door handle with his jacket sleeve. It opened easily onto a little porch and another closed door he knew would connect to the living room. The interior door was warmer, but not frighteningly so. At the last moment he remembered to close the outer door to avoid feeding fire with a blast of fresh oxygen and elbowed the inner door open and dived to the floor. People caught in fires die most often from smoke inhalation, the handsome fireman said. If you ever find yourself trapped in a room full of smoke, get to the floor, where any remaining oxygen will be. He kept one cheek on the carpet and crabbed his way across the room. Still the smoke was choking and blinding him. There was no way he could stay here for long. He rapped his knuckles on something hard; the leg of a sofa. He went around it and found another piece of furniture, a bulky armchair. On the floor in front of the chair curled the inert form of a small man. His chest moved. Unconscious, but still breathing? Tuk's mind raced. How was he going to get him out of here without raising his head into the smoke, where there was no oxygen to breathe?

A fire engine screeched to a halt and down leapt an officer in uniform. Laurel screamed to him for help while all around, neighbours yelled and pointed at the house, where the smoke was becoming more dense and now seeped ominously between the roof tiles.

'He's inside!' shouted Bobby Halcrow, holding tight onto his son.

'Who's inside,' said the fireman. 'Where?'

'My dad,' said Laurel. 'He's probably in the living room, in his chair by the fireplace. My friend went in to try and get him.'

The officer didn't look happy about this.

'How long ago? How long since your friend went in?'

Laurel couldn't concentrate.

'Less than a minute,' said Bobby Halcrow.

Members of the fire crew unrolled hoses, attached them to an underground water hydrant. To others awaiting instructions, oxygen masks at the ready, the officer spoke loud and clear.

'Two persons confirmed inside, first location to check is ground floor living room, near the fireplace.' He pointed to two of his crew. 'Go! Stick together!' A few seconds later, he sent another team inside. A hush descended on the gawkers. Laurel stood supported by one of her neighbours, silent with dread. The smoke only got worse, even as hoses swamped the roof with powerful streams of water.

A shout rang out from an onlooker. 'There!' One of the women supporting Laurel pointed.

Two firemen emerged sideways through the front door, Laurel's dad hanging between them like washing on a line.

Laurel turned to the senior officer.

'What about my friend?' she shouted, 'he's still inside.'

'Patience, love,' said the officer. 'If he's in there, we'll get him out.'

Laurel stared at the door. She didn't believe in god, never attended church services, but right then would have prayed to a flying spaghetti monster if it meant she could see Tuk emerge safely.

'Here he comes,' said the fireman.

Billowing smoke chased two more officers wearing oxygen masks out of the hallway. They lent support to Tuk, who walked between them under his own steam. With two arms, he did his best to contain the furious struggles of a fat ginger cat who fought her way to freedom and shot off around the back of the house.

'I don't believe it,' yelled a teenager. 'The big Chinky saved Maggie!'

Laurel huddled next to the paramedics who tended to her unconscious dad.

'Are you family?' said one of the paramedics.

Laurel tried to get closer to her dad, now laid out on a stretcher. He suddenly seemed smaller than some of the children who watched on. 'Dad!' she said.

'You're Laurel, aren't you?' said the paramedic.

She couldn't put a name to the face, but thought she knew the man from Anderson High. She nodded.

'What's your dad's name?'

'George.'

'Can you hear me, George,' said the paramedic. 'You're safe now, we'll get you into the ambulance and to the hospital to check you out. Your daughter Laurel is right here with us.'

'I've got a pulse,' said the second paramedic. 'He's breathing. No visible burns.' He fitted an oxygen mask over George's face and adjusted the straps to help it deliver oxygen efficiently without being too tight.

Tuk sat slumped on the pavement, his back to the garden wall. His breathing was coming back to normal and his eyes were no longer streaming. He managed to convince a concerned paramedic he was fine, in no need of treatment. Laurel's scooter lay on its side on the pavement, one mirror twisted at an odd angle. Suddenly he remembered leaning his guitar somewhere close to where the scooter lay. He jumped to his feet, panic setting in, as a small boy tapped his arm.

'Hey mister,' he said, pointing to a little girl so similar she had to be his sister. She clutched Tuk's guitar case protectively.

'My daddy says you'll be wanting this,' said the girl.

'Thank you. Thank you so much.'

'He said to get it out of the way before someone tripped over it and it got broke in all the fuss,' said her brother.

'Thank you. Please thank your daddy for me,' said Tuk.

'You're awful brave,' said the little girl, 'Putting your hands on Maggie.'

'Maggie?' said Tuk.

'Maggie the cat,' said her brother.

'Cat's name is Maggie?' said Tuk. 'Why Maggie?'

'My daddy says 'cos she's a bitch, just like Maggie Thatcher,' said the girl. 'We call her Maggie fucking Thatcher.' She glanced around as if scared to be overheard by an adult.

'Who is Maggie Thatcher,' said Tuk. They laughed.

'I don't have a Scooby,' said the boy.

Laurel arrived and wrapped Tuk in a tight hug.

'Your father?' said Tuk.

'The paramedics took him to the hospital to check him over. They say they think he'll be fine.'

The senior fire officer approached and put a hand on Tuk's shoulder.

'Maybe you should leave the firefighting to the experts and stick to playing your ukulele.'

'It is not a —' he stopped. The man grinned, and Tuk dipped his head in appreciation. Perhaps he was beginning to understand Scottish humour.

Twenty-nine

Apart from one cracked mirror, the scooter was undamaged. On the way to Sadie and Matt's house, Laurel pointed out the hospital's main entrance, where she told Tuk she would watch out for him later. When he got off the bike, they shared the briefest of hugs before she scooted off at speed to find out how her dad was doing.

The door opened before Tuk could find his key. News of the fire had reached his lodgings faster than a speeding scooter.

'Are you alright, son?' said Sadie, with motherly concern. 'I gather George is already in his hospital bed. No injuries, just a bit of smoke inhalation that will keep him in for observation. Not that his house is fit to go back to, though they tell me it was a stovetop fire they caught quite early, so the only real damage is to the kitchen ceiling. The rest is water damage from the fire brigade making sure the whole house didn't go up.' Her nose wrinkled. 'The smoke's clinging to you. Get yourself in the bath and sort out a change of clothes. Do you need something to eat? A wee cup of tea, maybe?'

Matt appeared at her side. 'More like a wee whisky to calm the boy's nerves,' he said.

Tuk went to his suitcase to pick out a change of clothes before heading to the bathroom. There, the hot tap roared as it filled the green plastic bathtub with water and the room with steam so thick it made him flash back to a living room full of smoke. He shivered, not from the cold.

As Laurel walked into the Gilbert Bain hospital she thought, not for the first time, of how dominant a role the building had played in her life so far. Twenty-five years ago, she was born in its maternity ward. Her entire life so far was spent within a few minutes' walk of the building she visited occasionally as a child for treatment to the cuts and bruises that went with growing up riding bicycles in a hilly town, or when taking fruit or flowers to ageing relatives who sometimes were not much longer for this world.

Upon leaving Anderson High just before turning eighteen, she decided the fevered rush to enroll in college or university on the Scottish mainland was not for her, and came straight to work in the Medical Records Office. She was at her desk on the day, five years ago, when her mum was brought to Accident & Emergency in an ambulance. Word quickly reached Laurel and she rushed over in time only to say goodbye. Mum was pronounced dead less than twenty minutes after admission, struck down at forty-three by an aneurysm doctors and nursing staff assured her nobody could ever have anticipated.

Staff turnover at the Gilbert was low, and now, after seven years interacting on a daily basis with people in almost every department, she was on first name terms with most of her colleagues. A few of them she wouldn't give a nod in the desert, but she counted others as valued friends; the rest she would happily exchange greetings or stop to chat with, at work or elsewhere.

In an instinctual move born of routine she clipped her ID card to the button line of her blouse. Not many people knew the proper name for that line of buttons, but Scrabble enthusiast Laurel knew it was a "placket". Something to be filed for occasional use in pub quizzes and the tackling of cryptic crosswords.

She had been signed off work for a little short of three weeks, a spell that at times felt like an age, at others like the snap of a musician's fingers. Her return to the building met with a warm reception, and without stopping, she gave thankful waves and thumbs-ups to expressions of welcome and best wishes from staff at the small reception desk and to well-wishers asking after her dad. By now everyone would know he was in Ward 3 – and understand she was in a hurry to get there.

Ginny Ward stooped over the desk at the nurses' station between two corridors. There was a wobbly swivel chair she seldom had time to occupy while updating the paperwork involved in maintaining scrupulous care of an ever-changing cast of patients. Sitting was not even an option, the chair creaking under the weight of a stack of papers awaiting attention.

Nobody knew this better than Laurel. As a filing clerk in the Medical Records Office, virtually every document in the entire hospital passed through her hands at one time or another. She counted Ginny Ward, known by her pals as

3 Ward because of her role as Senior Charge Nurse at Ward 3, as a friend and ally. When Ginny spotted her, she put down her pen and drew Laurel into a hug.

'How is he?' said Laurel, peering over her friend's shoulder to see if she could locate her dad. There, in a six-bed room, a wee balding head swallowed by a pillow, emaciated frame enclosed by blankets tucked tightly in place. Her practiced eye interpreted it to mean he was restless, and the nursing staff didn't want him catching them unawares with sudden moves. It was a professional nursing secret written nowhere. Carefully arranged bedding had useful straitjacket qualities.

'Not too bad, considering,' said Ginny. 'Mr Shah gave him a wee something to calm him down. The moment George realised he was in hospital, he tried to get out of bed and demanded to be let go, but that's not going to happen until Mr Shah is sure there are no complications from all the smoke he must have inhaled. I told Mr Shah I was a friend of the family, explained George is drinking a great deal, almost certainly every day. He added Librium to his script to reduce the chance of him suffering from withdrawal. We don't need the complication of him going through the D-Ts.'

'Thanks, Ginny.'

'We took bloods. Mr Shah thinks he sees signs of jaundice, wonders if his liver might be struggling. The tests should tell us more.'

Laurel consulted the clock on her mobile phone and did the calculation in her head. 'He can't have been asleep for long.'

'Only a few minutes, but he'll be out for a while. The "wee something" wasn't so wee.'

'I'll come back.'

'Anytime you like. What about you? How are you getting on?'

Laurel was reluctant to talk about it, but Ginny was a good friend, worried about her. She appreciated her concern, and didn't want to brush it off without an honest answer.

'I've been off work for three weeks now. The pills are helping, but every time I come back to the house feeling a bit better, dad seems to do his best to drag me down. We argued yesterday and I stormed out before I blew a gasket. I stayed at Louise's place last night.'

'Today must've given you a helluva fright. Don't you dare blame yourself for it. If you need a good listener…'

'You'll be the first person I'll call. Now, stop worrying about me, will you? Are you forgetting there are sick people here depending on you for the best care the NHS can provide?'

Ginny punched her on the arm. Playfully, but hard enough to hurt.

'See you in a wee while.'

Vivienne Nicholson, "Viv" to her friends, worked straight through her lunch break, feeding contentedly on a sandwich of home-baked bread with smoked Parma ham and tomato while churning through the never-vacant in tray at the front of her desk. She had mostly good people in her department, but being temporarily short-staffed meant even more work piling up on her desk.

She savoured the quiet of the office at lunchtime, but the reason for staying in was her Aunt Grace. Her late father's only surviving sister was an odd one, who made no secret of hating visitors turning up unannounced at mealtimes. If pushed, Grace would confess she didn't want folk thinking she ought to be feeding them. Viv knew the real reason: Grace was ashamed of being unable to cook anything more involved than an egg. Boiled or fried, those were the options. Which explained why Viv came out of the hospital's main entrance in the middle of the afternoon, on her way to spend time with her aunt, something she tried to do at least twice a week, always taking with her something nice for her aunt to enjoy for lunch. The poor old lass had no other visitors, if you didn't count religious mouthpieces. The only ones to make Grace pause were the young Mormons who, instead of trying to foist literature upon her, made a point of asking if there was anything they could do to help. Viv had popped over once to find two clean-cut young Americans, sharp white shirts with the requisite black badge on the left side of their chests, pruning rose bushes surrounding the wee patch of freshly cut grass in front of her aunt's terraced house. One other time, years ago, she arrived to find a young missionary ironing the frilly blouse Grace liked to keep for Sunday church services. The kid in charge of the ironing was the double of a young Donny Osmond, not so surprising when you learned he was the world's most famous Mormon's son, much discussed around Lerwick, and about whom nobody had ever been heard to say a bad word.

Viv often argued it was a mistake not to provide anywhere to sit outside the hospital's main entrance, even if she understood the reluctance to help smokers create a fog of carcinogens through which all visitors had to tramp on the way in and out of the building. It meant a low wall around the perimeter of the adjacent parking area was the only place for people to take the weight off, and Viv was surprised to recognise the nice young Asian man she had met on the Glasgow flight. She struggled to recall his name. Tuk, that was it. She took a slight detour to say hello. He removed his headphones.

'Do you remember me?' she said.

'I remember. On the bus.'

Of course, she thought. *After the flight from Glasgow, we shared the bus to town.*

She saw his guitar case, propped against the wall where he sat.

'Any luck?' she said. 'Luck with the festival?'

'No luck yet,' said a voice she recognised.

Laurel had come out of the building, spotted Tuk sitting on the wall, and her boss approaching him for a chat.

'Hiya,' said Viv. 'The jungle drums say you've had a hard day. How's your dad?'

'Mr Shah gave him something to knock him out for a couple of hours. Ginny says he's going to be OK.'

'Glad to hear it,' said Viv. 'I met Tuk yesterday on the plane from Glasgow and we came up on the same bus from the airport. No luck getting somewhere to play at the festival?'

'Not yet. We've been a bit too preoccupied to chase up Colin Drummond.'

'Good luck. He's awful busy.'

'So he says,' said Laurel.

'Listen,' said Viv. 'I need a quick word, a quiet word – about work.' She saw Laurel's eyes narrow. 'Nothing to worry about. The opposite, in fact.'

Laurel gave Tuk a palm-down, *wait here for a minute* gesture, and they wandered to the other side of a row of parked cars.

Thirty

'You must have had fish and chips before,' said Laurel as they walked from the chip shop carrying hot bundles wrapped in paper, the two of them enveloped in the aroma of hot vinegar.

'In Thailand, I like fish,' said Tuk. He held up his dinner to sample the smell coming through the paper. 'Maybe not the same fish.'

They took to a bench with a view over the inner harbour. Beneath them were the small sailing boats Tuk watched go out the other day, now wrapped in tarpaulins and hitched tightly to the floating pontoon.

Tuk was a bit more tentative about attacking the food than Laurel, but soon showed signs of enjoying the new dining experience. Thai food, fiercely spicy or not, was all about subtlety. This was different. Somehow bland but still delicious.

'I spoke to Colin,' said Laurel. The name didn't mean anything to Tuk.

'Colin, the Lerwick Blues organiser, Sadie and Matt's grandson.'

Now he understood. 'Yes?'

'He says he will know more tomorrow, but you might get a chance to play.'

'With Tyler Gray?'

She was beginning to wonder about Tuk's desire, maybe even his *need* to play with the star of the festival.

'He didn't say.'

'How about your father?' said Tuk. The abrupt change of subject made Laurel wonder. Maybe he was just being polite. Possibly not. He had already made her feel guilty by expressing genuine concern for her wee dad.

'Not too bad,' she said. 'He was asleep when I went in, but I bet he wants to thank you for saving Maggie.'

'Maggie?'

'The cat.'

'Oh yes. Maggie fucking Thatcher.'

Laurel giggled. 'Where did you hear that?'

'From the little girl holding my guitar.'

Laurel knew exactly who that would be. A wee neighbour who copied everything her foul-mouthed dad said, even while he stood by, beaming with pride.

'Your friend at the hospital. Viv?' *Another change of subject.*

'Yes, Viv. Short for Vivienne. She is my boss.'

'She has good news?'

Laurel was touched. He didn't miss much.

'Something that made me happy,' she said.

'Good. I like you to be happy.'

'Viv and I work in an office. We look after all the records.'

Tuk's eyebrows shot up in wonder mixed with confusion.

203

'Not music records, not long-playing records. Files. Paperwork. I have been off work for a few weeks. Sick leave. For depression.' She silently cursed herself for losing him again, worried about making him feel frustrated.

He fished smartphone from guitar case side pocket, opened the translation app, and handed it to her, screen smeared with vinegar and oil. After wiping it with a tissue, she typed: "*I have been off work for three weeks because I suffer from depression.*" He read the Thai translation solemnly.

'I understand,' he said. 'My mother has the problem.' He scrolled up the screen in search of the English word. 'Depression,' he said. 'Very difficult.'

A sadness overcame Tuk every time his mother came up. *Change the subject.*

'The thing Viv said that made me smile?' she said. 'She had good news. Another person in my office is leaving, so maybe I will get his job. A better job, more senior. A wee bit more money, too.' She typed "*maybe I will get a promotion to a better job with a higher salary*" into the app, and his eyes lit up.

'Good news,' he said. And he meant it. The delight on his face almost reduced her to tears.

Laurel decided not to ask the translation app to explain how the poisonous bastard who was leaving her office was someone she wouldn't piss on if he spontaneously combusted at his desk.

They rinsed their hands under a tap next to the floating pontoon. Laurel laughed aloud when Tuk jumped back from the water as if it was scorching. The boy from the tropics had never felt water so cold. Laurel couldn't remember laughing so hard in years. Certainly not in the five years since her mum died.

They left the scooter and helmets chained together on Victoria Pier. Tuk was beginning to grasp that in Lerwick, nowhere was far to walk, especially after they got to the famous Lounge, no more than a few seconds' climbing a skinny hill beside the Tourist Office. From street level the sound of violins and a piano warming up teased them from upstairs windows. Laurel led the way through an unremarkable door to a set of stairs so narrow and steep there was room only for one-way foot traffic. Tuk wondered about late at night, when drunks met each other midway on the stairs. Maybe Lerwick people were so polite that drunks found themselves in a dilemma. *After you – no, I insist, after YOU.*

It was as if the door at the top of the stairs was connected to a conductor's baton. The moment they pushed on it, the room burst into fast-paced traditional dance music. An elderly lady in tight grey curls and a two-piece trouser suit drove the beat on an upright piano with her left hand and countered it with chords from her right. The rhythmic clump-chirp kept the rest of the room in perfect time – no mean feat, considering there were at least twelve musicians being led. Seven violinists ranging in age from late teenagers to pensioners sawed away with competitive vigor while two guitarists, a mandolin, a tenor banjo, an electric bass and a flute did their best to be heard.

The scene immediately reminded Tuk of Irish music sessions in Bangkok bars. Never mind that the music was alien to him, he appreciated the warmth, the sense of community and the clear love they all had for what they played. The scene in the Lounge was the same.

Musicians occupied round tables laden with pint glasses under permanent threat from flashing elbows and swinging guitar headstocks. Tuk saw heads turn to see who the newcomers were, which made him feel self-conscious about the guitar on his back. This was no place for him to get the Gibson out of the case, even if his sore hand allowed him to play. He was thankful when he realised the attention was aimed at Laurel. Violinists in mid-flow winked and nodded at her. One guitarist suspended his metronomic chop for long enough to pull her into a one-armed hug, and they hadn't walked three steps into the crowd before someone pushed a drink into her hand, the bearer pointing at Tuk and doing the drink-to-lips-and-raised-eyebrows gesture. After some indecision Tuk, who wasn't much of a drinker, found himself clutching a half pint of Guinness. When Laurel giggled at the Guinness foam moustache from his first sip, he added to it and left it there, and she giggled some more.

The music was relentlessly fast-paced, violins playing in faultless unison, jigs and reels changing mid-flow as if they had all spent long hours rehearsing.

Tuk spotted faces he knew. Laurel's boss Viv saluted him with her cocktail glass from one table, and the other person he had met on the plane from Glasgow, Davie, did the same with a pint of lager from the bar. Henry the acupuncturist asked after the welfare of his injured hand; someone else tapped him on the shoulder, and he turned to find Lewis, the martial arts expert who saved his guitar from thugs in a back lane in Glasgow city centre.

'You made it,' said Lewis.

'Thank you for your good advice,' said Tuk.

'Have you spoken to the organisers to try and get a gig?'

'We are trying. No answer yet.'

Lewis scanned the crowded bar. 'No sign of Tyler Gray? Maybe not here yet, and probably not his scene.'

'I don't know,' said Tuk, who spotted someone else he knew. The busker with the long ponytail was taking advantage of a break in the music to tune up his guitar. Unbidden, he burst into Neil Young's *After the Gold Rush*. He was barely two bars into the opening phrase when the pianist added chord-perfect accompaniment. Half-way through the second line of lyrics, most of the bar were singing along. Everyone, but *everyone* was having fun.

When the busker drew the song to a close it met with cheers and applause from everywhere in a room of many corners. The busker reached for his case, contribution over, and Tuk became aware of people around Laurel urging her to take the floor. The tiny bit of floor between crowded tables and the piano.

'Your turn, Laurel! Any one of your favourites will do!' said a mountain of a man with green eyes staring happily from deep within a thick red beard and thicker eyebrows.

'Aye, come on, Laurel,' said a young woman holding a flute. 'None of your excuses. It's not as if you've been fighting fires all day.'

Laurel turned to Tuk. 'Can you play *Summertime* in A?'

'Of course,' said Tuk. 'But my hand…'

'Let's try.' She obviously wanted to sing. He could try.

The bass player fed a cable to Tuk, already plugged into a small amp near the piano. He pulled the 335 from its case, tuned up, played a soft A major chord – and Laurel burst into song, pitch-perfect, confident, her powerful alto voice filling the room. A murmur of appreciation gave her more encouragement and Tuk provided gentle accompaniment; his hand was sore, but up to the task of a few simple chords. After the second verse, Laurel surprised him with a gesture that could only mean one thing: guitar solo time; the noise in the room fell away in anticipation. He kept it subtle, finger-picking Chet Atkins licks around the melody that drew more murmurs from the audience; instead of taking up the vocals again as he expected, she gave him the rolling hand signal: *one more time*. So he obliged.

The cheers when they finished made the hair on the back of his neck stand on end. *This was why he played music; this was what he lived for.* He expressed his gratitude to Laurel with a clumsy, guitar-in-the-middle hug. Drinkers patted them both on the back and raised their glasses in appreciation. Laurel politely refused offers of drinks for them both. She was on a high, and it was time to go.

As they turned to leave, the door opened and festival organiser Colin came in, eager to find out what the fuss was about. Tuk gave him a hands-together *wai* greeting just as one of the audience yelled:

'Bad timing, Colin. You just missed something special. We all knew Laurel's got a fine voice, but jeez-oh her friend can play.'

Laurel pulled the scooter to a halt, front wheel touching the kerb outside Sadie and Matt's house. When he took off his helmet, she closed the strap and hung it around her arm.

'Thank you,' said Tuk.

'It's me who has to say thanks,' said Laurel, one hand resting on his forearm. 'You ran into a burning house without a thought for yourself. You led the firemen to my dad and saved Maggie. You accompanied me beautifully in the Lounge tonight. And you made me laugh. Thank you.'

When they hugged in the Lounge, the gesture was rendered impersonal by the guitar between them and the curious crowd watching their every move. Now, Laurel was perched on the scooter, balancing it on a steeply pitched hill. But the potential was there for something more than a hug, and they both leaned into it until a loud noise destroyed the moment. It came from upstairs, where Matt stood, elbows on the bedroom window ledge.

He farted again.

'That's better out than in,' he said. 'Sorry for the interruption. Carry on. Don't mind me.'

Thirty-one

Tuk woke to a voice pitched at little more than a whisper: 'Maybe he was on the beer last night.'

'How long have we been married?' said a second voice, a little more loudly. It was Sadie.

'I didn't know this was going to be a test,' said Matt.

'A long time. I shudder to think how many nights I shared a room with you after you had a "couple" of drinks with your pals.'

'And?'

'And, when you've been on the beer, the room stinks. There's no smell of beer in here.'

'Who are you today? Give me a clue. Sherlock Holmes? Detective Colombo? Hercule Poirot? Alright, maybe he's just tired.'

The loud ring of the wall-mounted telephone rendered the cheery dispute moot. Tuk squinted at the clock above the mantelpiece and was ashamed to see it was nearly 10 o'clock. He had lain siege to Sadie and Matt's living room for at least three hours too long. While he jumped into trousers and a long-sleeved shirt, he could hear Sadie talking rapid fire into the phone; he hardly caught a word other than his own name, which cropped up more than once.

Matt came into the room to carefully place a mug of tea on a side table at one end of the sofa bed. He shook his head in the direction of where Sadie was still on the telephone.

'If talking was an Olympic sport,' he said.

'I am sorry,' said Tuk. 'I didn't know..' he waved a hand at the light streaming in the living room window.

'Don't worry about it, son. Have a skinful last night, did you?'

'Excuse me?'

'Beers. Have too many beers?' Matt, whose normal voice boomed, bellowed even more loudly when Tuk didn't understand. All around the room, glass ornaments rattled.

'Only one,' said Tuk. 'Only one, how do you say, one half pint.'

'What did I tell you?' said Sadie as she returned just in time to hear her husband proven wrong. 'The lad was just tired, no wonder after the scary experience he went through yesterday.' Matt shrugged in good-natured defeat. He was used to it. She hooked a thumb towards the phone. 'That was Colin.'

'Yes?'

'He asked if you can come to the Mareel main auditorium in about an hour.' She explained: 'The Mareel. It's the pride of Lerwick. A big entertainment centre, theatre, even a recording studio and a café with a decent bowl of soup and good cakes. In fact, the whole building might have been modelled on giant slices of cake. It's where Colin's wee blues festival is happening. He hopes you can get there at eleven.

You'll find him in the main auditorium. Oh, and bring your guitar, he said.'

Half an hour later, he walked along the waterfront, belly heavy with a cooked breakfast he had pretended not to want, guitar on his back, strings dutifully checked; the indignity of turning up for an audition with a broken string only happens to a proud man once. He walked with Matt's instructions in mind. *Keep the water on your right side and it'll take a while, but you won't miss the Mareel. Modern place, like Sadie said, like big triangular slices of cake jammed onto a wee plate.*

The building was indeed angular and strikingly modern. Inside, he spotted a sign for the main auditorium. After a wrong turn sent him down a couple of empty corridors, he found himself in the wings of an impressive stage looking out over an equally striking array of banked seats. Voices reached him from out of sight near the front of the stage. Because he heard an argument raging, and since he didn't want to appear from an area he was probably never meant to set foot in, he held back for a moment. Through a gap at the inside of the curtain, he saw festival organiser Colin talking with an attractive young woman whom he thought might be the co-organiser Laurel talked of and a man wearing a 1975 Fender Strat on a rhinestone-encrusted strap, the guitar's headstock pointing towards the stage floor. Its neck was defaced with *Willie Duke* in big letters set into the fretboard. Sacrilege. Tuk had seen the name on the festival website. Duke tried hard to give off the blues musician vibe, but crusty jewellery, a russet headscarf, a frilled shirt and trousers and tight threaded pleats in his greying hair only made Tuk think he was trying too hard to be Keith Richard – or an extra in a pirate movie.

Duke was clearly not happy, no matter how hard Colin tried to get him on his side.

'I'm only talking about two or three songs,' said Colin, 'a surprise guest who came all the way from Thailand, a special guest. I hear the guy's good.'

'You *hear* he's good?' said Duke. 'What if he's rubbish? Two or three songs could screw up my set. You hired me and my band. What's the deal with this foreigner nobody ever heard of?'

'He's right,' said the woman, jabbing one finger at Colin's chest. 'If we make a mess of our first ever festival, we'll never get another chance to produce live events. There's no way this Thai guy plays without so much as an audition.'

They turned to Duke.

'Don't look at me!' he yelled. 'I'm not going to audition some wannabe to see if I'll let him steal a chunk out of my gig.'

Sadie saw Laurel pull her scooter to the kerb outside the house, so she knew who to expect when the doorbell rang.

'Hi, pet. How's your dad doing?' she said.

'A bit grumpy. The doctor won't let him go home before tomorrow at the earliest,' said Laurel.

'What's happening with the damage to the house?'

'Cleaning crew and painters are already working on it. My dad's been pals with Billy Douglas the insurance broker since primary school. Special urgent assistance for a mate. Is Tuk here?'

'No. Our Colin asked him to go over to the Mareel for eleven o'clock this morning.'

Laurel peered past Sadie at the big clock over the fireplace. Nearly two o'clock.

'Is he still there?' She knew it was unlikely.

'No, he came back a couple of hours ago, dropped off his guitar and went straight out again.'

'Are you sure?'

'I'm old, love, but I still have most of my marbles.'

'Sorry. No, I mean, are you sure about the guitar? He never goes anywhere without it.'

'It's right where he left it in the living room, still in the case.'

'Thanks, Mrs Drummond. I have to run.'

Before she put on her crash helmet, she used her mobile to dial a number from its list of contacts.

'Colin Drummond.'

'It's me, Laurel. Have you seen Tuk today?'

'He was meant to meet me at the Mareel this morning, but he didn't show. I thought I caught a glimpse of him in the auditorium, but things were kind of frantic, and when I went to find him a couple of minutes later, he was nowhere to be seen.'

'And?'

'And what? I thought I saw him, just for a moment.'

'Even on the phone I can read you like a book, Colin Drummond.'

'What are you getting at?'

'Out with it,' said Laurel. She waited for the few seconds it took Colin to consider lying to her, in the end deciding against it.

'OK, I feel bad about this. Me, Susan and Willie Duke, the guy who plays the headline spot tonight, were talking in the auditorium this morning. I tried my best to get your friend some time onstage with Duke, but he said no way he'd let Tuk even jam with them, and of course Susan took his side. I think Tuk overheard us. I went to talk to him, but he'd already gone. Hello? Laurel?'

Thirty-two

As she parked the scooter at the beginning of the track to the Knab, Laurel realised it was the first place she should have checked.

Colin had assured her there was no point in going to the Mareel; nobody at the Peerie Coffee Shop had seen him since their visit the other day; the chip shop was empty except for a cluster of newly-arrived birdwatchers, carbon fibre tripods and camouflaged telephoto lenses at the ever-ready, drawn all the way to Shetland by a rare British sighting that inspired the charter of two light aircraft from different points on the UK mainland. A radio news report said the bird had disappeared from the garden in Frakkafield the night before they arrived, but still the twitchers exuded optimism as they attacked their fish suppers. One of them stood well apart from the rest of the group. His body language suggested he wanted to keep his distance from his fellow enthusiasts. Friction among the small group, or factionalism to the point of bullying? Laurel was a bit of a loner at school and knew about being estranged from the in crowd. She stopped next to the loner.

'I heard you all got here too late to see the bird you flew up for?'

'Yeah, pretty sure we missed out,' he said in a dense Geordie accent.

Laurel indicated the rest of them with a tilt of her head. 'Not getting on with these guys?'

'Didn't know them before today when a pager alert went out saying they needed someone to make up the numbers on the charter flight,' he said. 'Won't want to hang out with them again. A cliquey shower of shite.'

'You'll be glad to get back home. I'm trying to find a friend of mine. A big-built Thai bloke. Seen anyone like that around?'

'Sorry, no.'

The last place she tried before heading south was the bench next to the small boat harbour, which was occupied by the busker, who said he hadn't seen Tuk since the Lounge the night before.

She found Tuk lying back against a lump of rock set into thick grass overlooking the south mouth and beyond to the Bressay lighthouse. She sat beside him, and though his eyes remained closed, she sensed he was awake.

'I thought I might find you here,' she said.

He opened his eyes. 'Very nice place. Good for thinking,' he said.

'I was worried about you.'

'Worried?'

'I spoke to Colin. He told me you heard them talking about you.'

'Yes. No chance to play with Willie Duke band. I don't even want to play with the guy. He destroys a wonderful 1975 Fender with his own name.'

'But it could have been your chance to play the blues.'

'Of course.'

'To play the festival, which is why you came all the way to Shetland.'

'I only came to Shetland for Tyler Gray.'

'But he's the headline act. Nobody here has even heard you play, except for one song in the Lounge. How could you get onstage with him?'

'I don't know. But it is important to try. For my father.'

It was Laurel's turn to not understand. Tuk went on:

'Only weeks before my father died, he got a new CD by Tyler Gray. Expensive for him to buy import CD from America. Made my mother angry. She looked at our apartment, old furniture, second-hand everything – and new album by Tyler Gray. Always money for his music, she said. Never money for his family. My father was sorry, seemed sad. She was right.

But we listened together every day. I learned guitar solos from Tyler Gray. 'One day,' my father said, 'One day.....'

I cry for my father who is dead for many years Tuk said, only seconds after he came to comfort her when she was bubbling her eyes out on a Victoria Pier bench. How could it be only two days ago?

Now he had a story he needed to share. She listened without interrupting as he told her of his father, of Tyler Gray, and how the two were enmeshed in a long tale that eventually brought Tuk to Shetland as he fled the latest misery he faced in Glasgow. Misery of his own creation, misery that wracked him with guilt at what he had put his mother through. A stranger drawn to a strange city in an even stranger country, by a woman who had never experienced a moment's thought for anything or anyone other than herself. When Tuk considered what he had done to his mother, was he any better?

He explained how his father was perhaps the most unusual man he ever knew, and how Tuk now realised his mother, despite how much she loved his dad, never understood him. Now her son was treading the same path as her dead husband. Still she grieved for her husband, and she couldn't begin to understand their son taking the same path.

Many years ago, after a trusted friend raved about Tyler Gray, Tuk's dad came home with yet another new CD to add to his already impressive collection. He and Tuk listened to it endlessly, and his father talked dreamily about the possibility of ever playing with someone so good as Gray. *One day, son. One day I want to share a stage with a fellow blues musician as good as Tyler Gray. You are smiling, but don't let people laugh at your dreams, son. Do you know why I admire musicians like Tyler Gray?*

Because he's handsome,' said Tuk.

Oh, he's handsome, but so am I, right?

Right, Dad.

I'll tell you why. Because people tell me – you're Thai, so you can't play the blues like Black Americans from the Deep South. You're not Black, you don't feel the pain of Black Americans who descended from slaves. Now, you're wondering, what about Tyler Gray? I'll tell you. OK, he's Black, but he's not from the Deep South. Maybe generations ago, his ancestors were slaves, but Tyler Gray is from New Jersey. His mother was a kindergarten teacher, his dad a car mechanic. He's got this new album because he's GOOD. I dream of the day I can play on stage with Tyler Gray. Show people a Thai can play the blues. You'd want to be there to see that, wouldn't you?

Sure, Dad, said Tuk.

It's a big world, son. It would be a shame if I never managed to play the blues abroad. Your mother will never understand, but one day you will.

Laurel watched as he gathered his thoughts, delayed his tale by sipping at a bottle of water he produced from a jacket pocket.

'A few days later my father played a small bar off Rama 4, a main road in Bangkok. It was rainy season and the bar was half inside half outside. A lot of water on the floor. I am standing in front watching, same as usual, while he gets ready to play. Something wrong with his microphone, he pulls it with his hand - and I watch him fall into the water on the floor. Already dead. Electric shock.'

Laurel shivered involuntarily at the realisation Tuk was talking about watching his dad drop dead when he, Tuk, was only a kid.

'That explains what you did yesterday,' she said.

'I don't understand.'

'Yesterday, at the fire. You ran into the house even when everyone else stood around watching. You didn't want me to lose my dad.'

'I want to help. I miss my father. I still dream of him. Every time, always the same. In the bar, and he falls down. I want to wake him but he never wakes up and a kind woman in the audience held me, stopped me from going too near. If I touch him, maybe I am dead too. I think about my mother if we are both dead.'

Laurel wanted to ask if he had received counselling, if medical professionals had considered the effect upon a young child's brain of watching his father die such a horrible, unexpected death and being unable to do anything about it. She had done a lot of reading about counselling in preparation for future work as a volunteer with the Samaritans – she was due an interview in Edinburgh in the coming months – and from her reading, she wondered if Tuk might be an undiagnosed victim of post-traumatic stress disorder, PTSD. Tuk interrupted her thoughts:

'But the festival is my chance. To do something for my father. He dreamed of going to other countries to play the blues with people like Tyler Gray. Yesterday I tried to help your father, and I failed. I try to play with Tyler Gray and I fail. My father worried about failing. Now I am failing. Failing my father, and failing for me, too.'

'Bullshit, Tuk.'

He knew bullshit, but clearly didn't know what she meant. She went on:

'You failed my father? Bullshit. You ran into a burning building to help him. Because you went first, and found him first, the firemen saw where to go, how to help my father. You helped save him. AND you saved Maggie Thatcher.'

'Maybe,' said Tuk. 'But still no way to play with Tyler Gray. That is me failing. Even Tod failed.'

'Your friend in Bangkok? How can he share the blame, how could he help?'

'He sent send emails to Colin. No results.'

Laurel knew her old Nokia wouldn't get a signal at the Knab.

'Let's walk and I will make a call.' Taking his hand in hers felt like the most natural thing in the world. She led him to where the scooter was parked, and where she knew her phone would work. When the signal returned on the little screen, she dialled Colin and spoke the moment the call was answered:

'It's me again….. I know, Shetland's impresario's a busy man. Listen, did you get emails from Tuk's friend in Thailand, a guy by the name of Tod? T-O-D Tod. He's sent you a bunch of emails in the last couple of days.'

'Nothing from Thailand, I'm sure,' said Colin.

'Can you check again? Check your SPAM folder.'

Colin was not impressed. 'You're still playing cheerleader for the guy I already got a place to stay where he's probably getting fed three times a day and his laundry taken care of for free? Need anything else done while I'm at it? It's not exactly like I have nothing on my to do list.'

'Tod promised Tuk, and he wouldn't bullshit his oldest pal. Do me one favour. Check again. They'll be there.'

'Alright. But first I have to get to the airport to pick up Tyler Gray and his A&R. Isn't that something. His record company sent an A&R man all the way over here to hold his hand at our wee festival.'

'I'm so happy for you,' said Laurel, who didn't have a clue what an A&R man might be.

They rode the scooter the short distance to Commercial Street. As they took off their helmets, the Nokia rang. It was Colin. She answered and listened for a few seconds.

'You're kidding,' she said. 'No wonder. Will do, thanks.' She thumbed the red button on the phone and turned to Tuk.

'Your friend Tod sent Colin about fifty emails, but because Colin's account gets swamped with junk, they all ended up in his SPAM folder. He's going to check them after he gets back from the airport. Tyler Gray arrives in a few minutes.'

'That's nice,' said Tuk.

'We're trying to help.'

'I know. Sorry.'

'Never mind. Now I need to get online. Your phone doesn't work without Wi-Fi, and this old heap of mine can't do the internet.' As she spoke, the sound of a mandolin introducing a slow blues came from a little further along the street. The busker Tuk kept meeting but was yet to put a name to caught his eye and nodded at his guitar. Tuk waved his injured hand, sore from last night's song with Laurel, but as an afterthought, pulled his harmonica from his pocket and tested it. The song being introduced was in G, and his was a C harp. Perfect for 12-bar blues in what harp players called "second position". The Busker broke into song:

Picked up my newspaper this mornin'
On the front it said June 29
Readin' ma paper this mornin'
On the front it said June 29
Took me back twenty long years
To a summer I near lost my mind

In twenty years did you ever
Meet me walking through your dreams

Or maybe did you wonder
Where I was or how I'd been

Did you ask yourself if only
How different things could be

Or in twenty long years -
Did you never dream of me?

Tuk received the signal he was waiting for and put in a well-received 12-bar lament on harmonica before the busker wrapped up the song with a repeat of the opening verse plus one more refrain. The crowd applauded loudly and coins flew at the open guitar case, eyed protectively by the busker.

He came over and introduced himself.

'I'm StewMac, bytheway.'

Tuk shook his hand, thinking Bytheway sounded like an odd name, one he had heard a few times lately.

'Stewart MacDonald. Stewart with a W. My dad could turn metal to a thousandth of an inch, but couldnae spell for toffee. That was a grand ending to my set. Let me buy youse a drink.'

In the Thule Bar, StewMac sent them to a table while he got the drinks, and returned with two half pints of lager and a whisky for himself. Neat, no ice.

'I'll have to be quick,' said Laurel. 'I need to go to my cousin's place to get online.'

'Something important,' said StewMac.

'Tuk's friend in Thailand sent some YouTube links.'

StewMac extracted a new iPad from his guitar case.

'Would you be wanting to see them in HD?'

'You have an internet account?'

'I'm a busker, darling, not a hobo dosser. How the hell else would I keep up with all the festivals?'

Laurel logged into her email account, clicked on a link in the new message from Colin and a YouTube window popped up. Tuk and *City Limits* playing in a crowded Bangkok pub. She turned up the volume and set the iPad on the bar. A small crowd gathered around them to watch.

Thirty-three

The Mareel had given Colin and Susan a little ante room in the auditorium to use as their office during the festival weekend. Blessed with good Wi-Fi, it gave Colin a chance to watch some of the YouTube links sent to him by someone called Tod, apparently a fellow member of the band Laurel's friend – and Colin's grandparents' temporary house guest – played with in Thailand.

The SPAM filter on his email account didn't have to be particularly effective for Tod's messages to end up there. They bore subject lines like "The Man's Best Performance!!"; "Bangkok Performance Rocks!"; "Best Live Action in Thailand!!; and Colin's favourite: "Thai Man Makes Girls Scream!!". Smiling at the titles, Colin plugged in his headphones and hit "Play" on the first video. Mid-way through the second stanza of a raunchy electric twelve-bar blues, a hand slammed so hard onto the desk it made his expensive new laptop jump.

He gently pressed the space bar, took off the headphones and turned to find Tyler Gray's A&R man playing the textbook intimidation game, standing over him to force Colin to look up at his visitor.

The internet had told him A&R stood for *Artists & Repertoire*. A&R men were record company executives who held key responsibilities over a label's performers and their music. This made them important, something that had not escaped Jack Murdock's vision of his place in the entertainment world. He wore a pressed polo shirt with the brand of a Long Island golf resort, chinos and soft leather boat shoes without socks. He had an image to sell, one that might have worked if he wasn't stuck with a forgettable face nobody would ever pick from a police lineout. The pushy bastard might have been difficult to recognise, but he was easy to dislike.

'We need to talk,' said Murdock. 'I said we need to talk.'

Colin tried for affable. It was a struggle.

'Sure, Jack. I meant to ask you if Tyler's planning to catch the show tonight? I'm holding a few good tickets for him and the band – and yourself, of course.'

'Won't happen. He's laid up with a bit of a cold. No wonder, the shit weather you folks have to live with. The rest of the band are going to give tonight a miss too. Probably can't be assed with fighting off autograph hunters, and I don't blame them. They'll see you tomorrow for the sound check, two o'clock sharp.'

'I was hoping to have a word with…'

'Whatever you do, make sure you get somebody half decent on the mixing desk for the sound check and the show. Tyler's a professional with standards.'

The hell with affable, thought Colin.

'You mean I have to tell my grandmother to leave the headphones at home, Jack Murdock says the job needs a pro to take care of his star performer?'

Colin watched it go in one ear and out the other. Guys like this were too busy to listen, too determined to compose and share their next words of wisdom.

'What are you doing, talking about your grandma? As far as having a word goes, anything needs saying, you say it to me. But I'm busy, so hurry up, man.'

'Forget it,' said Colin. 'Wouldn't want to distract you from your executive level multi-tasking.' *Whoosh whoosh. In one ear, out the other. Again.*

'I have a conference call with important people in New York and Nashville in ten minutes. These people are players, man, so I'm not going to keep them waiting while we nitpick over this amateur hour clusterfuck.'

'You must give me the name of your charm school,' said Colin. 'Tell Tyler I hope he feels better in the morning. Dickhead.'

'What did you…'

'Mind the door doesn't skelp your Ivy League arse on the way out.'

The Mareel was alive with the sense of excitement and anticipation that precedes a sold-out show. Laurel pointed at a Wi-Fi sign with the password in bold letters, along with a smaller sign asking audience members to PLEASE turn off telephones before the show began. Maybe the odd ring during performances outweighed the social media benefits of dozens or hundreds of excited posts and Facebook check-ins ahead of the curtains being pulled back.

'Connect to the Wi-Fi network in case you hear from Tod, but turn the sound off?'

She needn't have worried. Tuk had been the victim of a thousand mobile telephone interruptions at shows big and small, so he knew what to do.

Laurel showed him the two tickets Colin had sent over, by messenger, no less. More like an unpaid Anderson High intern, but who could blame him. And they were for good seats near the front.

'Why so unhappy,' she said.

'Not unhappy,' said Tuk. 'OK, just a little.'

'Worried you will not get a chance tomorrow?'

'I don't know. Don't know what might happen. I don't know why I hear nothing from Tod.'

'Maybe he's busy.'

'Maybe,' he said, as his telephone rang the moment he connected to the Wi-Fi. Which probably meant it was a Skype call. Maybe it was Tod.

'Might be Tod,' he said, and answered the call. 'Hello. Hello?' At first there was no reply, but as he went to disconnect the call, he heard a voice he was not expecting.

'Jo? What is wrong. Why are you calling?'

He listened for what seemed like a long time, Jo's excited voice, too muffled to understand, droning on. Tuk interrupted her:

'Maybe we can talk tomorrow. I am busy now.' He disconnected the call without another word.

'Who is Jo?' said Laurel.

'I told you about my girlfriend.'

'Jo is your ex-fiancée?'

'Thank you. Yes. Ex-fiancée.'

'The woman you say tricked you into coming to Scotland to open a blues bar paid for by her daddy, a plan that fell apart the moment you got here. You said she threw you out,' said Laurel.

'Now she says daddy changed his mind and so now she will open a blues bar in Glasgow.'

'Quite a turnaround! She needs you for her on-again-off-again bar and so now she wants you back?'

'She says she comes to Shetland tomorrow.' Tuk didn't seem too sure what he thought of that.

'And if she does come, it's OK with you?' said Laurel, unable to hide her disgust.

'I don't understand.'

'It's not just Jo who needs the bar in Glasgow, is it?'

'Sorry?'

'I'm curious. What did you love more. The fiancée, or the blues bar she promised you?' She thrust the tickets at Tuk. 'I don't feel like this anymore.' She headed for the exit without a backward glance.

Tuk followed her out and handed tickets for two of the best seats in the house to a couple of teenagers who couldn't believe their luck.

Thirty-four

Day two was already going well. Colin and Susan had set out a tight schedule with multiple acts changing places on the main auditorium stage throughout the course of the day. Shetland musical talent was thick on the ground across multiple genres, blues included. And with a decent number of people visiting the islands specifically for the festival, it presented an opportunity to highlight locals, who were given tight, thirty-minute slots between acts brought in from the UK mainland. Solid performances from Shetland acts spread via social media, increasing their chances of being invited to future events elsewhere in Britain.

Roadies and tech crew members busied themselves during a break between acts. Colin, Susan and Jack Murdock used the relative quiet to discuss what was bothering Susan and Murdock. Namely, Tuk.

'To be perfectly frank,' said Colin, 'I'm not asking much.'

'I'm not so sure,' said Susan. Not exactly supportive, thought Colin – situation normal.

'There is zero risk involved,' he said. 'The guy is good. The clips prove it.'

'It doesn't matter if he's good,' said Susan. 'People paid money to see Tyler Gray. He's the headline act, the biggest name on the poster and the website and on the tickets for tonight's show. HE's the reason people are here - and you want to put a nobody onstage during the climax to the festival? At the very least, you're taking a risk.'

Murdock was visibly pleased with Susan taking the lead.

Colin wasn't about to give up. 'Think about this for a moment. We tip off the news websites and the TV people. They're hungry for original storylines, especially ones with a feelgood factor. Stories like "Unknown Thai artist gets miracle break at tiny Shetland festival". The press will go apeshit for a happy story. We post a clip to YouTube right after the show and tip off every journalist on my contact list – and everyone in Jack's email address book. The media attention could make it go viral, and overnight a million people who never heard of Lerwick or Tyler Gray will know all about the festival and Tyler's successful appearance and the feelgood tale of the Thai musician who managed to play alongside his dad's hero. We keep the ball rolling with an announcement: Tuk is to feature on next year's bill. Gigantic PR coup, foundations already laid for next year.' Colin dried up, conscious he had gone out on a limb supported only by a couple of YouTube videos.

Murdock seemed to change his mind about staying quiet. He had had enough.

'Did you stay up all night writing your little speech? I got one word for you. Bull. Shit.'

'Christ,' said Colin, 'he's numerically challenged as well.'

'Ooh, careful you don't hurt my feelings. You're so far off base you're not even in the stadium anymore. You wanted

Tyler to grace your shitty little festival in the back of beyond here –'

'Tyler is here because he wants to be. Nobody forced him.'

'You can't get anything right. Tyler's career has been down a dark hole full of wasted spells in rehab for the last twenty years. My record company is taking a chance on bringing him back into the blues rock mainstream; he's here to see how he goes down with the European blues fans. Face it, even if he screws up here in chilly Nowheresville, who's gonna notice? But **we** made this happen. We paid most of the band's expenses - do you have ANY idea how much it costs to ship and insure all the gear they brought with them? Of course you don't. Around here, a big music night is your grandfather sawing away at a fiddle and a retard in a skirt banging a drum with a bone.'

Colin, fearful people nearby were beginning to sense the tension, lowered his voice and moved closer to Murdock.

'Are you too busy thinking up **your** next stream of shit to listen to what anyone else is saying? Think of the media. Stories in all the press and on TV. A series of carefully promoted YouTube clips going viral worldwide. Does this mean nothing to you record company executive types? Didn't they cover this kind of thing when you did your MBA? If Tyler is credited for giving this week's YouTube sensation a major break, is it going to hurt Tyler? Maybe it will drive new fans and former fans to listen to what he's doing now, after twenty years in obscurity.'

'He has a point,' said Susan, much to Colin's surprise. 'The Thai bloke could draw attention to Tyler's resurrection story. Everybody loves a good comeback tale, an artist who lost it all, but worked relentlessly to get his career back on track.'

'You had the cheek to ask what I learned in college,' said Murdock, his face red with rage, finger pointing aggressively at Colin's chest. 'I'll tell you exackly what they taught us. The client comes first, always. So when a jerk-off wannabe Big Time Promoter Man from the Arctic tries to pull a stunt to put our artist in the shade of a no-name nobody from Tibet or Timbuktoo - turning HIM into the story of the day instead of promoting Tyler Gray and the new album this whole festival appearance is all about – we say screw you.'

Colin's raised palms said *you've proven my case*. 'So all the stuff about the client coming first was shite. It's all about the record company.'

'Egg zackly, maestro. The same company who paid for your headline act to be here. The company who's not even a little interested in promoting some Asian kid with a few amateur clips online. This ain't *Bangkok's Got Fucking Talent*.'

Colin walked away, more angry than disappointed. In the space of a few hours the visitor from Thailand had, in Colin's mind, transformed from an unknown nobody to the guy who, with good social media promotion from Colin (with or without Susan), could transform the future fortunes of their festival, put it on the front pages of newspapers and television stations and websites around the world. Even if it was for only one day....

Watching this unfold from nearby in the wings, Tyler Gray's expression gave nothing away.

Thirty-five

Crossing the entrance hall of the Mareel, guitar on his back as usual, Tuk was accosted by a stranger. The guy wore neatly pressed beige chinos and a pale blue dress shirt, open to show off a gold disc on a chain around his neck. The shirt sleeves were rolled up to just below his elbows, letting all see a heavy gold Rolex on his left wrist and a chunky silver bracelet on his right. Gucci shoes and an almost painfully precise haircut finished off an unspectacular appearance the man had clearly put a lot of thought into. When he spoke, he revealed the dental perfection that exists only in American dentist waiting room catalogues.

'Are you Tuk?' he said in a voice combining equal measures of arrogance and aggression.

'I am Tuk.'

'I'm glad I found you.'

'You are?'

'Didn't I just say I was glad?'

'Why are you glad?'

'Because now I can tell you to take your guitar and fuck off.'

'Excuse me?'

'You speak English? You won't be needing your guitar anytime today. Tyler Gray works for me. My record company is calling the shots, and no way you get to steal the limelight from our artist. No fucking way. Get it? Understand?'

Tuk watched while the guy with the big mouth tried to add to the intimidation by closing the gap between them until their chests almost touched. Tuk's gaze was unflinching, completely without expression until finally, Murdock backed away, spun on a designer heel and strutted off, still muttering under his breath.

The bus service into Lerwick was cheap and reliable and, in an archipelago where it rained more than two-hundred-and-forty days a year, impervious to weather. A combination of slow-moving traffic, the frequency of stops, the quiet patience of the bus drivers and the casual, going-for-a-stroll manner in which departing and boarding passengers treated the walk to and from seats also made it painfully slow. Laurel sometimes imagined the distances between stops could be covered on foot faster than they took the bus. And, having forgotten her headphones, she was forced to endure what passed for conversation between teenaged girls in the seat behind her.

'Last night was probably like the best live gig I've ever been to,' said girl number one. 'It was like pure dead brilliant.'

'– brilliant,' said girl number two.

'An' ohmigod, Willie Duke. What a hunk.'

'– hunk,' said her friend.

'Did you see how he kept staring at me with those like gorgeous mysterious druggy eyes of? Ah swear to god, I like nearly wet my pants.'

'– pants.'

'I know he's not, like, not like a real rock star.'

'– rock star.'

'But I'd shag him.'

'Only after I shagged him first,' said girl number two.

Laurel's mobile rang.

'Colin,' she said, and listened. 'Hang on, I see him. I'm on the bus, near the Marlex; I'll call you back.'

Tuk suffered the indignity of having two locals think he was searching for somewhere to buy porn. A third person he stopped, a little woman with grey hair wrapped tight in a net and pulling a red tartan shopping trolley, put on her reading glasses and looked relieved at the words on his translation app.

'Goodness,' she said. 'For a moment there I thought you were asking for something else. There isn't a proper pawn shop anywhere in the town, but Walter's place might be the closest thing. He buys and sells almost anything. I often wonder how he manages to scrape a living. Some of the rubbish in his window has been there for years.' She gave Tuk careful directions to a shopping centre called the Toll Clock, only a couple of minutes away from the Mareel.

The Toll Clock was an odd little complex clad entirely in red metal, home to independent stores selling an eclectic selection of goods including Shetland knitwear, toys, greeting cards, gifts, cosmetic jewellery, electrical goods, beer and liquors, fitted kitchen cabinets and potted flowers. For those in search of food, it hosted a butcher shop complete with staff in funny hats and stripy aprons and a place to pick up sandwiches, soups and chocolate biscuits. In Scotland, so far as Tuk could work out, nobody was ever too far from sources of chocolate or beer or sausages or all three.

Deep in a darker corner, away from most of the foot traffic, sat Walter's Buy 'n' Sell.

Tuk put off what he was about to do by poring over the contents of the crowded window. This kind of display fascinated him. A miscellany of second-hand goods included twin-lens-reflex and SLR camera bodies and lenses and flash guns, antique clocks, a couple of barometers, velvet-lined box sets of bone-handled 1950s cutlery, individual items of fragile crockery celebrating the births, coronations or marriages of identifiable British royals and – much more interesting – a selection of battery-powered transistor radios from decades past. One corner held a rough F5 mandolin, a tenor banjo with three rusty strings and a school-grade flute crying out for metal polish. Webs tugging gently at the display suggested the window was home to more than one spider.

Walter pulled his nose out of a well-thumbed paperback and stood up when the bell above the door announced the arrival of a potential customer. Aged about fifty, Walter wore a Grateful Dead shirt stretched taut over a basketball-sized belly, and jeans so faded they depended on cris-cross sewing machine work to hold them together. The unusual sight of a young Oriental man, quite tall and carrying a guitar case on his back made him think of stories more than one friend had told of a young guy whose playing lit up the Lounge the other night. Maybe with Laurel Hughson?

'Good afternoon,' he said.

'Good afternoon,' said the visitor. 'Will you buy my guitar?'

Despite the fact his livelihood depended upon buying things from people who wandered into his shop, Walter was taken aback by the directness of the question.

'It depends on what you have in the case,' he said.

'It is a Gibson.'

'Not many Gibsons grace my wee store. Shall we take a look?'

Tuk laid the case on the top of a heavily scored glass counter over a shelf jammed with Scalextric cars, track and accessories. He unzipped it and removed his faithful 335.

'BB King replica ES335,' said Walter. 'Beautiful. But well used.'

'Played every day for nearly twenty years.'

'Are you here for the blues festival?'

'Not now,' said Tuk.

'Played already? Need some money in a hurry? Happens to us all sometimes. If it didn't, I'd be out of business.'

'I need to buy a plane ticket.'

'My friend might be able to help you. Two doors along, Beatrice Travel. I can give her a call to say you're coming.'

The sale was painful, but went smoothly. Walter pointed to many signs of the Gibson's hard life and explained he might have to hang onto it for months before the right buyer came along. In the end he agreed to pay five hundred pounds so long as Tuk threw in the case, which he knew would sell quicker than the guitar, thanks to giving the impression it was held together by faded stickers. Someone whose budget might never stretch to the guitar would love to adopt the case's back story.

Tuk took the money and ran his finger across the Gibson logo on the headstock one last time. He thanked Walter and left with tears in his eyes.

Next door but one, a woman in an embroidered dress the size of a family tent welcomed him to her shop.

'You'd be the bloke who just sold my boyfriend a guitar and needs a plane ticket?'

'Please. I need a ticket from Glasgow to Bangkok.'

'Going home?'

'Yes, home.'

'One way or return ticket?'

'One way.'

'Had enough of Scotland? Sorry – none of my business, I know. Any particular airline?'

'Cheapest ticket, please.' He fanned four hundred pounds out on the counter top. 'I have only this.'

Beatrice sucked air through her teeth.

'A bit tight, but I'll see what I can find you. Date of travel?'

'As soon as possible.' His gaze settled on a poster of an idyllic sun-kissed beach on Koh Phangan. The island where an evening with Jo on a beach hut hammock set this whole mess in motion. Reminded for the umpteenth time there was nobody to blame but himself, he dragged his gaze from the poster and watched Beatrice work the phones in search of a way to get him home without his dad's guitar.

From the doorway of what used to be a bookstore with a window display of faded cardboard constructions touting cookbooks by TV personalities, Laurel saw Tuk emerge from Beatrice's shop and tuck a plastic folder into his pocket as he shuffled, head down, towards the exit to the street. Outside the Toll Clock, raindrops bounced from car bonnets and roofs as grey skies unloaded a long-promised, merciless torrent of cold rain.

Thirty-six

The end of Colin and Susan's relationship came when Susan accused him of being unfaithful; they were living together happily in a flat above Commercial Street with views over the Bressay Strait, and no fixed plans to take things to any "next stage". This was despite pressure from both sets of parents counting the days before the sound of wedding bells or, at the least, a baby shower announcement. Colin had never in the two years they had been together considered being unfaithful, let alone played away.

The accusation hurt, but the lack of trust in how Susan acted on her unfounded suspicions – there was a German tourist Colin had met once, for coffee, nothing more, no hopes or intentions attached nor acted upon. One cup of coffee, openly enjoyed in a coffee shop only yards from where they lived without a thought given to the likelihood it would be reported on by anything up to a dozen folk who knew Susan, cost him – no, them – their relationship. Truth be told, three months on, Colin was glad, enjoying the freedom and absence of responsibilities that came with being single. It helped that he kept the flat after Susan moved back to her parents' place, even if it meant he drew daggers from unplanned encounters with members of her large family. And despite shoppers flocking to the bigger stores on the edge of town, there was still nowhere more likely to bump into people than Commercial Street.

None of which stopped him being pleased when she came around to his way of thinking on the matter of Tuk. When they split, they agreed their roles as festival co-organisers would remain in place. Nothing personal would get in the way of making their event the best it could possibly be, which is why her initial rejection of his suggestion about Tuk had bothered him. He had convinced himself of the viability of turning the Tuk situation into a marketing tool that, if they played it well, could draw attention from the traditional media, and maybe even go viral on the web. It could develop into the kind of PR money couldn't buy.

But after she initially took Jack Murdock's side, and after the mouthy American had stormed off to put a fresh crease in his chinos, she apologised for not keeping to their pledge. Now she had done an abrupt one-eighty and Colin had his chance to set things up, if only he could get Tyler Gray to play along.

If things went according to plan, right now Susan was massaging Murdock's prideful ego in the wings of a deafening show by a rather brilliant rockabilly band from Aberdeen who would have the audience dancing in the aisles. Their set was a beguiling mixture of original songs and covers and adaptations of hits from the Stray Cats and Elvis, Bob Wills and his Texas Playboys, Little Richard and even, for UK fans of a certain vintage, Showaddywaddy and Shakin' Stevens.

Colin tapped on the door of the dressing room assigned to Tyler Gray and his three-piece band. Gray himself opened the door and ushered him in. He too wanted to avoid getting on the wrong side of Murdock, at least for now.

Like a lot of showbiz folk who had successfully extracted themselves from the grip of chemical and other addictions, Tyler drank a scary amount of coffee. Susan had made sure fresh roasted beans from Brazil and Thailand sat prominent on a counter beside a quality grinder and a machine capable of satisfying the demands of a five-star hotel breakfast buffet. When Colin came into the room, he spotted its Perspex pot half-full and smelling good. Tyler poured two mugs, set them on the coffee table and sat down next to him.

'Thanks,' said Colin. 'Smells good.'

'Wasn't much of a rider we gave you, a decent coffee machine and some diet drinks,' said Tyler, 'but we appreciate it all the same. I take it you want to talk while our beloved A&R bozo is otherwise engaged?'

'He's busy having his ego seen to by Susan.'

'That ought to work. Conceited fool.'

'You heard us talking earlier about the Thai guy, Tuk?'

'Murdock the Mouth made it easy to catch.'

'Did you get what I was hoping for, trying to engineer a media thing that could help everyone out? You, the band, next year's festival – and the Thai guy?'

'And now you're going to show me why we should go along with it?'

Colin opened his computer, YouTube already cued up.

The band crowded around the computer. Colin cranked up the volume and set in motion a short, edited playlist of Tuk playing to an appreciative audience at a packed live music bar in Bangkok. To save time in case Murdock showed up, he had cut the songs to show off some of Tuk's best work, both on vocals and guitar. As the highlights played, he kept watch on the faces of Tyler and his band. If not obviously impressed, they were certainly surprised by what they saw. The playlist came to an end.

'Want to see more?' said Colin.

'That's plenty,' said Tyler. 'Now explain to me how letting this guy sit in for a couple of numbers could possibly become an internet sensation.'

'That depends on what you let us say.'

'About what?'

'About the years your career, ehm, *stalled* around the time Tuk's dad bought your first album.'

'Stalled. You're going easy on me. More like it went into freefall.'

Colin thought Tyler was deliberating how much detail to divulge, so he waited for him to go on.

'It's no secret I drank and snorted my career away, spent years bumming the use of friends' sofas, a few nights at a time. In the space of a few months, I went from a guest spot on Letterman beamed to fifteen million homes around America, to playing in front of a half dozen drunks in basement bars in Trenton, New Jersey.' He shook his head, sad regrets in his eyes. Opportunities lost, perhaps forever. Another thought occurred to him: 'What's the connection to Tuk's daddy?'

'He loved your album, told ten-year-old Tuk he should do his best to play with the best musicians he could ever join onstage, people like you. A couple of weeks later, he died in front of his son in an accident onstage in Bangkok, electrocuted.'

'Shit, that's heavy, man. And Tuk's here to fulfill his daddy's dying wish?'

'It's a no-brainer that's how the media will run it. You saw the videos,' said Colin. 'If he wasn't any good, I wouldn't try to make this happen. I'm thinking in terms of headlines that almost write themselves, and might get picked up all over the world.'

'When you put it like that, it might not hurt,' said Gray. *'Thai musician fulfills daddy's dying wish when comeback trail Tyler invites him onstage at obscure festival.'*

'Exactly,' said Colin. 'Maybe without the bit about "obscure"'. He had another thought. 'What about Murdock? Won't he blow a gasket?'

'The mofo will go apeshit. But if it all goes to plan, he'll claim that it was all his doing from day one, nobody else had the foresight to think of it or the guts to pull it off.'

Thirty-seven

Tuk took advantage of the pass Colin gave him to catch the end of a rockabilly set. It was joyous, filled with energy, the packed audience and the seven-piece band sharing an obvious love for the music. It made him think of a Bangkok rockabilly band who scraped a living by playing two or three sets a night, often in two or three different bars, six nights a week. Many of their performances were in front of audiences barely into double figures, yet they could compete with these guys. He wished they could be here to enjoy the show with him. Hell, he wished any number of his friends on the Bangkok music scene could be here to enjoy it with him.

Next to impress him was the stage production crew. At the end of the rockabilly encores, the curtains closed on the main stage to let the roadies quietly set up for another band while out front, a singer-songwriter walked to where a microphone rose from beneath the stage floor, only a couple of metres from the front row of the stalls.

He was obviously well-known in these parts, but an announcer introduced him anyway, to loud applause from the full house. Shetland's own man (Tuk thought maybe he was called Steven) played acoustic guitar with occasional breaks on a kazoo taped to its top. The music was about as far removed from any definition of blues as you could find, but his casting and his placement on the schedule were inspired. Light relief, even comedy, from a confident one-man act who brought the pace and the volume down to an intimacy that set everyone up for big acts to follow.

Anecdotal monologues between songs delivered in a near-impenetrable Shetland dialect must have left visitors to the islands in the dark, but were met with glee by the locals. His humour was infectious, the audience responding in roars of laughter, glances of shared delight firing back and forth among friends and partners, tears rolling down faces. One song people were clearly anticipating, a parody of Steve Earle's *Galway Girl*, drew hilarity loud enough to drown out the performer's kazoo solos.

It was first-rate entertainment, but a bit too happy for Tuk.

He left the building, walked towards town and a few minutes later found himself perched next to a centuries-old cannon pointing from the ramparts of Fort Charlotte. When Laurel brought him here on the scooter, she explained how the cannons once directly faced the harbour. The cannons were never fired in anger, but with a lot of help from the translation app on Tuk's phone, told him how they were used in one grisly act of mischief in 1855. In the depths of winter, young men relieved boredom by commandeering two of the cannons to fire dead cats out to sea. What the app could never explain was why they did it, but as an image in Tuk's mind it rendered tame memories of *Loi Kratong* candle-powered paper lanterns floating silently upwards from the banks of Bangkok's Chao Phraya River.

Hunger pangs were dealt with by a bag of chips soaked in vinegar, eaten while he walked. He couldn't guess how food so patently unhealthy could taste so delicious; but he could assert with some certainty that the chips would taste even better with a liberal application of *sot pik,* Thailand's staple, sweet-but-spicy sauce. It was for good reason big orange bottles of *sot pik* graced the tables of almost every diner back home.

He got back to the Mareel's main auditorium in time to watch the second half of the set by British harmonica legend Paul Lamb and his band. Thirty-plus years at the top of his game, he played the crowd like a personal cheerleading section. Tuk had accompanied dozens of harmonica players who, in his experience, occupied a range in ability from poor to awful, though the occasional guy would appear who was not only able to contribute something, he knew when to shut up. For the first time since he came to Scotland, he remembered a little chubby Scot he sometimes invited up for a couple of numbers at Saxophone Pub. So long as Tuk and the band stuck to twelve-bar-blues standards like *Hoochie Coochie Man* or *Sweet Home Chicago*, Ron did a decent enough job of filling the gaps and keeping quiet when others stepped forward. After visibly relishing his slightly predictable 24-bar solo, he would step back to warm applause from the audience. The modest pleasure the little guy took from his short spell in the spotlight always made Tuk feel good.

Paul Lamb was of course in another league, his mastery of the harmonica amply illustrated when he set off on an encore featuring an exquisitely executed Sonny Terry-inspired solo, whoops and all.

Thirty-eight

Tuk made himself scarce as Paul Lamb's band brought their encore to a close. A lesson was learned years ago at his first big festival in the coastal town of Pattaya. *City Limits* filled a slot low on a crowded bill headed by Thai folk-rock heroes Caravan, and festival organisers somehow hadn't fully taken into account Pattaya's proximity to eleven million people in Bangkok, only two hours away by road. The result was a beach area lightly cordoned off for a few hundred ticket holders who were completely overrun by ten times as many day trippers from the capital.

Even when *City Limits* took to the stage hours before Caravan arrived in town, it made for a memory that still made the hairs on the back of Tuk's neck stand on end.

Much later in the day, he was in the wings to watch a band play the last set before Caravan were due onstage. The crowd was already restless.

Second top billing went to a Bangkok-based blues band led by Irishman Keith Nolan. Outsiders could be forgiven for thinking it an odd spot on the bill for a band more used to playing in front of fifty or a hundred people in Bangkok bars and clubs, but Cannonball were there because no Thai band would dream of possibly upstaging Caravan (or, almost as bad, being blown away by them).

Tuk had played with Keith and Cannonball many times, subbing for regular lead guitarist Daniel. When Keith came off the Pattaya stage to polite applause from a crowd calling out for Caravan, he shook Tuk's hand and said:

'Don't stand here, man.'

'Why?'

The stage was already under attack from roadies and stage crew tasked with preparing the performance area for Caravan. Keith hooked a thumb at them.

'They work for *Caravan*. Mick Jagger and Stevie Wonder could stand here, and they'd still walk all over them.'

A few years and a few thousand miles away from Pattaya, Tuk made himself scarce while the crew set things up for Tyler Gray's band. Thankful for the *Access All Areas* pass hanging from his neck, he wandered freely through the complex until he found an exit. Outside on the street, he was surprised by how fast darkness had fallen and intrigued by a stream of people making beelines for the back of the complex, so of course he followed them. As they came out from the lee of the Mareel the cloud covering opened up and the growing crowd emitted a collective gasp. Overhead, the blue-black sky was crystal clear, jammed with more stars than Tuk ever saw above light-polluted Bangkok. Closer to the northeastern horizon, it was alive with vast, interweaving curtains of green, yellow and scarlet. A light show like no other.

'Aurora borealis,' said a voice. He turned to find Lewis, the guy who saved his guitar in Glasgow and who planted the idea of coming to Shetland.

'The Northern Lights,' Lewis explained. 'I've always wanted to experience them. It's unusual to see them this early in the year, so I can't believe our luck. Shetlanders call them the Mirrie Dancers. Don't ask me why.'

All around them, people jostled in search of the best angle from which to capture the scene on their smartphones. Tuk's phone stayed in his pocket as he stood, awestruck.

He re-entered Mareel via a backstage door guarded by a bored youth in a luminous security vest. The poor kid had to be a long way down the pecking order to get stuck with an outdoor assignment so far from the action of an indoor music event. Not for him lording it over pretty girls in the front row, no enjoying the music with his back to the band. Out here he was lucky if he could pick up the thump of a bass drum.

Tyler Gray's band were pumping out a spirited version of the Tommy Tucker hit Hi-Heel Sneakers when Tuk resumed his post just behind the edge of the curtain, where two surprises awaited him. The first was how the hall had been re-arranged for the headline act. All the downstairs seating was gone, revealing a standing-only area for a few hundred happy, mostly young souls. The second surprise was Laurel, who pointed up at the far side of a U-shaped balcony where the only seating remained. A souvenir program waved at him, Sadie and Matt enjoying prime spots almost within touching distance of the performers. Tuk waved back. Matt toggled his finger between Tuk and Laurel and gave him a wink combined with a suggestive thumbs-up and side-to-side pantomime smooches. Tuk glanced at Laurel, who might not have noticed, and seemed preoccupied. He hoped she wasn't still angry about the night before when he took the call from Jo.

With the booming sound from the PA, there was no need to keep their voices down, but they spoke in murmurs just the same.

'He's great, isn't he?' said Laurel.

'Just like I remember when I listened to him with my father.'

'How does that make you feel?'

'Sad, but happy,' said Tuk. 'Sad my father cannot be here with me, but happy I can see one of his heroes from so close. Thank you, Laurel.'

'Here comes trouble,' she said, angling her head at Susan, cutting a course from the shadows behind them. But Susan wasn't here to bother them.

'I'm glad you got your passes,' she said, waving her hand at the laminated rectangles hanging from their necks.

'Thanks to you and Colin,' said Laurel, as Susan left without another word. Maybe she had more important things to take care of. They went back to watching the band, who broke into an up-tempo Chicago blues shuffle. Tuk stepped closer to the edge of the curtain, where he could see some of the crowd. He saw Lewis edge through to the front, polite but determined.

'Who are you trying to find?' said Laurel.

'Nobody.'

'Your ex?'

'No. The last time I saw Jo was in Glasgow.'

'And still you're searching for her.' Laurel handed him a paper flyer. 'Did you see this? She's giving them out all over town.'

Tuk was aghast. The flyer had a big colour photograph of Tuk playing his Gibson. He recognised the shot from a show *City Limits* played at Saxophone Pub, a few weeks before Jo left Thailand. The flyer had a breathless announcement about a GREAT NEW BLUES BAR opening soon in Glasgow. THE NEW ADHERE BAR.

'I didn't see this,' said Tuk. 'How can Jo –'

'She seems pretty sure of herself. You honestly didn't talk to her?'

'I didn't. I don't want to talk to her. You helped me understand. Jo is not my problem - I am my own problem. I came to Scotland to escape from my life in Thailand, playing small bars, making little money. My father's dreams are important, but I forgot about my good life there, the good life like my father had. Fine music, good friends. When Jo wanted me to come with her to Scotland, I followed her. I was stupid and it was my mistake. She did not make me come here. Jo was selfish, but now I know I was selfish, too. You helped me understand I came to Scotland for the wrong reasons. But now, I am here, thank you. I am grateful to you. Tod will never believe I got close to Tyler Gray for a live show. Thank you, Laurel.'

It might have been the longest string of English he had ever put together, and was certainly the longest utterance he had ever shared with Laurel. It disappointed him when it didn't seem to make much of an impression. They stood in silence while Tyler Gray and his band worked through a tight setlist in front of a few hundred Shetlanders dancing with joy, arms raised, smartphones taking selfies and recording shaky unwatchable videos destined for the delete button.

As the applause softened at the end of a song, Tyler Gray did the palms-down signal for the audience to let him speak.

'Thank you, ladies and gentlemen. Thank you so much. Now we have a special treat for you, a special guest, so special he's not even on the bill.'

The reaction in the crowd was part curiosity, part frustration at a possible threat to the flow of a show they were already enjoying quite enough, thank you very much. Near to where Lewis stood, Jack Murdock was seriously pissed off. Tuk was scanning the crowd trying to identify a guest when Tyler spoke again.

'This man has come a long way to be here, folks, all the way from Bangkok. Let's hear it for Tuk Blues. Yes, you heard me right. All the way from Bangkok, Thailand!'

The crowd clapped sparingly. Jack Murdock appeared on the verge of a stroke. Tuk remained rooted to the spot.

'Go on!' said Laurel. 'It's not your own blues bar in Glasgow, but it's your chance.'

'You know about this?' said Tuk. She must have. Tuk still didn't move even as Tyler Gray gestured from centre stage.

'I can't,' said Tuk, to Laurel. He stepped sideways as if to escape her gaze or even to escape into the wings. She matched the movement, blocking him.

'You told me all you want to do is play the blues. You told me you wanted this more than anything, not just for you, but for your dad. You came here with a dream. Here's your chance. Now take it.'

'I don't have a guitar.'

'Borrow one.'

Why was she smiling?

He still didn't move. The crowd started a slow hand-clap as the situation threatened to degenerate into a fiasco. Jack Murdock waved his way past a security guard as he made for steps at the side of the stage. Tyler Gray stopped him with one pointed finger. Murdock thought about ignoring him, but they locked eyes.

'Stay the fuck outta this,' said Tyler, into the mic. The crowd didn't understand what was going on, but they laughed anyway. Murdock froze, face rigid, as if he had never done anything to deserve this.

Tuk, too, remained frozen.

'I can't watch this any longer,' said Laurel. She disappeared into the backstage shadows as the slow handclaps gathered power.

Thirty-nine

Later, when he replayed in his mind the minutes that followed, a recurring phrase kept interrupting his thoughts. *An out of body experience.* But it was much more. No matter how many times he thought it through, this couldn't be framed in a dreamy cartoon image of Tuk hovering, watching himself walk from the shadows of the wing towards the glow of centre stage. He once watched a TV producer friend at work in the PCR, the Production Control Room of a Thai TV show, broadcast live, with a cast of dozens; musicians, back-up singers, dancers, announcers, the requisite transgender presenter lashed with circus clown quantities of make-up, stray, cosmetically frozen-eyed TV stars there to be seen if not heard – a producer's nightmare displayed in the PCR on a couple of dozen flat screen monitors, camera operators reacting instantly to the producer's rapid-fire instructions in their headphones.

Tuk saw himself from multiple angles, walking tentatively towards centre stage, appearing from dark shadow to be instantly picked up by a sharp operator on the lighting gantry who nailed him to the stage with a spotlight so strong it cast a moving shadow across the rest of the band and the forest of electrical hardware involved in putting out a live show at ear-shattering volume.

The standing area where once the stalls were located was not too densely packed, certainly not the stuff of mosh pit dives. As his eyes adjusted, he began to see faces he knew. Lewis, of course, doggedly hanging onto a front-of-stage spot. Walter the pawnshop guy arm in arm with his girlfriend Beatrice, the travel agent; Henry the acupuncturist who wanted Tuk to show him around the herbal medicine stores in Bangkok's Chinatown; Elma the fortune teller, who seemed to be cosying up to the guy whose puppy had almost licked Laurel and Tuk to death at the Knab; and, bouncing on the spot like she had springs in her heels, Jo. They locked eyes momentarily and she let out a squeal. Next to her, Brendan grinned broadly and gave him two thumbs up. Tuk wasn't sure there was any room for Bren's optimism. He didn't even have a guitar.

A roadie appeared from the other wing carrying one, and Tuk did a double take that would have made Oliver Hardy jealous. Not just any old spare guitar. *His* Gibson ES335. What was going on? He took it gratefully from the roadie, who had already plugged it in. The roadie pointed to the tuner clipped to the headstock and gave him a thumbs-up. It was even tuned, primed ahead of Tuk's hesitant emergence from the shadows.

Tyler Gray patted his shoulder warmly.

'What do you want to play, man? It's your call.'

'I, I don't know,' said Tuk.

Not what Tyler expected, let alone wanted, to hear or see. An expectant audience already skeptical about the unknown arrival, and the guest artist rigid with fear. He turned to his band and shouted out: 'Shuffle in C.' Tuk heard him, and joined in an up-tempo 12-bar-blues shuffle of a sort that, at a hundred blues jams in dozens of pubs and clubs around Thailand, he had routinely helped turn into something special.

Except tonight it died out in painful slow motion as Tuk waved the band down to a clumsy disjointed fadeout drawing complaining groans from the audience and scowls from the band. Even Tyler was looking pissed off, but Tuk turned to the microphone and, softly picking out a slow blues in E which Tyler and the band immediately backed, spoke gently to a crowd which was in two minds whether it was going to pay attention – or boo him from the stage.

Tuk held up the Gibson.

'This was my father's guitar. He died seventeen years ago. Today I thought I lost it, but tonight my friends bring it back to me. My father taught me to play the blues with this guitar. He sang love songs when I was so young, and I thought he was singing to me. Of course he was.'

Now they were listening. Tuk's eyes scoured the crowd as he played an intro full of blue notes that, by virtue of its seamless technique and steadily rising volume, by now had their complete attention. He saw StewMac appear from an emergency exit, a guilty expression on his face, but he couldn't spot the one person he wanted to find. He spoke again into the mic:

'Sometimes the blues is sad, but other times it is about how someone can help you when you are sad. Someone special. Today I start to write a song about someone special. Someone I want to sing to. I am sorry for my English.'

Accompanied by his own guitar work, and by Tyler's band adjusting their volume to suit, he began to croon in a throaty baritone voice to make a young BB King smile.

'One day you'll really need somebody – believe me

Movement from near the entrance. Tod and a two-man film crew. Tod stopped and spread his arms in delight. Tuk, every bit as delighted, continued to scan the crowd and to sing:

One of these days you'll really need someone – you'll see

Stage left, where Tuk and Laurel stood earlier, Willie Duke and Susan seemed enchanted.

Someone to chase away your sad, lonesome blues

There. Laurel pushing through the crowd to stand near the front. Tuk locked eyes with her.

And believe me when I say – that someone is you.'

Jo's face went from delighted to sour at the sight of Tuk staring lovingly at some woman she'd never seen before. Beside her, unaware or unconcerned, Brendan cheered.

Tuk ripped into a wailing solo that sent hands into the air, smartphone flashlight apps gleaming, a swirling show of illuminated arms swirling around Laurel. Tod's sound man and cameraman moved in near the stage for close-ups. The audience no longer had any doubts about the new arrival.

Jo fought the tide as she made a rush for the nearest exit, Brendan refusing to heed her order to leave with her. In the balcony, Sadie and Matt stood with their arms over their heads, synchronised waving in not-quite perfect time.

Tyler took over with a soaring 24-bar solo that kept the audience on their toes, and followed it by coaxing Tuk into a lengthy exchange of four-bar call-and-answer slots where ideas and themes played off one another as if they had been making music together for years. By the time Tuk brought the song to a close, the audience were already crying out for more – and not a single soul appeared to notice that he had pulled off a one-verse song. One solitary verse without even a chorus. It can happen when you invent a song on the fly – not that he had ever managed it before.

Forty

As a live music venue, the layout of an Asian shophouse is impractical at best. Designed to be crammed side-by-side along short strips of retail property, the traditional shophouse is shaped like a shotgun barrel. At the street end, the narrowest of pavement shopfronts provided rudimentary access to a long, uniformly skinny interior. Somehow, Adhere the 13th blues bar turned being only ten feet wide into an asset. It forced the band to play interlocked like moving puzzle pieces on a tiny rectangular patch of carpet midway along one side of the barrel. A thin walkway separated the band from a single row of tiny round tables tight against the opposite wall. The result was one of the most intimate music venues Tuk and *City Limits* had ever played.

Ever the showman, Tod waited just long enough to allow Adhere's long-suffering waitress to thread her way past him carrying a full tray of drinks before he leaned out until his microphone cable was in danger of sweeping away glasses on the table opposite. Perched on shaky stools and loving every second of this were Tuk's mum, her partner Khun

Jiraporn – and Laurel, grey with fatigue from her first ever brush with jet lag.

Tuk watched his mum and Laurel exchange amused looks at Tod imitating Mick Jagger's pseudo-American accent, stretching out the vowels of the chorus to *Honky Tonk Women*. The way the two had bonded almost immediately did a lot to salve Tuk's conscience over putting his mother through so much in recent months; and if mum's acceptance of his new partner helped resign her to Tuk continuing in his quest to be a musician, he would call that a win. As he looked at Laurel, she turned her iPad around to show Sadie and Matt, faces so close together on the screen they almost blended into one. Their expressions when they saw him and waved excitedly earned them a return wave and a big smile. How lucky had he been to meet them?

While Adhere co-owner and house band leader Pong enjoyed a break from performing and used his smartphone to stream a live broadcast of the goings-on in the unofficial best small blues bar in the world, partner Nong presided over the tall bar, where StewMac chatted animatedly with English Phil, continuing a heated debate over whose music was best. While they stood united in their dislike for everything Phil Collins did post-Genesis, namesake Phil was devoted to Frank Zappa while StewMac was more of a Lou Reed guy. Next to them, an envious Brendan watched Lewis enjoy the undivided attention of two beautiful Korean backpackers.

Tuk followed the end of *Honky Tonk Women* with an intro to a slow minor blues the band recognised immediately. As the bass played softly and the drummer switched from sticks to brushes, Tod slotted the microphone into a stand in front of Tuk and headed for the bar. Nong had a cold Lao Beer waiting for him.

Tuk could hardly believe he was back home in Bangkok, playing the blues, with his mum and Laurel contentedly watching his every move. Life was good.

Seven weeks had passed since he was eventually coaxed into joining Tyler Gray onstage at Lerwick Blues. What was initially meant to be a guest appearance for one or two songs turned into Tuk becoming Tyler's sideman for the rest of the show, happily launching into solos whenever Tyler gave him the nod, solos the audience responded to with thunderous applause and which Tyler answered with inspirational musical soliloquies of his own. Along the way, the Lerwick Blues weekend's closing act turned into a greater success than anyone, with the possible exception of Colin, could possibly have foreseen.

Precisely as Colin had dreamed, and with the help of professional-grade footage rapidly whipped into shape and supplied by Tod, YouTube clips from Tuk's Lerwick appearance went instantly viral. Local, national and international TV stations picked up on the heartwarming tale of the unknown blues guitarist from Thailand being invited to play alongside his late father's hero. The publicity generated was so far-reaching, within 48 hours, Colin and Susan announced the dates for Lerwick Blues II were confirmed – with *City Limits* promised a slot high on the bill. Attempts to get Tyler Gray's name on a contract for next year were on the back burner only because his newly installed management team were flooded with requests for Tyler's band to appear at blues and rock festivals all over Europe and North America.

Press and internet exposure saw sales of Gray's new album soar overnight, much to the delight of Jack Murdock who, precisely as predicted by Tyler, did his best to hog the credit for making Gray's Shetland appearance such a success.

Not that Murdoch was interviewed anywhere nearly as often as he wanted. TV stations in the UK and abroad were much more eager to fire softball questions at Tyler Gray and his new best friend, Tuk Blues from Bangkok. While Tyler talked endlessly about Tuk, he never uttered a single word of praise for Jack Murdock, even on rare occasions when they were interviewed side by side. Relations between the two became toxic. When Murdock tried to pour shade on Gray with the studio bosses back home, they blew him off. Top management were only interested in keeping on Tyler's good side, rendering Murdock's views irrelevant. Within a week, his area of responsibility shifted to taking care of an unknown Texas bluegrass combo.

Thanks to Tod's networking efforts, Thailand's entertainment world woke up to the story of a Thai musician being courted by media across the globe. Bangkok record labels started a bidding war to get Tuk's signature on a recording contract, with signing-on fees rising at an unprecedented rate. Tuk told them if they didn't want his band's names on the contract, he wasn't interested. Within weeks, *City Limits* had the recording deal no label would have entertained giving them only months before, Bangkok studio time was reserved and Tuk, who was still in Lerwick, spent hours every day on Skype, working with Tod on writing original songs for the upcoming album.

In their free time, he and Laurel went for long walks or scooter rides, binoculars to the fore, adding to their life lists of birds spotted. In the evenings, he either joined jam sessions in the Lounge or the Marlex or gave blues guitar lessons (free of charge; he still had no work permit, remember) to grateful Shetlanders between the ages of twelve and eighty.

Laurel went back to work, where her boss Viv immediately approved a request for long service leave. After a memorable goodbye party in the Lounge, Laurel and Tuk flew with their hangovers to Glasgow for a gleeful reunion with Bren that they were careful to make sure happened on a Tuesday so Tuk could join in the blues jam at the State Bar, with Lewis in attendance. A few days later they flew to Bangkok, where a welcome home gig at Adhere the 13th Bar awaited *City Limits*.

The slow minor blues that drew a hush over the tiny Adhere crowd was a number one chart hit for Albert King in 1972.

Looking across the tiny gap separating him from his mum and Laurel, Tuk sang *I'll Play the Blues For You*.

The End

Ron McMillan began writing in Seoul, South Korea when he became a freelance journalist and photojournalist in the fevered run-up to the 1988 Seoul Olympic Games.

During a decade based in Hong Kong, he travelled throughout Asia on assignment for magazines in North America, Europe and Asia, visited Mainland China almost fifty times and made five 'tourist' visits to isolated North Korea. As well as appearing prominently in *Time*, *Newsweek*, *L'Express Magazine* and the *New York Times Sunday Magazine*, his photographs gained notoriety in North Korea. To this day, visitors are watched to ensure photographs of the giant statues of the Great and Dear Leaders never cut them off below the knees.

Ron later wrote and illustrated articles in travel, airline and business magazines and Sunday newspapers before travelling around the Shetland Islands in the autumn of 2005. *BETWEEN WEATHERS, Travels in 21st Century Shetland*, the first travel narrative about Shetland since Victorian times, was published in 2008 by Sandstone Press..

In 2010, Sandstone Press published *Yin Yang Tattoo*, a crime novel that earned the unusual distinction of having its invitation to the Hong Kong Literary Festival rescinded. '*Altogether too highly coloured for our kind of festival*,' said the festival chairman. *Yin Yang Tattoo* and two Thailand-set crime novels, *Bangkok Cowboy* and *Bangkok Belle*, are available as eBooks and paperbacks on Amazon.

Also on Amazon is *Don't Think Twice*, the first in a crime series set in Scotland in the 1990s.

Independent authors are heavily dependent on reviews posted by readers on Amazon and Goodreads. I would be very grateful if you could please take time to post a brief review. Thank you.

Acknowledgements

I owe a debt of gratitude to a considerable number of friends who have been generous with their help and advice and patient feedback during the writing of *Still Blue*. If I fail to thank you all individually, forgive me.

Keith Nolan in Bangkok advised me on matters related to playing the blues in Thailand. Micheal Woods in Chiang Mai, Thailand, Mark McTague in Baltimore, USA, Ute Zahn in Minneapolis, David Donald on Koh Samui and Rose Sloan Ford in Shetland were very helpful; and Davie Gardner and Ryan Leith in Shetland exhibited the patience of saints in the face of strange requests for information or verification of facts and obscure locations and flora and fauna in Shetland.

And Louise Aylward in Totnes, England did a wonderful job adding polish to a rough manuscript, along with valued encouragement to keep going when spirits or confidence were flagging.

While this is most definitely a work of fiction, music fans should be assured that Adhere the 13th Blues Bar and the Saxophone Pub in Bangkok are genuine homes of the blues in Thailand – and every bit as fine as they are depicted in the story. Blues fans visiting Bangkok should use social media to seek out Keith Nolan's band, the Cotton Mouth Kings, for top-quality, earthy, piano-driven blues. Likewise, the Tuesday blues jam at the State Bar in Holland Street, Glasgow, is not to be missed.

Printed in Dunstable, United Kingdom